Praise for Jennifer Bohnet

'A thoroughly charming, captivating read.'
— *Reviewed the Book* on *The Little Kiosk by the Sea*

'A wonderful escape, overflowing with secrets. I couldn't have loved this more.'
— *Becca's Books* on *The Little Kiosk by the Sea*

'Simply wonderful, I enjoyed every moment.'
— *Welsh Annie* on *The Little Kiosk by the Sea*

'Beautifully written, the perfect summer holiday read.'
— *The French Village Diaries* on *A French Pirouette*

'A lovely romantic read. I got lost in it completely.'
— *AJ Book Review Club* on *A French Pirouette*

'A wonderfully fast-paced story that whisked me away to the French Riviera.'
— *Rachel's Random Reads* on *You Had Me at Bonjour*

'Delightful chick-lit, a great story to escape into!'
— *Splashes Into Books* on *You Had Me At Bonjour*

Jennifer Bohnet is originally from the West Country but now lives in the wilds of rural Brittany, France. She's still not sure how she ended up there! The saying 'life is what happens while you're deciding what to do...' is certainly true in her case. She's always written alongside having various jobs: playgroup leader, bookseller, landlady, restauranteur, farmer's wife, secretary – the list is endless but does provide a rich vein of inspiration for her stories.

Allergic to housework and gardening she rarely does either, but she does like cooking and entertaining and wandering around *vide greniers* (the French equivalent of flea markets) looking for a bargain or two. Her children currently live in fear of her turning into an ageing hippy and moving to Totnes, Devon.

To find out more about Jennifer, visit her website at jenniferbohnet.com or chat to her on Twitter at @jenniewriter

ROSIE'S
Little Café
ON THE
RIVIERA

**A summer
of taking chances…**

Jennifer Bohnet

ONE PLACE. MANY STORIES

HQ
An imprint of HarperCollins*Publishers* Ltd.
1 London Bridge Street
London SE1 9GF

This paperback edition 2017

1
First published in Great Britain by
HQ, an imprint of HarperCollins*Publishers* Ltd. 2017

Copyright © Jennifer Bohnet 2017

Jennifer Bohnet asserts the moral right to be
identified as the author of this work.
A catalogue record for this book is
available from the British Library.

ISBN: 978-0-00-824607-5

Printed and bound by
CPI Group (UK) Ltd, Croydon, CR0 4YY

Also by Jennifer Bohnet

To my husband Richard with love and thanks
for being there.

Chapter One

'*Bonne chance*,' the notaire said, counting the large wad of euros Rosie had given him before pushing a bunch of keys across the desk towards her. 'The Café Fleur is now yours.'

Five minutes later and, juggling the keys happily, Rosie walked along the ancient ramparts edging the Mediterranean towards the beach and the Café Fleur. Day one of the rest of her life was here at last and it felt oh so good. It had seemed to take forever, but one of her lifelong dreams was about to become a reality.

Owning and running her own successful café had been her number-one dream for several years now. Her other dream of being married and having a family by the time she was thirty had been foiled by her own seeming inability to build a long-lasting relationship with any man.

It was after a wine-fuelled thirtieth-birthday hangover that she'd decided enough was enough. Life was passing her by. Okay, she'd failed to meet and marry Mr Right, but owning her own café was still within her grasp. So, Dream Target No. 1 became saving enough money to open her own beach café in the South of France. Now, a couple of months before her thirty-fifth birthday, she was about to realise her dream.

Glancing across the bay to where several boats were making their way to the marina entrance, her smile faded. She recognised the hull of the boat leading the way, flying the English ensign. *A Sure Thing*, the yacht she'd been chef on for the past few years, while she squirrelled away enough money to gain her independence, was returning to port.

Briefly she wondered if Antoine, the skipper, had forgiven her yet for deserting her. He'd been less than happy when she'd told him her plans.

'*Sacre bleu*, Rosie, Charlie's going to be furious when he finds out you've left. He'll probably make William fire me for letting you go. Rosie, please, for me – one more summer?'

'No. Definitely not.' Rosie shrugged. 'He already knows I've left but, Antoine, *do not*, under any circumstances, tell Charlie the whereabouts of my restaurant. Understood?'

Antoine had given her a resigned nod and wished her well, knowing when he was beaten.

Rosie sighed. She could only cross her fingers and pray that the message had got through to Charlie that she wasn't interested in a relationship, however much he wanted to rekindle their long-ago college affair. She had enough to do getting the Café Fleur ready to open without having to deal with him as well.

Hopefully the yacht was coming into port to take on fuel and stock up with food supplies and wouldn't be staying long. Maybe they had plans to motor across to Corsica, one of Charlie's favourite places. Corsica would be good. Go to Corsica, Rosie silently willed.

The longer she could keep the location of her new business from Charlie, the better. The scene he was sure to make when he realised what she was doing was not one she looked forward to. Not that she cared these days what he thought, but no way did she want him turning up at her opening party next week. He definitely wasn't on the guest list.

Tansy, ex-stewardess on *A Sure Thing*, her best friend and, as of today, her sous-chef, waitress and chief washer-upper, was waiting for her in the car park at the back of the restaurant. 'Signed your life away?'

'Yep – and I've got the keys to prove it,' Rosie said, stretching to raise the security grill before putting the first key in a lock near the top of the door and turning it. Another large, old-fashioned key went into a lock in the middle of the door and finally she bent down to insert a small, gold-coloured key into the lock six inches from the bottom, before turning the handle and opening the door.

'I guess the last guy had a security obsession,' she said. 'At least, I hope that's all it was.'

Inside, dusty tables and chairs were arranged in neat rows, a pile of parasols leaned haphazardly against the far wall and faded curtains hung limply at the sides of the shuttered windows. In the kitchen a huge, old, white-doored fridge, which looked ancient enough to have graced Elizabeth David's kitchen fifty years ago, held centre stage. Its presence dwarfing all the other, equally old, utensils. Rosie prayed it would all be in working order once she and Tansy had cleaned things.

No way could she afford to buy a lot of new equipment. Paying the notaire had seriously depleted her bank account. She needed to be open and putting money into her new business account as quickly as possible. Otherwise she would be in trouble financially before the season even got going.

'Right, let's get the shutters open and make a start,' Rosie said.

'What's behind that door?' Tansy asked, pointing to a door at the side of the bar.

'Stairs to a store room,' Rosie said. 'I didn't take much notice, to be honest, I was more interested in down here. Come on, let's get scrubbing.' She handed Tansy a pair of pink rubber gloves before pulling on a pair herself.

While Tansy got to grips with the kitchen, Rosie went through to make a start on the restaurant. Sliding the bolts back on the front door, she stepped out onto the terrace to fold back the shutters with their peeling Provençal blue paint and stood for a few moments, visualising it busy with customers. *Her* customers. Eating outside on the terrace was an essential part of her plan for the café. People loved eating al fresco.

Two large eucalyptus trees gave some perfumed shade where the terrace ran down to the beach. The French phrase *pieds en mer* – feet in the sea – described it perfectly, Rosie thought, looking around. Oleander bushes already budding up. Yachts sailing in the distance. A woman and a young girl beach combing. Shimmering sea.

A vine with a thick, tree-like trunk covered the loggia running along the length of the restaurant. Rosie sighed. It really was an amazing location come true for her dream. It had to be a success for so many reasons. Not least because it was her final chance to make something of herself. And of course there was the little matter of being bankrupt if she didn't make it work. She took a deep breath. Failure was simply not an option.

The Beach Hotel next door was undergoing a seasonal spring clean too, judging by the number of men carrying ladders, paint, new equipment, etc. who were swarming all over it. Rosie watched enviously as three men struggled to manoeuvre a large La Cornue range through a narrow door on the side of the building. That was a stove to die for. Pity her budget didn't allow for gadgets like that.

What couldn't she do to this place if she had a 'no limits' budget? New tables and chairs – some of those comfy, Paris bistro-type ones indoors, teak ones outside. New modern equipment in the kitchen. An up-to-date range. Different crockery and cutlery, pretty tablecloths, a florist to come in every day with fresh flower arrangements, rather than the silk ones she was planning to use. Original paintings on the wall – ah, but she was going to have those. Tansy knew someone who wanted to hang some paintings of local scenes, and a few exotic ones, with a view to selling them, so hopefully every few weeks the paintings would change.

A man sitting on the rocks down by the shoreline smiled and raised a hand in greeting. Rosie hoped he didn't make a habit of sitting in front of her café – with his bare feet, tousled, sun-bleached hair, cut-off jean shorts, and a pink T-shirt bearing the faded word MUSTIQUE, he didn't exactly fit the image she had of the customers she wanted in her café. Like he'd ever been there. Neither did she want his presence to attract any undesirable friends he might have.

Rosie politely raised her hand in acknowledgement but didn't make eye contact, hoping he'd take the hint she didn't want to talk. He didn't.

'Hi, I'm Sebastian. Seb to most people,' he said, walking towards her and extending his hand, the leather friendship bracelets around his wrist tangling as they dropped forward. Reluctantly Rosie shook his hand. She didn't want to be rude but she didn't intend to encourage him to hang around.

'I'm Rosie.'

'Restaurant reopening soon? The old place could do with a makeover.'

'A week today,' she said.

'Have you got all the staff you need? I might be able to help if you haven't.'

His English was impeccable but tinged with a faint accent some people might have described as sexy. Did he want a job? Or was he just asking, making conversation? He probably didn't even have any suitable work clothes and, while the dress code during the day in her restaurant might be casual, she certainly wasn't going to allow the staff to dress tattily. In the evenings, dress would definitely be smart casual.

'All organised, thank you,' Rosie answered quickly. He didn't need to know Tansy was the only staff she could currently afford. Looking at Seb's tanned, olive skin and the general air of casualness that hung about him, she guessed he'd be more of a drifter than a steady nine-to-five-type guy.

'Look, I'm sorry, but I really do have to get on,' she said. 'So much to do.' This time he took the hint.

'Yeah, right. See you around,' Seb said with a smile and wandered off along the beach.

'Good luck,' she called out, feeling unexpectedly guilty about not being more friendly towards a guy who was clearly down on his luck. If he came back, she would definitely offer him a couple of small jobs – cleaning the windows or washing the terrace down, something like that.

Seb didn't turn round at her words, merely waved his hand in the air in acknowledgement.

Back in the restaurant, Rosie set to work. She pushed the old upright piano in the corner by the French windows into the centre of the room, making a mental note to check the piano tuner was still coming Saturday morning. Musical lunches and suppers were all part of her plan to create a different ambience in the restaurant. And live music for the party was a definite necessity.

Three hours later, when Tansy made them both a coffee from the newly cleaned espresso machine that had sprung miraculously, if noisily, into life when she switched it on, they were both fit to drop.

'Rob said he'd give us a hand painting tomorrow if you'd like him to,' Tansy said, smothering a yawn.

'Great,' Rosie said. 'I was going to make a start this evening but...' She glanced at her watch. 'I think I'll just make a list of things I've got to get at the cash-and-carry on Thursday. Rob still okay about us borrowing his van?'

'I've got to drop him off at the marina first, then we've got the van until three o'clock. Right, I'm off. See you in the morning.'

Closing the door behind Tansy, Rosie stood by the kitchen window for a few moments watching the continuing activities at the hotel. A large poster had been placed in one of the upstairs windows overlooking their car park: GRANDE RÉOUVERTURE BIENTÔT.

Just how grand would their opening be? And how soon was soon? Would she be open before they were? Was she about to find herself in competition with a top-notch chef right on her doorstep? Would their food be better than hers? Rosie shook herself. She would not think negative thoughts.

The advertisement she'd arranged on the local English radio station would hopefully bring a few ex-pats her way and kick-start a word-of-mouth buzz about the Café Fleur before the summer tourists started to arrive.

She'd worry about the competition next door when she knew more about it.

Chapter Two

Locking the shop door of The Cupboard Under the Stairs, Erica ran down the narrow street behind the church before turning left into the town's main square and dashing into the boulangerie. Thankfully, only two people were waiting to be served and Erica was on her way to the school gates two hundred yards down the road as the town-hall clock struck midday.

She let out a deep breath as she reached the school. Made it. Cammie panicked when she was late meeting her and she hated being responsible for dredging up feelings of fear in her daughter. Cammie's panic attacks, like the nightmares, were on the wane, thank goodness, and Erica wanted more than anything in the world for them to disappear totally. For her daughter to be happy again. For her own hurt to be healing.

Everyone had told her it would take time, lots of time, but she couldn't help wishing she could speed things up. She hated the thought of Cammie's childhood being blighted indefinitely by the events of last year.

'Hi,' she said now as Cammie ran to her. 'Picnic on the beach today okay?'

'Cheesy baguette? Yummy,' Cammie said, slipping her hand into Erica's.

Five minutes later, as Cammie tucked into her cheese baguette, Erica asked, 'How was school this morning?' She held her breath, waiting for the answer.

Cammie had been like a zombie going to school for the last few months – zero interest in anything, just listlessly doing anything she was told to do. Last week, though, during the weekly telephone call the school had instigated to keep Erica in the picture about her progress, her class teacher had said there were a few hopeful signs starting to appear.

'It was okay. We have to find stuff to make a collage with for next week. I'm going to do a beach one so I'll need shells, seaweed, pebbles – oh, lots of stuff.'

'We'd better have a walk when you've finished your lunch and start collecting stuff then,' Erica said, trying not to sound too pleased that Cammie was looking forward to getting involved with a project. Was it a real sign that she could finally be coming out of the terrible lethargy she'd sunk into after Pascal's death last August? Starting to come to terms with what had happened.

The walk along the beach, filling their pockets with shiny pebbles and shells, engrossed them both and time was forgotten. It was only as they passed the café and Cammie said, 'Can I have an ice cream please?' that Erica looked at her watch and realised Cammie's lunchtime – all two hours of it – was almost finished.

'No time. We've only got five minutes to get you back to school. Besides, it isn't open yet,' she said, glancing over at the Café Fleur. Seeing the shutters open and a woman moving around inside, she added, 'Maybe they'll be open next time. Now, let's run or you'll be late.'

Back at the shop, Erica opened the mailbox and took out the day's post. Among the usual promo leaflets there was an envelope with the notaire's name stamped across it. At least the sick feeling in the pit of her tummy no longer pounced when she received envelopes like these.

She was getting better at handling things. Things she'd never anticipated having to deal with.

Her heart did flip though, when she read the latest letter and saw the final amount of Pascal's estate – including the insurance money. Her life with Pascal was now officially over – all formalities tied up and she was free to move on. Make a new life without him.

The problem though, was she didn't want a new life courtesy of Pascal's insurance money. She would prefer to have him around, for Cammie's sake as much as her own. Thoughtfully, she emptied her pockets of beach treasures and put them to one side for Cammie to sort later.

She didn't have a clue as to the kind of life she wanted to live for the next few years while Cammie grew up. But having such a large sum in the bank – she'd have to do something with it. Providing for Cammie had to be top of her priorities. Pascal would expect her to do that. Invest it in something. Bigger shop premises? Mentally she shook her head. No. The Cupboard Under the Stairs worked as it was – a tiny space crammed with a mixture of unexpected things. A bigger layout would move it away from her original premise.

The Cupboard Under the Stairs worked as a bijou vintage shop selling an eclectic mix of new and second-hand stuff, from vintage clothes and handbags to kitchen paraphernalia, kitsch of all descriptions, pottery, cushions, books, even the occasional art-nouveau piece when Erica was lucky enough to find one. She'd made The Cupboard Under the Stairs into the kind of shop, in fact, that she'd always loved to discover and browse in, full of irresistible bits and pieces.

Maybe she should spend the money on a bigger house? A villa with a swimming pool. Cammie would enjoy that. But would she want to move from their townhouse with its memories of Pascal? She'd have to talk it over with her. If she liked the idea, they could add house-hunting to their weekend itinerary along with *vide greniers*, looking to buy stuff for the shop.

Erica turned the shop sign to open. Not that she expected many customers. This time of year was all about stocktaking and gearing up for the coming season rather than making lots of sales. This year, too, a real spring clean was called for after her neglect of the past few months.

Everything looked a bit sad. She'd begin this afternoon by giving the place a thorough clean and rearranging the shelves. Start the summer season all spruced up.

Life had to go on, so the quicker she could get back into a proper routine the better. She had to make the best life possible for herself and Cammie.

Chapter Three

Rosie's days flew past in a haze of painting, organising, cooking, panicking and not a lot of sleeping. By late Saturday afternoon, when she and Tansy hung the final painting on the wall of the restaurant, she was exhausted.

'Is that level?' Tansy asked, nudging a flamboyant modernistic painting, with its clashing red, mauve and blue colours, into a better line.

Rosie nodded, wondering how she was going to get through the next few hours of partying. 'I can't believe everything is done. I need a coffee – actually I need sleep but coffee will have to do. People will be here soon.'

As Rosie pushed open the swing door into the kitchen, James looked up from putting the finishing touches to the party food. 'You look like you need a drink.'

'Later. Right now a double espresso will fit the bill,' Rosie said. James had appeared two days ago looking for work. 'Antoine said you might need someone,' he'd said. 'I've trained as a sous-chef and want a job on a yacht but apparently I need more hands-on experience.'

'I hadn't planned on taking anyone on for a few weeks,' Rosie had told him. 'Tansy and I are used to working together and until the restaurant takes off I can't afford to pay anyone else. Not even me. Maybe come back in a few weeks. Or you could try the hotel next door,' she suggested.

'I'll work for free for a few days,' James offered. 'Antoine says you're really good and I'd learn a lot working for you.'

Amused by his blatant flattery, Rosie had smiled. 'Okay. You free to help Saturday afternoon and stay for the evening party?'

'What time?'

'Two o'clock.'

'I'll be here.'

And he was. Everything she'd asked him to do in the past couple of hours, he'd done quickly and efficiently. Now, as she watched him work the coffee machine, she hoped she'd be able to employ him officially in the next couple of weeks. He'd be a real asset. She must remember to thank Antoine the next time she saw him for sending James in her direction.

'You've put enough champagne in the fridge?' she asked now, taking her coffee. 'And rosé?'

'Yes,' James said. 'Drink that and then go and change. Tansy and I have everything under control.'

Resisting the urge to make a sarcastic rejoinder along the lines of, 'Well, of course you've got everything under control – you're practising to be a typical bossy man,' Rosie flew into the Ladies' loo.

With less than half an hour to go before people arrived, there was no time to do more than change her clothes and slap on some make-up. She pulled on her white jeans and a spaghetti-strap black top and slipped her feet into her one pair of Jimmy Choos. No time to do anything with her hair other than push it up into its usual style with a huge glittery clip. Slipping on her amber ring, so big it dwarfed her hand, she was ready. She took a deep breath – time to party and raise the curtain on Café Fleur.

James was already handing round champagne to the early arrivals. Tansy was in the kitchen doing some last-minute food prep and waved her away. 'Go circulate.'

Rosie began to work her way around the room greeting people, accepting their congratulations and their Good Luck cards.

The pianist, playing a medley of jazz, smiled at her as she placed a glass of champagne within his reach, before standing to look around 'her' restaurant.

People were helping themselves to the plates of finger food laid out on the bar. Smoked-salmon blinis, fois gras on crisp toast, slices of quiche, individual *pissaladières* and lots of bowls of nuts, crisps and peanuts were scattered around. For those with a sweet tooth there were tiny individual *tartes abricots* with rosettes of crème frêche piped on top, demitasse servings of chocolate mousse and a bowl of fruit salad.

Tansy had placed the cheese board, with its selection of Brie, Roquefort, Boursin and Cantal on a separate table. And Rosie knew that, out in the kitchen, a cauldron of home-made parsley soup stood on the stove, ready to be heated at the end of the evening as people left.

An hour later the place was buzzing. Her pile of business cards on the bar had shrunk and the reservations book by the till had several bookings pencilled in. Rosie allowed herself a secret smile of satisfaction. Café Fleur was on its way.

The lights were dimmed, couples were wrapped in each other's arms, swaying to the romantic jazz. Rosie sighed. It was years since she had danced with anyone like that. Working on the yachts it was impossible to have a shore-based relationship with anyone. Away at sea for weeks at a time, particularly after William had bought *A Sure Thing* eighteen months ago, her days off were invariably spent alone in whichever port they were currently moored in: Saint-Tropez, Monaco, Corsica.

All of which sounded far more glamorous and romantic than it was, with no one special to spend time with. And now, if she was to make a success of the Café Fleur, she had to continue to put any ideas of meeting someone and having a serious relationship out of her mind. All her energies had to be focused on the Café Fleur...

A scream pierced the babble of music and general noise as the restaurant was plunged into darkness. The emergency lighting in the kitchen and behind the bar area flickered weakly before fading completely.

'Any idea where the fuse box is? And do you have a torch?' James asked.

'Cupboard in the cloakroom,' Rosie said. 'And no, sorry, no torch.' Mentally she added torch and candles to the ever-growing 'essential items' list still hanging on the board in the kitchen.

Helpful guests started to give quick flashes from their cigarette lighters and James was able to find the trip switch in the cupboard and flip it up. Nothing.

'I'm sorry, folks, but it looks like the party's over for this evening,' Rosie said. 'Thank you for the support and Café Fleur will...' Her voice trailed away as Seb walked in through the open terrace doors carrying a lit candle.

'I'm guessing you haven't got a supply in yet,' he said, placing a bundle of candles on the bar before lighting a couple from the flame of the one in his hand and carefully positioning them on the counter. 'Any food left?'

'Yes, of course. Thank you,' Rosie said, grabbing a plate and filling it with a selection of nibbles. 'Champagne?' She poured a large glass and handed it to him.

As Tansy and James placed more candles in strategic places, the pianist started playing again and people drifted back to the small dance floor, arms around each other.

Rosie poured herself a glass of champagne and sipped it as she looked at Seb. Not so scruffy tonight – the shorts had been changed for a pair of fashionably torn jeans, and a plain white T-shirt accentuated his tan. His hair was still tousled, though.

'I can't thank you enough for the candles. I definitely owe you,' she said.

Seb shrugged. 'This is good. Did you make it?'

'What…? Oh, the mackerel pâté, yes.' She glanced at him. 'So, did you make a special journey to bring me candles?'

'Yep. All twenty metres of it.' Seb pushed his empty plate away and held out his hand. 'Dance?'

'Uuh…' But Seb had already taken her by the hand. 'Twenty metres – but… that's the hotel? You work at the hotel?'

'I own it.'

Rosie stood still. 'But I thought…'

'I know what you thought,' Seb said. 'You thought I was a down-and-out.'

'You could have said. I was going to offer you some odd jobs when I saw you again,' Rosie said. 'I feel so stupid.'

Seb shrugged. 'You shouldn't. You weren't to know. But you shouldn't judge people so quickly – especially down here. Millionaires often dress like tramps.'

'You're a millionaire?'

'You saying I was dressed like a tramp?' Seb countered, shaking his head. 'No, I'm not – yet.'

'But you own the hotel. So we're competitors? When does your restaurant open? Just don't tell me you've got a Michelin-star chef lined up.'

'There's room for both of us. I don't see us as competitors – we're aiming at two different markets. And yes, I expect a Michelin star within the first year.'

'Oh, good,' Rosie said. A crash from the kitchen made her jump. 'Look, I'm sorry but I'd better go check that out.' Grabbing a candle from the bar, Rosie made her way into the kitchen.

Bloody typical. Just when she was beginning to think Seb was an okay bloke, he had to spoil things. Her cooking was as good as anybody's – why didn't he think she was capable of aiming for a Michelin star, too? Oh, not in their haute-cuisine section – she wasn't that daft – but in their bistro section, where they highlighted the less pretentious places.

Tansy was scrabbling about in the candlelight picking up cooking tins and baking trays that had fallen onto the floor when a shelf had collapsed.

'You okay?' Rosie asked.

'Fine. Who's the candle guy?'

'Seb. Owns the hotel,' Rosie said, handing Tansy half a dozen trays to put on the work surface. 'And he has Michelin aspirations for his restaurant when it reopens. That's all I need – a bloody Jean-Christophe Novelli on my doorstep.'

'Your cooking will get the punters in,' Tansy said. 'You know you can cook as well as any poncy chef.'

'But I'm not a poncy *French* chef. Maybe I am being naive.' Rosie sighed. For the first time she began to feel doubts creeping in about the Café Fleur being the success she wanted. 'I know there's a lot of competition out there. Let's face it, every other building down here houses a restaurant or bistro. I just didn't expect to have a major competitor right next door to me on the beach.'

'Well, it's a bit late now for second thoughts,' Tansy said. 'Think of the money you've already invested. You can't just throw that lot away without even trying to make this place work – and it will work. Look at the reservations already in the book.'

Rosie took a deep breath. 'You're right, of course.'

She really did have to think about all the money she'd already invested. 'Right. Back to Plan A – making the Café Fleur *the* place to eat and be seen.'

Determinedly, Rosie pushed all traitorous thoughts of sexy hotel owners to the back of her mind, where she intended to keep them for the foreseeable future. This was not the time to let any man hijack the plans she now had in place for her life.

Men always wanted to be in control, do things their way, no argument. But the worst thing about men, in her experience, was they were totally unreliable. Charlie was living proof of that – and her father, of course.

This summer she was going to focus all her energies on making the Café Fleur the best beachside restaurant on the coast. No way was she going to let any local competition distract her from pursuing that plan.

Chapter Four

Escaping the office was always a bonus, especially on a sunny day, and Georgina George smiled happily to herself as she settled on one of the picnic benches at the Café Fleur. Her summer office was open.

Her normal desk in one of the most prestigious estate-agent's offices in town was an expensive necessity. One she needed for official meetings and for keeping her name 'out there'. It made her legitimate in the eyes of clients. Never mind that in summer she did most of her paperwork on the laptop sitting at a café table. Bringing clients somewhere like this for an initial discussion over a relaxed coffee was always a good move, too.

At least the place was looking a bit more presentable this year. New name. New owner. The grapevine around the office was saying the new owner was English. She'd introduce herself when she ordered her coffee, find out for herself. With luck, the prices wouldn't have gone up. Her budget was even tighter than last year, thanks to Hugo raising the rent of her official desk.

A toasted sandwich and coffee for lunch was still a cheaper option than actually buying food and cooking it, though. As long as she had that at midday, she could survive on cereal at home.

'Bonjour. What would you like? I'm afraid we don't have a vast selection of food just now. Mainly baguettes, soup or toasties.' The woman standing at her side, order pad poised, looked about Georgina's own age.

'Hi. Are you Fleur?'

'Yes – although the name is really Rosie. Rosie Hewitt.'

'I'm Georgina George. Yep, I know my parents had no imagination! Most people call me GeeGee.' She smiled at Rosie. 'A large coffee right away, please. And a croque monsieur in about half an hour – with another coffee. Thanks.'

While she waited for her coffee, GeeGee wrote an email to Stan, the sleazy landlord of her studio flat, reminding him she was waiting for the renewed lease to sign. Should have been sent over a week ago. As she pressed send, Rosie reappeared, with her coffee.

'You're a lifesaver,' GeeGee said. 'Need my coffee fix. How are things going with the café? I'm one of the regulars here, by the way.'

'Fine so far,' Rosie answered. 'Looking forward to a busy season. You live around here?'

GeeGee nodded. 'Out on the Cap d'Antibes. I've been down here eight years now and I can't think of anywhere else I'd rather be – even if things have gone a bit pear-shaped recently.'

'What do you do?' Rosie asked.

'I'm an estate agent and live off commission – which makes life a tiny bit scary at times.' GeeGee picked up her coffee and took a sip. 'Right now there's a bit of a slump, but the signs are it's slowly picking up. I've got a sale going through this month. And an apartment viewing this afternoon, which I have high hopes of selling.' She didn't add that she'd be in desperate straits if she didn't sell another villa or an apartment in the next couple of weeks.

'Bit like me then,' Rosie said. 'Not that I work on commission only, but I've sunk all my savings into this place and need it to start earning me some money ASAP.'

'Oh, it will,' GeeGee said. 'This place is a honey pot in season. Some days it's impossible to find a spare table. My friend Erica and her daughter are always down here, too. We'll spread the word for you, but trust me, you won't need it.'

'Thanks.' Rosie smiled. 'I'll be back soon with your lunch.'

GeeGee sipped her coffee and watched Rosie go, before returning her attention to the spreadsheet she'd opened on the laptop and its rows of figures.

Twenty minutes later her concentration was broken as an email pinged into her box. Jay. She stifled a sigh.

'*Bon appétit*,' Rosie said, appearing with her lunch and another coffee.

'Thanks. This looks good,' GeeGee replied as she closed the laptop down. Reading another of Jay's happy-happy missives wasn't what she wanted right now so it could wait until this evening – if she didn't delete it unread before then. Right now she was going to enjoy her lunch.

***

An hour later, GeeGee waved goodbye to Rosie, left the beach and made her way through town to meet her client, Marc, and show him a new property on her list. A top-floor apartment in one of the oldest townhouses on the coast road.

Marc and another man were waiting for her on the opposite side of the road to the house, their backs to the sea, looking at the four-storey terraced house with its pale-green shutters. Both men were in their early thirties, and both wore the regulation uniform of the 'yachties' who crewed on the large luxury yachts: smart bermuda shorts, polo shirts with their yacht's name embroidered discreetly on the pocket, and sockless feet in deck shoes.

It was Marc who had contacted her and booked the viewing, so she assumed he was the buyer and the other man was there to give him some moral support. Clients often brought friends along to voice their unbiased opinions and to help them decide about a property. Sometimes, of course, the friends were being just plain nosey. Or maybe Marc and his friend were an item and they were looking to buy together?

'Hi. Not late, am I?' she said, searching in her bag for the keys.

'No, we just thought we'd come and spy out the lie of the land first,' Marc said. 'This is Dan... my financial adviser,' he added, laughing.

GeeGee held out her hand. 'Nice to meet you, financial adviser Dan,' she said, smiling at him.

As her hand was taken in a firm grip and shaken, unexpected tingles shot up her arm and she was glad when Dan released it.

'Love the position of the house,' he said. 'Must have wonderful views.'

'It does and it's a really lovely apartment. The sort that's on my personal wish list,' GeeGee said. 'Despite the fact it's on the fourth floor and there isn't a lift,' she added.

'How many apartments in the building?' Marc asked as they made their way up the stairs.

'Three apartments and a couple of studios. 4c at the top is the nicest apartment – and the most expensive.'

GeeGee could tell from the moment she opened the door to the apartment that it was Dan who really loved the place. Marc didn't seem that enamoured of either the recently decorated sitting room or the slightly old-fashioned kitchen with its original butler sink and blue-and-yellow tiling on the walls. The 'Juliette' balcony off the sitting room with its French doors and sea view was, in his opinion, too small to be of any use.

Finally she led them up the spiral stone staircase into the room that opened onto the pièce de resistance as far as she was concerned – the roof terrace. The first time she'd seen it, she'd immediately pictured it with urns and pots full of plants and tumbling geraniums and hidden lights dotted around. A perfect romantic hideaway for two.

After warning Marc that the apartment had only been on the market a matter of days and the owner wouldn't consider an offer – he wanted the full asking price – GeeGee stayed up on the terrace while Marc and Dan had a wander downstairs on their own.

Standing there by the railings, watching the people down below making their way along the narrow coast-road pavement, she longed to own a place like this. Romantic suppers in the moonlight with a loved one. She sighed. Maybe one day.

Downstairs, Marc and Dan were talking too quietly for her to make out what was being said, but her gut instinct told her that Marc wouldn't be buying the apartment. She turned to face them as they joined her on the terrace.

'Have you seen enough?'

'Yes, thanks,' Marc said. 'It's a lovely apartment but—'

'I'll pay the asking price,' Dan interrupted. 'Where do I sign?'

Surprised, GeeGee looked from Dan to Marc. 'I thought *you* were the one looking to buy?'

Marc shrugged. 'We both are. But, to be honest, this place is much more Dan's style than mine. I'd prefer a penthouse studio in one of the modern blocks with a swimming pool.'

'That's because you've no soul,' Dan said. 'Who needs a pool when you've got *that* twenty yards away...' And he gestured towards the Mediterranean.

'Right, Dan. I'll contact the owner. Then you'll have to sign the first part of the contract and you'll need to notify your notaire,' GeeGee said. 'You do have a seven-day cooling-off period if you want to change your mind. But after that the notaire will start things moving.'

'Right,' Dan said.

'I can give you the names of a couple of mortgage brokers?' GeeGee asked. 'They'll make sure you get the right deal for you. Oh, I forgot, you're a financial advisor so you'll have your own contacts.' She grinned up at him, waiting for him to say Marc had called him that as a joke. But he didn't.

Instead he said, 'I'll have the funds in place by next week.' He held his hand out. 'All business deals need to be sealed with a handshake.'

As her hand was again enveloped in his, GeeGee said, 'Thank you.' And prayed he couldn't feel her trembling.

Chapter Five

Rosie bought a box of candles and went across to the hotel with them to say a proper thank-you to Seb.

She knocked tentatively on the side door, which was ajar. 'Hi. Anyone here? May I come in?'

No answer, so Rosie pushed open the door and walked in. The empty kitchen was gleaming with stainless-steel equipment, copper pots by the dozen hung in rows and huge refrigerators lined one wall. Close up, the range Rosie had seen being delivered last week was even more beautiful. God, did she covet that stove.

The saloon-style service swing doors were just too high for her to see over so, clutching the box of candles, she pushed her way through into the dining room. 'Anyone here?'

A smell of paint still hung in the air from its recent decoration, and tables and chairs were arranged haphazardly, but even so, the room still managed to give off an air of luxury. Helped by the ceiling frescoes and the gold leaf that was literally everywhere. Round one – decoration and ambience – definitely went to Seb, although the Café Fleur being on the beach had to be worth some Brownie points.

Rosie was still standing there trying to take in all the details to tell Tansy later, when Seb appeared and caught her snooping.

'Seen everything you want?'

'Umm, yes, thanks. These are for you.' Embarrassed, Rosie thrust the box of candles into Seb's hands. 'The door was open. I did try to find someone. I'd better go.'

Seb shrugged. 'No worries. Have a coffee.' He moved back towards the gleaming espresso machine in the kitchen.

'Sugar? Milk?'

'Neither, thanks.' Rosie watched as Seb placed a plate of tiny, delicious-looking pastries alongside the coffees on a tray.

'We'll take this through to Reception. The chairs are comfy out there. Follow me,' he ordered. Rosie followed meekly, wondering how long before she could leave. On a scale of one to ten of embarrassment, being caught snooping was a definite ten.

The reception area was pristine and clearly ready for the grand reopening. The requisite glamorous receptionist was already behind the desk, working away industriously. She glanced up as they approached.

'Meet Miranda, my PA,' Seb said. 'She's getting Saturday's opening bash organised. Remind me to give you your invite before you go.'

'Sorry,' Rosie said. 'I've got reservations for Saturday evening.'

'It's from eight till late so come over when you finish,' Seb said. 'I'll make sure there's a bottle of champers left for you.'

He was clearly a guy who didn't accept a No easily – a bit like Charlie in that respect. Rosie decided it would be churlish to argue so she just shrugged and muttered, 'Okay – if I'm not too tired.'

Sitting there, eating his delicious pastries and drinking coffee that was way too strong for her taste, if she were honest, she began to feel an obligation to be polite to Seb. She needed to stop feeling awkward at being caught snooping around the place and at least make an effort to socialise politely. The guy had rescued her, after all, arriving like some gallant knight with candles. He didn't deserve her cold-shouldering him – even if he was an annoying mix of sexy charm and arrogance.

She took another pastry. They really were divine.

'Is this your first stab at running a hotel? Or have you done this kind of thing before?' Rosie asked.

'It's my first time. I've been in the restaurant business for years but I fancied the challenge of a place of my own. And what about you? Fed up with the yachts, I gather?'

Rosie looked at him. How did he know that?

'I love cooking and having my own beach restaurant has been my dream for years. Besides, I couldn't live the nomad life for ever.'

'Like the name Café Fleur, by the way,' Seb said. 'Good idea to change it – sends a message to the locals that this summer it's not the place it was.'

'What d'you mean?'

Seb shrugged. 'The local gendarmes took exception last year to drugs being dealt on their patch.'

Rosie gazed at him appalled. 'Drugs?' No wonder there were all those locks on the door.

'Don't worry about it. The people involved are enjoying a holiday in Marseille courtesy of the Republic. The gendarmes will be keeping an eye on you.'

'I hope you're right.'

'I'll get your invitation for Saturday,' Seb said, before walking over to Miranda.

The embossed card he handed Rosie was impressive.

'Thank you. Will your chef be here in time for Saturday?'

Seb nodded. 'He's here already. He made those pastries you evidently like,' he said, glancing, amused, at the plate.

Rosie pushed the plate, with its single remaining patisserie, towards him. Moreish didn't begin to describe how delicious she'd found them.

'So is your chef somebody I'm likely to have heard of? My biggest fear is that you've managed to entice Jean-Christophe Novelli back to the land of his birth to work for you. If you have, I'll just give up now. I mean, there's competition and then there's Jean-Christophe.' Rosie laughed as she said it, but deep down she was serious – and worried about his answer.

Seb shook his head. 'You can stop worrying. It's not him. But do you seriously think your little beach restaurant is going to compete with this place and the chef's reputation?'

'My cooking is as good as any chef,' Rosie said, standing up. He'd put her biggest fear into words and she didn't really want to hear what else he had to say. 'Thank you for the coffee and pastries. I'd better go now.'

'Have you heard of The Recluse restaurant? Head Chef Sebastian Groc. He earned two stars for that place within four years.'

'The Recluse in Monaco?'

Charlie had taken her there last year as a birthday treat. It was certainly a special place and the food had been superb. These days, though, Rosie tried not to think about the evening they'd spent there and the way it had ended.

Seb nodded. 'That's the one.'

'Hang on a minute – what's your surname? You're not Sebastian Groc, are you?' Rosie's voice trailed away as Seb nodded.

Oh, brilliant. Not just one but two bloody Michelin stars in his last restaurant. And now he was next door to her and the Café Fleur. So much for not worrying about the competition.

Chapter Six

The bord de mer was busy with traffic despite the early hour as Rosie made her way to the local market for her fresh vegetables. She'd planned her plat-du-jour menus for the week and now she quickly picked up the potatoes, onions and fresh garlic that were basic to so many of her recipes.

She hesitated over bunches of new-season asparagus. Her favourite – gently steamed and served with hollandaise sauce. Expensive stuff to waste but she could always make soup, she decided, placing five bunches in the basket before moving on to the cheese counter.

Back at the café she switched on the espresso machine and opened the shutters. The beach was deserted. Things were quieter over at the hotel, too. No hordes of workmen rushing in and out. Just the occasional glimpse through a window of chambermaids moving from one room to another, preparing the newly decorated bedrooms for their first guests of the season.

Tansy, when she arrived, looked at the party invitation Rosie had pinned to the noticeboard in the kitchen.

'You going?'

Rosie shook her head. 'Planning on being too tired.'

'Might be fun?'

'You can have the invite if you like.'

'Any other Saturday night, I'd love it,' Tansy said. 'But Rob's taking me clubbing when we finish here.'

The café phone rang and Tansy moved across to answer it.

'Hi, Antoine. Table for two tomorrow? Fine. You'll probably have the place to yourselves as it's still quiet. See you at seven-thirty then.'

'Who's he bringing?' Rosie mouthed at Tansy.

'Antoine, who...? Sorry, he's hung up,' Tansy said, looking at Rosie apologetically.

'It had better not be Charlie, that's all,' Rosie muttered, savaging the potato she was supposedly peeling.

As a busy morning turned into lunchtime, Rosie was pleased to serve half a dozen plates of *daube provençale*, her plat du jour, to a group of walkers on their way to the Cap d'Antibes.

Tansy left at three o'clock. 'I'll be back about six-thirty. Make sure you have a rest this afternoon. Go for a walk on the beach or something. We're all organised for this evening.'

'I want to check upstairs first. See if there is any way we can make use of the place,' Rosie said. 'See you later.'

Locking the door behind Tansy and turning the sign to CLOSED, Rosie turned the key in the door by the bar and began to climb the stairs. Steep and clad in threadbare carpet, they weren't the easiest to negotiate and Rosie was glad when she reached the room.

It was larger than she remembered. There was even a walk-in shower in one corner. A halfway decent sofa bed covered in boxes was against one wall and there was a kettle on a wooden table. The whole set-up reminded Rosie of her very first bedsit at college.

The windows were curtainless and, through the back one, she looked directly into the conservatory sitting room of the hotel. Lloyd Loom chairs and matching small coffee tables were dotted around, palm trees in pots and Seb working on a laptop. Rosie stepped back out of view. The last thing she wanted was for Seb to look up and catch her watching him. He'd probably accuse her of spying on him after the way he'd caught her snooping around the hotel.

Rosie pulled at the lid of one of the boxes on the settee. Beautiful wine glasses. Mentally she made a note to remember them for special functions. The rest of the boxes, though, were filled with kitchen equipment well past its sell-by date. Rubbish really.

Back downstairs, Rosie locked up and set off for a walk along the beach. Strolling along inches from where the Mediterranean was gently lapping at the sand, enjoying the warmth of the sun, the temptation to paddle was strong. Her feet, though, were nice and snug in her trainers and she decided she wouldn't torture them by placing them in water that was still certain to be on the cold side.

The gentle breeze that blew in her face was invigorating and by the time she returned to the Café Fleur the exercise had banished her tiredness from the busy morning.

A dog was lying under one of the terrace tables when she got back. 'Hello. Where's your owner?' Soulful brown eyes that tore right into Rosie's heart looked at her but the dog made no attempt to move.

'You're very thin,' she said, gently stroking the dog's head. She wasn't wearing a collar, so no helpful name tag and address. 'Stay there,' and Rosie went into the kitchen to get some of the mince she had left over from the lasagne.

When she'd eaten and drunk, the dog managed a few wags of her tail before curling up under the table again and going to sleep.

Black-and-white, she reminded Rosie of the collie dogs her Aunty Elsie had kept on her Somerset farm. Whenever Rosie had visited with her parents there had always been at least two dogs bounding around for her to play with. And just once there had been a litter of puppies.

That litter of puppies had caused a family row Rosie had never forgotten when she'd begged to be allowed to take one home. Olivia, her mother, had said yes, but her father had said no, and however much Rosie had cried and begged, nothing would make him change his mind.

Rosie remembered shouting at him through a blur of tears. 'I hate you. When I'm grown up I'm going to live in the country and have six dogs.'

Of course it had never happened – living in the country or the six dogs. Maybe the dog turning up unexpectedly was some sort of sign? Could she keep her?

Gently, Rosie examined the dog's ears. Every French dog was supposed to have a number tattooed in their ear. No tattoo. Which probably also meant no micro ID chip, either. Rosie sighed. The lack of both would mean the paperwork would be immense and would probably mean the dog went straight to 'death row' at the local dog pound. No way could Rosie bear the thought of that.

There was only one thing for it. Tonight she'd take the dog home with her and, if nobody claimed her in the next few days, she'd keep her – and christen her Lucky. With the French being so laissez-faire about dogs in restaurants it was unlikely to be a problem.

Chapter Seven

'Why are you looking at houses, Mummy?'

Erica jumped. She'd left Cammie engrossed in her beach project at the kitchen table while she'd sneaked into the sitting room to look at some houses on the Internet. No time to close the laptop now.

'GeeGee was telling me about some of the lovely houses she gets to sell and I thought I'd take a look,' Erica said evasively.

'You'd have to be a princess to live in that one,' Cammie said, pointing to the decorative turrets on the house Erica was looking at. 'Like Rapunzel. Does GeeGee know a princess?' she asked, her eyes opened wide in wonder as she looked at Erica.

Erica laughed. 'I don't think so but you never know.' Would this be a good moment to talk about selling this house? She'd planned to introduce the subject casually one afternoon when they were walking back from school. Drop it into the conversation and wait for Cammie's reaction. Now she felt unprepared and caught out.

'If we didn't live here, what kind of house would you like to live in?' she said casually, thinking she might as well make the best of the opportunity and see how Cammie reacted.

'One like Madeleine's,' Cammie said instantly. 'With a big garden so I could have a dog.'

Erica pursed her lips and blew a soft whistle. Given that Madeleine's parents lived in a belle époque villa in one of the most desirable areas of town, her daughter had good taste. And why the sudden desire for a dog?

'A house like that would be too expensive for us but lots of villas have nice gardens – even swimming pools. How about…?' She scrolled quickly through a couple of pages. 'Something like this?'

Cammie shook her head. 'It's not very pretty.'

Erica clicked on another page and started to scroll through. Cammie stopped her when she reached a typical Provençal villa with a terracotta roof, olive-green shutters and a vibrant bougainvillea clambering over the walls.

'That's pretty.'

'You like that one?'

Cammie nodded.

Reading the description and seeing the price, Erica took a deep breath and said, 'We could sell this house and buy that one. Would you like that?'

'Could I have a dog if we lived there?'

'Possibly,' Erica said as her phone rang. Amelia, her mother-in-law, making her weekly 'I'm not checking up on you, I'm just keeping you in the loop with family news from up here' telephone call. This time it was a bit more. Amelia was planning a weekend visit next month.

'That's great,' Erica said. 'Already looking forward to it.' She and Amelia had got on from the moment Pascal had introduced them. Both had been equally heartbroken when he died.

'Is there any chance of you and Cammie coming up here for a visit before?' Amelia said.

Erica sighed. Amelia asked the same question every time she phoned, and every time Erica shied away from telling her the truth. She couldn't face it yet. The thought of being in Pascal's family home without him made her want to cry.

She tried to soften her latest refusal: 'I'm busy getting the shop ready for the summer at the moment.'

Amelia didn't push her, saying simply, 'I'll see you both in a couple of weeks then. Take care.'

'You, too. Give our love to everyone up there,' Erica said, ending the call, knowing she'd hurt Amelia with yet another refusal.

Slipping the phone into her pocket she turned back to Cammie. 'So, shall we ask GeeGee if she can find us a new house?'

Cammie looked thoughtful, before saying slowly, 'Yes. But we will take Daddy's things with us, won't we?'

* * *

GeeGee poured herself a bowl of muesli, added a generous dollop of fromage frais, and mixed it all into a glutinous mess before slicing the last five strawberries onto the top. A delicious supper. It would fill her up and then she could have a glass of rosé later.

Bowl in hand she opened the studio's French doors and stepped out onto the minuscule balcony – so tiny, one wrought-iron chair almost filled it, leaving no room for a table, but it was a good place to sit and relax at the end of the day.

A small ginger-and-white kitten was curled up on the chair. 'Hello, Trouble,' GeeGee said. 'You here again? Your real home next door too noisy with all those children around?'

The kitten simply stretched its legs before curling up in a ball again, closing its eyes and ignoring her. GeeGee didn't have the heart to disturb it so stayed standing to eat her supper.

There was a tantalising glimpse of the sea through the trees and shrubs that covered the acre of grounds that surrounded the villa. Grounds that she had no access to; grounds she was never invited to walk around. But nobody could stop her enjoying the smell of the night-scented jasmine that mingled with the lavender drifting on the air up towards her and she sniffed appreciatively.

Erica was always telling her there were nicer studios out there – with nicer landlords, too – but this location was perfect, giving her the solitude she'd craved when Jay had left. The fact that none of the wealthy neighbours were interested in making her acquaintance was an added bonus. Something that would have infuriated Jay. He did like to mix with what he called 'the right set'.

Since Jay had gone and she'd moved here, coming home, closing the door and losing herself in her own space had been wonderful. Nobody to hear her crying.

Last year, when he'd upped and left with practically no warning, she'd been devastated. Her home and boyfriend both gone in a single stroke. There was no way she could afford to stay in their apartment.

In those first dark, lonely weeks she'd read and reread his infrequent emails, looking for any sign that he was missing her. That he'd made a mistake leaving. That he was coming back. Mostly, though, he said he had to find himself.

Gradually, as his emails became full of news about people she didn't know, and waxed lyrical about both his work and social life in London, GeeGee started to skim-read and then stopped automatically replying to them. She couldn't bring herself to tell him to stop writing to her; she just hoped her silence would give him the message.

Over the past couple of months the emails had been more subdued. Almost as though he was tiring of his new life. Which, knowing Jay's low boredom threshold, wouldn't surprise GeeGee at all.

Today's email had been shorter than usual. Maybe he'd noticed she wasn't replying to every one he sent. There was no point. He wasn't coming back. The relationship was clearly over – time to move on. It wasn't as if Jay had been the love of her life. Working together, they'd simply drifted into a relationship.

Absently GeeGee spooned the last of the muesli mixture into her mouth. She was on her own now. A state of affairs she was beginning to enjoy, even feel happy about. Time to begin making plans for herself.

Tomorrow there would be some money in the bank when the sale of a small villa in Cannes La Bocca completed and her commission was paid. Mentally she ticked off the bills waiting to be paid: a month's rent on the studio; a quarter's desk rent to Hugo; a month's car-lease payment – plus petrol in the tank.

She'd need to do a supermarket shop, too, see if the English hairdresser's in Antibes could fit her in... stop! It wasn't that much commission. Anything else she wanted, needed, would have to wait for the next commission payday which, fingers crossed, was due in about a fortnight if the notaire was on the ball. And then Dan's purchase of apartment 4c would be the next in about six weeks.

Ah, Dan. He was so... so nice. An overworked word but one that described him perfectly. She'd seen him again briefly when he'd come into the office to sign the first of the official papers and she'd been struck by his old-fashioned manners and courtesy. Before leaving the office he'd thanked her profusely for her help and asked if he could buy her a coffee.

Smiling, she'd agreed and had been reaching for her tote when his mobile had rung.

'GeeGee, I'm sorry, I'm wanted back onboard. We'll have to do coffee another time. Completion day maybe?' And he was gone. Now things were in the hands of the notaire there would be no need for him to contact her again; the notaire would answer all his questions.

Music and sounds of laughter from the grand villa on the corner of the road drifted on the air. The new owners had moved in then. Russian, Hugo had said when he'd gleefully told her he'd made the sale. A sale he'd virtually snatched from under her nose and for which she had yet to forgive him. The commission on that property alone would have set her up for the summer.

The buzz of the bell made her jump. Nobody ever visited her here, not even Erica.

'Evening, babe,' sleazy Stan, her landlord, said as she opened the door. 'Beginning to think I'd have to use my master key.'

'I hope that's a joke,' GeeGee said.

'You'll never know will you, doll?'

GeeGee gritted her teeth. No way was she going to let him rile her tonight. 'You bought my new lease for me to sign?'

'Nope. There isn't one. Don't know why you thought there would be. Studio's a winter let only. Always has been. You've had an extra month as it is.'

Dumbly, GeeGee stared at him. She'd gone through that lease several times. It had been a standard six-month renewable tenancy agreement. Nowhere had it said anything about it being a winter let.

She'd wanted a year's lease but Stan had said take it or leave it. Desperate at the time, she'd signed. She'd been stupid enough to believe that renewing every six months would be automatic. Should have realised what the scumbag was up to.

'But you have to give me a new lease.'

Stan shook his head. 'No, I don't. I've got holidaymakers coming in here soon. You can come back in October if you want but I want you out of here by the end of next week. And make sure you take that cat with you.'

GeeGee didn't have the energy to say the cat wasn't hers. What the hell was she supposed to do now? Finding another place needed money for a deposit, rent in advance, etc. Money she didn't have.

Chapter Eight

In the lull between closing the restaurant after lunch and reopening for dinner, Rosie sat at one of the tables with her laptop, planning to try and catch up with some of the restaurant paperwork – being French, it was breeding at an alarming rate. Lucky lay across her feet sleeping. Nobody had come looking for the dog and she'd shown no inclination to wander off. Stretching her hand down to fondle her ears, Rosie whispered, 'I guess it's you and me from now on.'

Rosie smiled to herself as she heard the Café Fleur advertisement play on Riviera Radio. Fingers crossed it was worth it and would bring more people down to the beach. She must try to remember to ask people where they'd heard about the Café Fleur when they booked. See if the ad was worth the money.

At six o'clock Rosie left Tansy preparing a tomato-and-mozzarella salad and went through to the restaurant to make sure everything was in order 'front of house' for the evening. She enjoyed this side of things – meeting and greeting her customers. After years of working in a galley hidden from view onboard the yachts, it was a welcome change.

Antoine's table for two had been joined by another three bookings. She and Tansy would manage just fine – the team were used to cooking and serving dinner for up to sixteen guests on *A Sure Thing*. They'd even cope if there were some unexpected customers off the beach. Though how she'd cope if Charlie came with Antoine she refused to even contemplate.

As she lit some table candles, Rosie glanced out through the windows. Shame it was still too cold to eat out on the terrace in the evenings. She was looking forward to the long summer evenings when the place would be full of people enjoying her food. Maybe next year she'd be able to invest in some of those outdoor gas heaters.

Rosie glanced at her watch. Antoine was late. Charlie's fault? He was a terrible time-keeper. When Antoine did finally arrive, accompanied by a fellow yacht skipper, Rosie felt the tension leaving her body and succumbed happily to a bearlike hug. No Charlie to spoil the evening.

By the time Antoine had been out to the kitchen to see Tansy and decided they all needed glasses of champagne, the guests for the other tables had arrived. For the next hour or two things were busy and Rosie had very little chance to talk to Antoine.

As she handed him his favourite dessert, he said, 'James not working tonight?'

'I can't afford him every day. Wish I could,' Rosie said. 'I meant to thank-you, too, for sending him my way.'

Antoine shook his head. 'Not me.'

'But James told me what you said about me.'

'He asked my opinion, that's all.' Antoine looked at his dacquoise. 'I wish you'd tell our new chef how to make this. Her dessert dishes aren't a patch on yours. How am I going to survive next week's trip to Sardinia without a decent dessert?'

'You're off to Sardinia?' Rosie asked, delighted to know Charlie wouldn't be around for a few weeks. No chance of him popping uninvited into the Café Fleur.

'William wants Charlie to spend a couple of days over there with him. He reckons there's a good business opportunity there.' Antoine glanced at Rosie. 'Talking of Charlie – he sends his love.'

'Does he?' Rosie said. 'That's nice.' A sudden thought struck her. 'He knows about this place? That you're here tonight? Oh, Antoine, you promised.'

Antoine held his hands up in defence. 'I didn't tell him. But hell, Rosie, out of season it's like a village down here. Everyone knows what everyone else is up to. And you've advertised on the radio. You can't seriously have expected him not to put two and two together.'

Rosie sighed. 'I suppose not. At least he'll be out of the way for a few weeks in Sardinia.'

***

Busy serving customers out on the terrace Friday lunchtime, Rosie smiled in welcome as Erica and Cammie arrived. She'd liked Erica the moment GeeGee had introduced them, sensing a kindred spirit behind Erica's quiet demeanour. Erica had been back to the beach several times since then, both with and without Cammie, and was turning into a real friend rather than just a customer.

'Hello, you two,' Rosie said. 'You're just in time for the last table. Not sure why we're quite so busy today. I think people must have the weekend feeling early.' She quickly wrote down their lunch order and returned to the kitchen.

Ten minutes later, taking Erica and Cammie's croque monsieurs out to them, Rosie smiled. Cammie was playing with Lucky and squealing with delight.

'I'll be pestered even more now to get a dog,' Erica said. 'Still it's good to see Cammie laughing.'

'I haven't seen GeeGee for a few days,' Rosie said, stopping briefly to chat. 'Do you know if she's all right?'

'I expect she's busy with clients,' Erica said. 'The property market usually picks up as the summer gets underway.'

'There's definitely more people around this week,' Rosie said. 'Enjoy your lunch.' And she made her way back to the kitchen.

When James stopped by for a coffee, Rosie asked him to stay and work for a couple of hours and also to work at the weekend. 'I'll even pay you this time,' she promised.

Later that day, an exhausted Rosie stroked Lucky, thoughtfully. Would she make a guard dog? There had been a couple of dodgy-looking young men buying stuff from the takeaway this morning – portion of chips each, then ten minutes later one would come for a drink, followed in five minutes by the second one. When they returned for a third time for one flapjack, Rosie, remembering Seb's mention of last season's drug bust, began to seriously wonder if they were casing the place. Having a dog around might be a good idea.

Lucky had been no trouble during the day; in fact, she'd shown every sign of settling in, wagging her tail as she greeted customers on the terrace, as well as playing happily with Cammie and any other child who happened to be around.

Saturday evening there were several reservations and even some casual passing-by trade. When the last couple walked in at half past nine, Rosie knew it was going to be a late night. It was James who stayed to help Rosie clear up when Tansy left to go clubbing with Rob at nearly midnight.

'Are you ready to party next door, then?' James said.

Rosie shook her head. 'I'm way too tired. If you want the invite, you take it.'

'I've got one of my own, thanks,' James said. 'My new stepbrother is a friend of Seb and wangled me one.' He shrugged his shoulders into his denim jacket. 'D'you want me to stay while you lock up?'

'No, you get off. And thanks for your help. See you in the morning,' Rosie said.

As James left, a blast of music drifted over in the air from the hotel. The party was clearly going strong. Lucky was curled up outside on the terrace and thumped her tail as she saw Rosie before getting up and wandering over to her.

'You ready for supper?' she said, bending down to gently stroke the dog.

Lucky lifted her head from the bowl of minced meat that Rosie had put down for her on the kitchen floor then growled as there was a knock on the door before Seb entered.

Tonight, dressed in smart black jeans and a crisp white shirt, a single woven leather bracelet on his right wrist, he was less of a drifter, more of a suave party animal. Even his hair had been subdued into behaving.

'Nice dog. Is she yours?'

'Yes. She turned up a couple of days ago and nobody seems to want her, so I'm keeping her. I've always wanted a dog. I've called her Lucky,' she said, glancing at Seb. 'I'm hoping she'll be my good-luck mascot as well as a deterrent.'

Seb raised his eyebrows.

'There were a couple of scruffy men – boys, really – hanging around earlier,' Rosie said. 'Probably perfectly innocent but...' She shrugged. 'Anyway, what are you doing here? Shouldn't you be at your party?'

'I've come to collect you. Your champagne awaits.'

'Seb, I'm sorry but I've had a busy evening. I'm tired – besides I'm not dressed for a posh party.' She glanced down at her smart, but plain, little black dress.

'You look fine to me,' Seb said. 'Maybe comb your hair. Bit of lipstick. Come on, Rosie. Just the one glass. There are a few people over there who could be potential customers. Come and do a bit of networking.'

Rosie looked at him dubiously. 'You keep telling me we're aiming for different parts of the market.'

'They might want to slum it one evening,' Seb said.

Rosie gasped at his cheek before seeing a smile twitch his lips and realising he was joking. A bad joke but a joke nevertheless. Maybe she should go. He had, after all, taken the trouble to come and find her. It was just a drink with a neighbour. Be churlish not to go.

'Okay. One glass,' Rosie said. 'Then I'm really going home to bed. It's been a long week.'

'You can bring Lucky if you want,' Seb said.

'No, I'm not sure how she'll behave,' Rosie said. 'She can stay on her blanket in the restaurant. I'll come back for her after I've had that glass of champagne.'

The party was in the conservatory Rosie had spied from the studio room upstairs and was packed to overflowing. Sipping the champagne Seb had poured for her while he went to fetch some nibbles, she looked around.

Seb was obviously well connected. There were a few, if not exactly famous, then certainly well-known,

Riviera faces and a couple of minor A-list celebrities she recognised. And GeeGee was here, too, Rosie was pleased to see. She raised her glass in her direction when she saw her glance across, but before she could make her way over to her, James appeared at her side.

'Seb changed your mind then?'

Rosie nodded. 'Just having a quick glass. So, which is your stepbrother out of this crowd?'

'He's... over there,' James said, turning to look around the room. 'You should recognise him.'

'Why should I?' Rosie said as she followed his gaze. 'Oh...'

'How long has he been your stepbrother?'

'My mum married his dad a month ago. Oh, he's seen us. He's coming over.'

'Rosie. How lovely to see you. I do miss not having you onboard. How's the Café Fleur going?' And Charlie leant forward to kiss her cheek. He sighed as Rosie averted her face and he kissed air.

'What are you doing here? You're supposed to be on your way to Sardinia.'

'We're leaving at the crack of dawn Monday. I hope James is behaving himself and being useful?'

Rosie stared at Charlie as realisation dawned. 'You sent him, didn't you? To spy on me!'

'To help, Rosie. To help.'

Furious, Rosie turned to James. 'You're fired! I'm leaving. Goodbye.'

Rosie was still fuming when she got into bed that night. As far as she was concerned, sending James to spy on her was a step too far even for Charlie the control freak. Furious didn't start to describe her feelings that, after all these years, he expected her to like having him back in her life.

If she'd had any sense she'd have walked off *A Sure Thing* the moment she'd heard the name of the new owners fourteen months ago. Unfortunately, there'd still been a year of her contract to go and the agency had refused to release her even when she'd begged them to let her go. So she'd thought of the money and prepared to be a good employee until she could legitimately take her money and run.

She'd been busy preparing a lobster for dinner the first time Charlie had strolled into the galley and asked for another bottle of champagne to be sent up to the aft deck. If it hadn't been such a standstill moment, Rosie would have laughed out loud at the look on his face when he saw her. As it was she just said, 'Right away, sir.'

She'd genuinely believed him when he'd sworn he didn't know she was the chef onboard until the moment he walked into the galley. When he learnt that she'd known the name of the new owner and had chosen to stay on, he decided it was because she wanted to see him again.

'Believe me, Charlie, I'd have left if I could. I had no choice – the agency insisted I honour my contract. But don't worry – I have no intention of renewing it. Once it finishes, I'm off.' Even as she'd said the words she could see he didn't believe her.

The more Rosie protested, the more determined he became that their youthful relationship should be revived and given another chance. Rosie was equally determined against it. So, during the season she made sure she was always too busy to take more than the occasional day off and then she made sure there was no chance of Charlie being around, insisting they spend it together.

Out of season, when Rosie lived ashore, it had been more difficult to keep her life separate from Charlie's. She had hoped the evening in The Recluse, when they'd had what she'd hoped would be the row to end all rows, would bring Charlie to his senses. Make him give up and go find himself a proper girlfriend.

No such luck. The moment he heard the agency were sending a replacement chef for William to interview, he redoubled his efforts to try and stop her. Telling him 'no' and leaving the yacht had failed to get the message across that she could never forgive him for letting her down all those years ago in college. He didn't seem to understand how his action all those years ago had changed the course of her life.

Turning out the bedside light, Rosie sighed. How the hell was she going to get him to butt out of her life once and for all?

Chapter Nine

Erica took her cup of coffee up to the roof terrace of the townhouse she and Pascal had bought before they were married. Early Sunday morning and the remains of a light mist hanging over the town were giving way to the sun.

She and Pascal had loved to sit up here together in the evening, sipping a glass of wine, happy to be spending time with each other. She'd barely been up here recently. She'd got used to the rest of the house feeling empty and lonely without Pascal around but the roof terrace had been a special place. Up here the memories were still raw. Even now, all these months later, she had to fight back the tears.

Facing inland away from the coast, the terrace had a view out over red-roofed villas and their swimming pools, stretching away in the distance to the boundaries of the town before merging into the beginning of the hinterland Provençal countryside. Pascal had fixed a low trellis around the three walls and between them they'd created a small, perfumed oasis where the two of them had relaxed and entertained friends.

Looking at the trellis now, with its rampant passion flower and honeysuckle tangled together, Erica realised how much she'd neglected things up here. Her beloved Italian glazed pots, too, were full of weeds strangling the spring flowers that had poked their way through.

Pulling a few weeds out from under the honeysuckle, Erica decided she and Cammie would do some pruning and tidy things up later. Get ready for eating al fresco in summer – their first proper summer without Pascal.

Besides, if she was serious about selling the house, it would need sprucing up. This morning, though, she'd promised Cammie they'd go to the *vide grenier* being held in the huge car park on the edge of the beach.

Erica smiled to herself. Cammie was as much a magpie for 'treasure' as she herself was and was already developing a good eye for what was rubbish and what was good in among all the tat that was always on offer.

As Erica pulled weeds out of the pot containing her favourite rose, the church bell tolling for eight o'clock Mass broke into her thoughts. Cammie's Sunday morning alarm. Time to go back downstairs and prepare for the day and the long walk to the *vide grenier*. Erica sighed.

Ever since the accident, Cammie had refused to get in a car; had screamed and shaken violently on the couple of occasions Erica had tried to force the issue.

All these months later and they were still either walking or catching the train or bus to wherever they needed to go, with Cammie showing no sign of losing her phobia over cars. This morning, with no convenient train or bus going in the right direction, walking was the only option.

An hour later they set off, Cammie pulling the empty wheely shopping bag behind her and Erica lost in her thoughts about the past and what the future would bring them. By the time they reached the *vide grenier* it was in full swing with people jostling around the hundred or so stalls.

'Right, young lady, you know the drill. You stick close to me and no wandering off,' Erica said. 'But in case we do get separated, you don't talk to strangers and you come and stand by the entrance here and wait. Understood?' Erica looked at Cammie intently as she waited for her answer.

Cammie nodded. 'I promise. I won't wander.'

Erica took charge of the shopping trolley and together they began to explore the various rows with their laden tables. Buying bits and pieces here and there, Erica carefully placed their purchases in the bag before they stopped in front of a stall devoted to art-nouveau collectibles.

So much stuff here that would be good in the shop, but Erica was drawn to a magnificent, stained, leaded-glass table lamp. Never mind about putting it in the shop, she'd love it for herself. Too big and precious to be put in the shopping bag, it was also too cumbersome for her to carry all the way home. She glanced at the woman behind the stall. 'Any chance you could deliver this for me later today?'

The woman shook her head. 'No can do, sorry. We've got a tight schedule today. We've got to get down to Saint-Tropez for an evening sale when we leave here.'

Erica turned away and caught Cammie by the hand. 'Fancy getting a taxi home later?' She knew the answer before she asked the question really.

The quick withdrawal of her hand and the shuttered look that came down over Cammie's face confirmed it.

'Never mind,' Erica said quickly. 'It doesn't matter. Come on, let's explore the next row.'

To her relief, Cammie for once was easily distracted and was soon engrossed in looking at a table of children's books and toys and surplus ornaments –

including a foot-high pottery lighthouse the base of which was badly chipped. When Erica pointed this out, Cammie said, 'It doesn't matter because it's not "treasure". I just want it for my beach project.'

'Wasting your pocket money again, Cammie?' a voice behind them said, and Erica turned to see GeeGee standing there, a big grin on her face as she gave Erica a hug.

'You're thinner than ever,' Erica said now as she returned the hug. Rosie mentioning she hadn't seen GeeGee for a few days should have rung alarm bells in her mind. She knew GeeGee skipped meals when commissions dried up and money was tight. 'How's things?'

GeeGee shrugged. 'Things are so-so.'

'Want to come back with us for lunch?' Erica said. 'And before you say, "No," I could do with talking to you.'

'Lunch would be great.'

'Actually,' Erica said as a sudden thought struck her. 'There's something else, too. Have you got your car here?'

'Yes.'

'Brilliant. Fancy an ice cream?' And Erica led the way to the picnic area and the catering van. She handed the shopping basket over to GeeGee before giving her a ten-euro note. 'You two have whatever you want and wait here. I'll be back.'

Finding the stand with the tiffany lamp took Erica some time, and when she did finally find it she had to wait for the woman to finish serving an elderly man who wanted to discuss the provenance of a glass plate he was buying. Erica crossed her fingers while she waited, hoping he wouldn't want the lamp as well. He didn't. Fifteen minutes later, the lamp was wrapped in protective bubble wrap and Erica was making her way carefully back to Cammie and GeeGee.

'You can take everything back to the house in your car while Cammie and I walk back, okay?' she asked. 'I'll pick up a roasted chicken in the market.'

'Don't forget the sautéed potatoes,' GeeGee said, knowing Cammie loved them but Erica rarely bought them.

'Here's the house key. There's a bottle of rosé in the fridge. Help yourself. I'll see you in a bit.'

Chapter Ten

Sunday morning, when Tansy arrived for work, Rosie was tired and grumpy having tossed and turned more than she'd slept.

'James not in yet?' Tansy asked.

'Not coming in.'

'Why?'

'I fired him. Those carrots need peeling,' Rosie said, slamming the oven door closed on the rib of beef.

'I'm not doing another thing until you tell me what's happened.'

Rosie sighed. 'I went to Seb's party last night. Charlie was there.'

'How is he?' Tansy had a soft spot for Charlie and had never understood Rosie's reluctance to get involved with him again.

'Antoine forgot to tell us that Charlie's dad, William, got married recently. It turns out that Charlie is James's newly acquired stepbrother. He sent James to spy on me – so I fired him. End of.'

'Oh. But James is so good. Just what we needed.'

Rosie shrugged. 'I can't really afford him at the moment anyway. We'll find someone else for later in the season. Now, can we please get on with preparing Sunday lunch?'

Tansy shrugged. 'Okay.'

Rosie left her to it and went through to the restaurant to open up and set the tables ready for customers. Keeping busy kept Charlie out of her thoughts. She placed the reserved tags on the five tables already booked for a total of fifteen people. Not bad for a Sunday so early in the season. People were out and about on the beach, too, so hopefully there'd be some passing trade.

Three hours later, when a tired but happy Rosie was saying goodbye to the last of her lunchtime customers and about to close the door, Charlie walked in and sat at one of the window tables.

'Hi again, Rosie.'

'What d'you want?'

'Sunday lunch, of course. And don't say I'm too late.' This as Rosie glanced at her watch. 'I know last orders are at two and it's only ten to.' He picked up the menu.

'I'll have the asparagus soup followed by the beef. Oh, and tell Tansy the usual, easy on the veg but the more roasties the better.'

Wordlessly Rosie turned and marched away.

'And open a bottle of decent red for me, would you, please?' Charlie called out after her. 'And bring a glass for yourself.'

'One soup, one beef, heavy on the roasties, lose the veg,' she said to Tansy through gritted teeth.

Tansy glanced up from the soup she was pouring into a fresh bowl ready for the fridge. 'Charlie's here?'

'Yep, and he wants me to open a decent red for him,' Rosie replied, standing in front of the wine rack. 'He wants decent – I'll give him decent.' And she opened the most expensive Château Margaux currently on her wine list.

She ignored the request to take another glass for herself. No way was she going to have a drink with him. Carefully, she poured a taster into Charlie's wine glass and waited for him to take a sip.

'Nice. Can I afford it?'

'Sure you can.'

'Where's your glass?'

'I don't drink with the customers.'

'I don't see any customers,' Charlie said, looking around the empty restaurant. 'Only me, and I reckon I rate higher than a mere customer anyway.'

Tansy appeared with Charlie's soup and a basket of bread rolls. 'Hi, Charlie. Good to see you.'

Rosie glared at her.

'Thanks for sending Jamie our way. Can you now please persuade Rosie to unsack him? I could do with some help around here and he was good,' Tansy said, ignoring Rosie.

'I'll fire *you*, too, if you don't stop interfering,' Rosie threatened. 'Kitchen?'

'You can't fire me – you need me too much. Okay, I'm going...' And Tansy disappeared back into the kitchen.

'I am not having one of your relatives spying on me in my own kitchen,' Rosie said. 'Talking of relatives – tell your dad congratulations from me. I hope he's very happy.' She liked William and was pleased he'd met someone new. She knew he'd been lonely since Charlie's mum died a couple of years ago.

'I'll pass the message on. But he'll be down soon and you can tell him yourself. He's sure to drop in for lunch – if you're still in business then.' Charlie paused. 'I didn't send James purely to spy on you. He does genuinely need the experience and I thought you could do with someone keen to learn from you. He's really upset you don't want him any more.'

'He should have told me the truth then... What d'you mean, – if I'm still in business next month?' Rosie demanded.

Charlie shrugged. 'Oh, come on, Rosie. You know how prejudiced the French are about "les rosbifs" and their cooking skills. They're not going to be rushing to support an Englishwoman. I wish you'd talked to me before you took on this place. I could have saved you a lot of money.'

'Well, I'll just have to be the exception to that rule, won't I?' Rosie said. 'My cooking will get them in. And if the French don't come, the English will.'

'The French don't care who cooks their lunchtime frites for them, but at dinner they want the whole gourmet experience, which they believe only a Frenchman can give. Nobody English in their right mind opens a restaurant in France – not without employing a French chef, anyway.'

'I'll get the staff to call me Fleur and start speaking with a French accent then, shall I? You could be more supportive,' she added quietly. 'You know this is my dream. What I've been working towards all these years and the reason I stayed working on the boats for the last five years. Besides, I'm thirty-five this year, so if I don't do it now...' She shrugged.

'Cooking on the yachts is a totally different ballgame, Rosie. Sorry, but I just don't see this place working. I know you're a good cook but...' Charlie said. 'But with Seb Groc right next door...' He shook his head.

'Different markets,' Rosie said. 'Seb and I have already discussed it. Finished your soup? I'll get your main course.' And she snatched the bowl away the instant Charlie replaced his spoon in the empty dish.

'Main course ready? Good. You take it out,' she told Tansy. 'Make sure he's got everything he needs – and don't talk about me. I'll start the clearing up in here.'

Rosie pulled the lever that sent the large, old-fashioned dishwashing machine whirling into action down with a bang.

'Temper. Temper. It won't last the season treated like that,' Tansy said, picking up the roasties and the veg in the serving dishes to accompany Charlie's beef.

'Here, you've forgotten his favourite horseradish sauce,' Rosie said, thrusting the pot towards Tansy.

Surreptitiously, Rosie watched the pair of them through the small hatchway between the kitchen and the bar area, envying the way they could still laugh and joke together like she had in another life – before everything had changed between her and Charlie.

Rosie turned away and vigorously set to cleaning the roasting tin until it was pristine and the ends of her fingers could take no more from the sharp shrouds of the shredded-steel wool. Tansy came back as she rinsed the tin and left it to dry on the draining board.

'No prizes for guessing what Charlie wants for dessert,' Tansy said. 'And please, will you join him for coffee?'

Silently Rosie opened the fridge and took out a tiramisu – Charlie's absolute favourite dessert.

'I let Lucky in, by the way. Like a true female she made a beeline for Charlie and is now worshipping at his feet,' Tansy said. 'You going to take this out to him?'

Rosie nodded. 'Okay.' She couldn't hide in the kitchen for ever, and now Charlie had had his say about the Café Fleur, maybe they could at least be civil to each other.

'Have I ever told you, you make the best tiramisu?' Charlie said.

'Once or twice,' Rosie said, determined to keep the conversation on an even keel.

'I think I might have overreacted last night,' she said, bending down to stroke Lucky. 'Tell James if he wants to come back – ten o'clock Tuesday morning.'

'Will do,' Charlie said as he spooned the last vestiges of cream from the bowl. 'Have you still got that beaten-up mini you call a car?'

Surprised by the question, Rosie shook her head. 'No.' The car had gone for a few hundred euros to add to her pot of money for the Café Fleur. 'I figured I could live without one for a while. Working here seven days a week in summer, I'm not going to be going anywhere.' She was blowed if she was going to tell Charlie the truth – that she couldn't afford a car until the restaurant was a success.

His eyes narrowed. 'How about getting home at night?'

'I walk.'

'I don't like the thought of that.'

'I've got Lucky now,' Rosie said. 'And it's not far.'

'Well, that's something, I suppose, but it's a bloody good fifteen-minute walk,' Charlie said. 'I'd prefer it if you took a taxi.'

'And I'd prefer it if you minded your own business. How I get home is nothing to do with you – besides, it's not fifteen minutes away. It's five. I'll get your bill,' Rosie said, forgetting that Charlie was unaware of the fact that she'd moved – another economic necessity. The rent for the apartment in one of the new gated blocks overlooking the sea had been an expensive luxury even when she was working on *A Sure Thing*.

To Rosie's relief, Charlie paid his bill, included a generous tip, and kissed Tansy goodbye. 'Any time you want a job, you know what to do,' he told her. 'Ciao. I'll be seeing you both.'

Rosie, safe behind the bar and out of Charlie's kissing reach, muttered 'Ciao' and held her breath until the door closed behind him.

'Thank God he's going to Sardinia tomorrow out of the way,' she said. 'Right, that's the door locked. I've had enough for today.'

She glanced at Tansy. 'I did ask him to tell James he could come back, if he wants to. I can't believe he said that to you about wanting a job. Cheek. He seems to think this place is doomed because I'm English.'

'He's worried about you losing all your money, that's all,' Tansy said.

'So am I – that's why I intend to work flat out to make sure this place is a success,' Rosie said. 'Here's the tip he left for you.'

'Half each?' Tansy said.

Rosie shook her head. 'No, you take it. I'm sure Charlie meant it for you, anyway.'

'Thanks – generous as ever,' Tansy said, taking the euros. 'Right, I'll see you on Tuesday morning, bright and early. Don't work too hard tomorrow. Remember it's supposed to be your day off as well. If nothing else, take Lucky-dog for a walk.'

***

Rosie pottered around after Tansy left, tidying up and putting some leftover food in her basket to take home. The bottle of wine she'd opened for Charlie was still half full, so she stuck the cork back in and put that in her basket, too. She'd enjoy a glass tonight while she did the week's accounts and worked on her laptop.

'Right, Lucky, time to go home,' she said, looping a piece of thin rope around the dog's neck. 'Tomorrow we'll buy you a collar and a proper lead but this will have to do again for now.'

Satisfied the door was securely locked and the security grill down, Rosie turned to walk through the car park and out onto the main road, where she came face to face with Charlie.

As the basket was taken out of her hand and he fell into step alongside her, Rosie said, 'What d'you think you're doing?'

'Seeing you get home safely.'

'It's not dark, it's Sunday afternoon and I don't need an escort.'

'Maybe not, but I want to see where you're living now.'

Ah, so he *had* picked up on her 'five minutes away' remark.

'Well, we turn left here and it's at the end of this street. The converted villa. See, literally five minutes.'

'You going to ask me in for a glass of my wine?' Charlie asked, looking at the basket.

'N... oh, all right. I'm on the second floor.' And Rosie pressed her code into the pad at the side of the ornate front door. Damn, why had she just agreed to that? Guilt, probably. He'd paid for the wine so was entitled to drink more than just the one glass he'd had at lunch.

Charlie followed her up the marble staircase. 'Sad to see these old places converted like this really. Imagine what they must have been like in their heyday.'

'At least this way more people get to live in and enjoy them,' Rosie said, unlocking her own door.

She released Lucky from her makeshift lead and the dog made straight for the end of the sofa she'd taken as her own.

Charlie placed the basket on the kitchen counter. 'Glasses?'

Rosie indicated the glass-fronted cupboard. 'I'll be back in a moment.'

From her perch on the loo, Rosie studied the small bathroom. The linen basket, filled with a week's worth of washing, overflowed onto the floor and the paper holder was empty. Feverishly, Rosie stuffed the clothes deep into the basket and pressed the lid on, slid the last roll of loo paper onto the holder and swished water around the sink. No time to do more. With a bit of luck, Charlie wouldn't need to come in here, anyway. Once he'd had his glass of wine, he was out the door.

'I've put the other stuff in the fridge for you,' Charlie said, handing her a glass of wine. 'Cheers. You sure you're eating enough? Fridge is practically empty.'

'Cheers. I don't eat here much,' Rosie said. 'No point. So, what's this business proposition that's taking you to Sardinia?' Not that she wanted to talk to Charlie; she wanted him gone, but they had to talk about something over their wine.

'Agrotourism.' Charlie shrugged. 'I suspect it's going to be a waste of time but Dad wants me to investigate the possibilities.'

William was the head of an environmentally 'green' company with interests in property and farming. Charlie was his right-hand man and would eventually take over. Rosie knew that both father and son were committed to trying to promote a 'Fair Trade' policy.

'Will you spend the day with me when I get back?' Charlie asked. 'For old times' sake?'

Rosie shook her head. 'No, I can't. The season is just starting and I'm going to be busy. Besides, our "old times" are just that. In the past. If William hadn't bought *A Sure Thing* we'd never have met up again. We move in totally different circles these days.'

'I'd be more than happy to move in yours,' Charlie said.

'Well, I wouldn't be happy in yours.' Rosie stared at him.

Charlie drained his glass. 'When I get back, I promise you I'm going to do everything possible to make you change your mind.'

'Back off, Charlie. Go meet someone else.'

'There is no one else, Rosie. I—' The ring of his mobile interrupted him. He glanced at the caller ID. 'Excuse me, I have to answer this. Hi, Sarah. How's things?'

Rosie stroked Lucky as she tried not to eavesdrop on Charlie's conversation, which was impossible. And just who was Sarah?

'What? Okay, I'm on my way. I'll be there as soon as I can.' He snapped his phone shut and turned to Rosie, his face white.

'Sorry, Rosie. Emergency. Got to go.'

'Not William, is it?'

'No.'

Before she realised his intention, Charlie leaned in and kissed her. 'You take care. And don't fire James again because I've told him to walk you home after work every night. Ciao.' And he was gone, the door slamming behind him.

Absently, Rosie topped up her glass. Whatever the emergency was, it had at least got Charlie out of the apartment. Getting him out of her life for a second time, though, was proving harder than she'd anticipated.

When would he realise she was serious when she told him she didn't want a relationship with him or any man? She'd learned a long time ago that relationships that worked were few and far between and personally she didn't intend to let one cloud her judgement ever again. Café Fleur was her baby and her life now.

Chapter Eleven

GeeGee sighed contentedly. For once, Sunday had turned out to be the way she always thought Sundays in France should be – but in her case rarely were.

A leisurely lunch around Erica's large kitchen table followed by coming up here to the roof terrace and lazing around for an hour before she'd jumped to her feet. A bit of payback time was needed.

'Come on, let's give this terrace a makeover.'

For the next couple of hours, Erica, Cammie and GeeGee weeded and watered the pots, before sweeping the terracotta tiles and setting up the small, white, cast-iron table and chairs. Erica had found some candles for the lanterns that were now, together with the setting sun, casting a gentle ambience over the place. A perfect place to unwind.

Cammie was tucked up in bed and Erica had gone down to fetch a baguette and the remains of the lunchtime rosé for supper. So far, she hadn't mentioned whatever it was she'd said she wanted to talk about. GeeGee smiled to herself. Knowing Erica, it could have just been a ruse to get her here and feed her. She knew her friend worried about her not eating enough.

GeeGee enjoyed food as much as anyone; it was just that, after paying the rent, the phone bill, her quarter's rent for her desk, putting petrol in the car, etc.,

etc., there was so little left over. And now, on top of everything, she was about to be made homeless.

When her next commission came in she'd treat both Erica and Cammie to... she sighed. Her next commission payment was spoken for even before it arrived. Not to mention the next two, or five. She'd struggle to even afford an extra coffee at Café Fleur for the next few months. Maybe Rosie would let her do the washing-up in exchange for lunch?

Hearing Erica coming back upstairs, GeeGee determinedly pushed all financial worries to the back of her mind. With a bit of luck there would be a flurry of sales in the next couple of days, she'd find an apartment she could afford and all would come miraculously right in her world. Well, she could dream.

'I ought to be thinking of going home,' GeeGee said.

'You don't have to. You can always stay,' Erica said, placing the tray of food on the table between them. 'You know there's always a room here for you.' She glanced across at GeeGee. 'I know everything down here is based on appearance and money rules supreme and your clients are super-impressed when you casually tell them where you live.' She shook her head. 'You might live on the Cap d'Antibes but your actual studio is like your landlord – the pits.'

'But my clients don't know that,' GeeGee said. 'They think I'm uber-successful living in that location. And clients like dealing with successful people.'

'You know, though, that you could get a better place for less money away from the Cap and have enough money for food.' Erica glared at GeeGee. 'I wish you'd move in with me and Cammie.' She handed GeeGee a glass of wine. 'You'd get to eat regularly and I'd be a better landlady than the snake you've currently got.'

'Cheers.' GeeGee hesitated. 'Actually, I might need to take you up on that offer. Stan's given me notice to quit.'

'What?'

'Have to be out next week. There's nothing remotely suitable on the rental side at work – even if I had the money for all the upfront fees, deposit etc. Which I haven't.'

'Why the hell didn't you tell me before?' Erica demanded. 'Right. No argument. You move in here tomorrow.'

'Thanks. I'll try not to get in your way. As soon as I get some money in the bank I'll find another place. I've got a villa in Antibes due to complete soon and an apartment on the coast road that should go through quickly. Just need some more clients to find their forever homes.'

A huge sigh of relief escaped her lips. 'I seriously owe you one,' she said, taking a sip of her wine. 'So, what did you want to talk to me about?'

'Selling this house.'

GeeGee choked on her wine, before turning to look at her. 'Really?'

Erica nodded. 'I want you to put it on the market for me.'

'But...' GeeGee hesitated. 'You sure selling up is the right thing to do? You've made a lot of memories here – for Cammie, too. You and Pascal were so happy here.'

Erica fiddled with her glass. 'That's part of the problem. I still keep expecting him to bound up the stairs looking for me. Everywhere I turn in this house he's there. I'm sure it's the same for Cammie – which in the long term can't be healthy, can it? I so want the rest of her childhood to be happy. Not one clouded with ghosts from the past.'

GeeGee regarded her friend silently and waited.

'I'm not talking about forgetting Pascal – how could I? But living somewhere that isn't associated with family memories in every room must be easier. Up here I can see him wheeling the bar-b-q into position, busy organising an evening with friends.' Erica glanced at GeeGee. 'I'll still have the memories of how happy we were. How perfect life was before the accident.'

'Have you mentioned moving to Cammie?'

Erica pulled a face. 'Sort of. She favours a house like Madeleine's so long as we can take Pascal's things with us. Oh, and she wants a dog if we move! She's slowly coming out of the melancholia she sank into after the huge trauma of Pascal dying. And I don't want to risk that progress so we'll have to take it slowly. We still have this ongoing phobia about cars to deal with, too.' She downed the last of her wine. 'I just feel a new home would give us both a fresh start and hope for the future. No shadowy presence hovering in any room I happen to be in.'

'You want the same area?' GeeGee said.

Erica nodded. 'Cammie's school and, of course, the shop both need to be within walking distance.'

'Not many cheap properties in this area these days,' GeeGee said.

'Pascal's insurance means I don't need ultra cheap,' Erica said. 'I just want somewhere Cammie and I can learn to live and be happy again – oh, and a pool would be nice.'

Chapter Twelve

Tansy was waiting for Rosie Tuesday morning when she arrived at work. 'Am I late or are you early?' Rosie asked.

'I'm early. I need to talk to you before we get busy.'

'Sounds ominous,' Rosie said. 'You're not taking Charlie up on his offer and going back to the boats, are you?'

'Of course not. Rob and I have set a date for the wedding.'

'Oh, that's brilliant. Congratulations.'

'You mightn't think so when I tell you it's in August and we want to hold the reception here.'

'Seriously?' Rosie said.

Tansy nodded. 'Last Saturday of the month. Late-afternoon wedding – evening reception party.'

Rosie could feel the problems running through her brain: the beach would still be busy; she'd have to close to other customers; she'd need more staff; it would be hot hot hot; Tansy would go away on...

'Honeymoon?'

'We can't afford one straight away, so we're going to delay it and go skiing in the New Year.'

Well, that was something. 'How many people?'

'Not many and very informal,' Tansy said. 'No receiving line, no sit-down dinner. Good food, dancing on the beach, maybe some fireworks at the end of the evening, and lots of champagne. A big beach party, really. What d'you think?'

'I'm not sure,' Rosie said. 'I love the idea but wouldn't you rather have someone like Seb organise things for you?

Tansy shook her head. 'I doubt we could afford Seb's prices. I'm hoping you'll do me a good deal, pretty please?'

'Tansy, I really don't know. I do want to say yes, but part of me says it will be too much when it's hot and the beach is busy.'

'If we have a really simple menu?' Tansy pleaded. 'I can do some of the stuff when I'm not working and freeze it. And it would only mean no dinner bookings for the one night. If you close at three and the party starts at, say, eight, there'd be five hours to get things out and organised. Please?'

Rosie sighed. 'I hope I don't regret this... Okay. But only easily prepared buffet food – not a sit-down meal. Do you want a cake?'

'Yes – but you can knock that up now while we're quiet,' Tansy said blithely. 'Fruit cakes need lots of alcohol and time to mature. Thanks a million,' Tansy said, throwing her arms around Rosie and hugging her.

By the time Rosie opened the restaurant doors and shutters the sun was shining. Lucky-dog instantly bounded across the beach and made for Seb sitting on the rock that Rosie was beginning to think of as 'Seb's Place', he sat there so often. He raised a laconic hand in greeting while stroking Lucky with the other.

'Hi. Sorry you left early Saturday. Are you over your hissy fit now?'

Rosie laughed at his words. 'Hissy fit? Well, that's one way to describe it, I suppose,' Rosie said. 'It's just that Charlie... I'm sorry. I don't think anyone missed me, though.'

'I did,' Seb said quietly. 'I still have the bottle of champagne I saved for you.'

'I'm sure there were plenty of people who would have willingly shared it with you,' Rosie said. 'The place was swinging when I left.'

'Do you have bookings for tonight?'

'Two tables so far,' Rosie said. 'Why?'

Seb shrugged. 'I thought we could meet here and open the champagne tonight after we finish work. Toast the season – wish ourselves all the best – before we both get too bogged down with customers.'

'D'you mean to say you've come round to thinking I'll actually have some customers wanting to buy my food this summer?' Rosie said. 'Well, that's more than Charlie does.'

Rosie shrugged as Seb looked at her. 'Oh, he quoted me the standard thing about the French not liking English cooking, etc., etc. Thinks I'm going to lose all my money.'

'True, that is a possibility,' Seb said. 'But this first summer you'll be a novelty. The crunch will come next season when we French will have decided whether you can cook or not and whether we love you or hate you.'

'Great,' Rosie said, shaking her head and smiling despite herself.

Seb stood up. 'But this evening we should both be free by ten. I'll see you here then – I'll bring the champagne – you bring the glasses. Okay?'

Rosie smiled. 'Okay. Come on, Lucky, let's go.' And Rosie made her way back into the Café Fleur.

The day turned out to be a busy one with crowds of people enjoying the beach in the sunshine. Lots of nice things were said about the food, with people promising to return regularly, and Rosie took several dinner bookings for the coming weekend. The two bookings she'd told Seb she already had for that evening had been joined by a table of five.

Tansy made no secret of the fact that they would have been hard-pushed to have managed without James. 'Thank God, you saw sense and told James to come in today. You are going to offer him a job for the rest of the season now, aren't you?' she asked Rosie as they began to prepare things for the evening menu.

'I was going to see how he felt when he got back this evening,' Rosie said. 'He's a definite asset, for sure. I just wish he wasn't related to Charlie.'

James, when he returned, was delighted with the offer of a permanent job for the season.

'But it will be a mixture of everything – not just cooking,' Rosie warned him.

'That's great,' James said. 'And it'll certainly make it easier for me to follow Charlie's instructions to see you get home safely every night,' he said, grinning at Rosie cheekily.

'If you're working for me, you follow my instructions, not Charlie's,' Rosie said. 'So you can forget that particular instruction – and any other ones concerning me that he gave you. Understood?'

James nodded. 'Of course, Boss.'

Rosie glared at him. Was he taking the mickey? 'Anyway, he's gone to Sardinia. I saw *A Sure Thing* setting off this morning.'

'You haven't heard about the change of plan then? William and Mum have gone to Sardinia but Charlie's gone to the UK,' James said.

At least he was out of the country. No chance of him popping in unexpectedly. 'Talking of William, has he got a PA called Sarah these days?' Rosie asked. 'Or is she Charlie's?' Even as she asked the question, she wondered why. It was of no interest to her.

James shrugged his shoulders. 'Neither. And before you ask, I don't know why Charlie has gone haring back to the UK either. Some sort of personal emergency. Right – I'll just go and check the bar over, shall I? Make sure there's enough nuts and things.'

'Damn. Here's hoping Charlie stays in the UK for a bit,' Rosie muttered. 'Right, tonight's desserts are calling. Where's the cream for the syllabubs?'

The evening turned into a busy one with a couple of extra tables occupied by people coming in off the beach, and it was gone ten o'clock before Rosie said 'Goodnight' to Tansy and James. Picking up two champagne glasses, she locked the door behind her and with Lucky-dog went to join Seb, who was already sitting on his rock. A bottle of champagne was cooling in the sand at his feet.

'Sorry I'm late. We had a busy evening in the end.'

Seb shrugged. 'A busy evening is good news. We just had the hotel guests to feed tonight. I think word is still getting about that we're open.'

Skilfully, he opened the champagne with a gentle plop and carefully poured the golden liquid into the glasses.

'Santé. Here's to the Café Fleur,' he said.

'Here's to the Beach Hotel,' Rosie said, clinking glasses with him. 'May we both have a good season.'

'D'you and Charlie go back a long way?' Seb asked.

'We were at college together years ago. We met up again when William bought the boat.' No point in telling him any more. It was all in the past now.

She took a sip of her drink before asking, 'You?'

'Few years.' Seb shrugged.

'I wouldn't have thought you two had much in common,' Rosie said. Damn, that sounded as if she was fishing, but she had to admit to being curious about Seb's past.

'Backgammon,' Seb said briefly. 'D'you play?'

Rosie shook her head. 'No. Charlie tried to teach me once. We both decided Monopoly was more my kind of game.' She glanced at him. 'You still play?'

'Not in the casinos any more. It got a little bit too addictive – and expensive. So I quit.'

'Just like that?'

Seb nodded. 'This place is a big enough gamble for me right now. I need to spend all my money and energy here.' He took a packet of cigarettes out of a pocket and offered one to Rosie. She shook her head.

'No, thanks. Ever thought about giving that up?' Rosie asked. 'You'd save money that way, too – and be healthier.'

'All the time – maybe this summer I will. And you, Rosie, do you have any vices? Secret or otherwise?' As he spoke he put the cigarettes back in his pocket.

Rosie shook her head. 'Sorry to be boring, but no. I'm rather too fond of very dark chocolate, and I buy too many books, but other than that nothing – unless you count betting on the occasional horse race?'

'No – you have to be down the local Pmu Café every day gambling for it to count.'

Rosie laughed. 'I haven't got the time or the money for that.' She smothered a yawn. 'Sorry. I'm tired. It's been a long day. I think I need to go home.'

'I'll walk you back,' Seb said, downing the last of his champagne.

'Honestly, there's no need,' Rosie protested. 'It's not far and I've got Lucky-dog.'

'But it's late. I can't allow you to walk the streets by yourself.'

'I'll just put the glasses back then,' Rosie said. She was too tired to make an issue out of it. She just hoped none of her neighbours were around to see her being escorted home by two different men in as many days.

Seb said a simple 'Bonne nuit' at the front door of the villa and was gone. Rosie sighed and shook herself. She was sure she wasn't imagining it – there'd been a definite spark between the two of them this evening. The last thing she wanted or needed right now. No way was she going to complicate her life with a relationship with anyone for the next few weeks, only for it to fade away at the end of summer.

The red light was flashing on the answer-phone when she let herself into the apartment. Lucky made straight for the end of the sofa she'd adopted as her own and flopped. Rosie pressed the Play button on the machine and listened to her mother's voice.

'Darling, I'm coming for a visit. I've booked a flight for later in the week, so I'll see you on Friday.'

Rosie groaned as the machine clicked off. She loved Olivia to bits but there were times when her mother drove her to distraction.

'Flight times, Mum?' she muttered. 'How long are you staying? Any info would be good.' But typically, Olivia hadn't bothered with any such details.

Chapter Thirteen

Rosie glanced at her watch. She knew it had been a mistake to book a morning appointment. If Lucky didn't get called within the next few minutes to see the vet, she'd have to leave. As it was, she was going to be far later getting back to the restaurant than she'd planned.

Just as she was getting up to go, Lucky's name was called and they went into the consulting room. To Rosie's relief the vet was happy with Lucky.

'She's a bit on the thin side but that is better than being fat, anyway; a few months living with you at the restaurant and I'm sure she'll put weight on. I'd say she's about three – needs a tattoo and a micro-chip – I'll do that now – and what about spaying? Shall I book her in for next month?'

Rosie shook head. 'Can we make it early September? The next couple of months are going to be busy – I won't be able to give her the time she'll need after an operation.'

Half running, half walking back to the café, with Lucky bounding alongside on her lead, Rosie tried to marshall her thoughts into organising the next few hours. A sunny day meant they would be busy with takeaway food as well as restaurant meals.

Hopefully, Tansy would have prepared the plat-du-jour ingredients, James should have organised the baguettes and sandwiches, and between them they should have at least started to prepare the potatoes and veg for both the lunch and evening dinner reservations.

She must remember to phone next week's meat order through to the butcher this afternoon. And this evening, after they'd closed, she'd stock up on some desserts.

Turning into the restaurant car park, Rosie stopped short. Two gendarme cars and a van plastered with the words Hotel de Ville and the town shield on its side were parked beside the back wall of the kitchen. 'What's happening?' Rosie asked, opening the kitchen door.

'Thank goodness you're back,' Tansy said. 'Monsieur Douce from the Health Department is in the restaurant with James and these two gendarmes are anxious to talk to you.'

Rosie glanced through to where the health inspector was busy studying the inside of the bar fridge and decided to talk to the gendarmes first. She needed to get the restaurant open and policemen with guns prominently displayed in their holsters standing around the place wasn't a good image for a friendly family restaurant.

To her relief it seemed to be a routine visit, 'Establishing contact,' was how one of the gendarmes put it. They didn't mention drugs and neither did Rosie. She offered them both coffee, agreed with them about not wanting to encourage troublemakers, and confirmed that, yes, she was English, but she could cook, and no she didn't serve frites with everything.

Finally, they left and she went through to the restaurant where James was now showing Monsieur Douce the two cloakrooms. There appeared to be several items written on official paper attached to the clipboard he was holding.

'Ah, Mademoiselle Hewitt – we need to talk.'

Rosie's heart sank. Something was clearly wrong. From experience she knew these inspectors had the power to make life very difficult. Taking a deep breath, she smiled and said, 'James, two coffees, please. And then please open the restaurant doors.'

Turning to the health inspector, she said, 'We'll take our coffee out on the terrace, shall we, while you tell me the problems?'

The problems turned out to be: a) the bar fridge wasn't cold enough; b) there were too many loose wires everywhere; and c) the shallow step from the restaurant onto the terrace needed white paint so people would see it and anticipate it. All easy enough to fix and Rosie began to relax.

The fourth problem, though, literally took her breath away.

'What? You're not serious?'

The inspector nodded his head. 'Very serious, mademoiselle. Food poisoning is a big problem – for me and for you.'

'I've only been open ten days. I haven't had time to poison anyone.'

'It is a very quick complaint,' Monsieur Douce agreed. 'Usually, we 'ave more problems when it is 'ot.'

Rosie sighed. If word got out that the food at Café Fleur was suspect, her reputation would be gone before she'd started.

'When am I supposed to have poisoned somebody?'

'Saturday. Two people. They were too ill to fly home the next day. I understand their lawyer will be in touch asking for compensation. Now, I finish inspecting your kitchen.'

Rosie followed him thoughtfully into the kitchen. Saturday night had been the night of Seb's party. They'd been busy for sure. But everything had run smoothly – no long delays, no panic in the kitchen and all the food had gone out looking good and appetising.

After the inspector had condemned the ancient fridge – 'Unacceptable condition. Replace it before my next visit' – and left, there was no time to do anything but try and catch up with the day's chores. James, busy dealing with the takeaway orders, was soon shouting for 'More salad baguettes. Running out of flapjack. And can we do six fish and chips to go?'

'Honestly,' Rosie muttered. 'Food-starved chimps doesn't begin to describe people today.' The tables on the terrace were already overflowing with people as the restaurant itself started to fill up.

'Need more help,' Tansy muttered as she struggled to keep up with the cooking. 'What time is Olivia arriving?'

'I don't know,' Rosie said, 'but if you're expecting her to help, forget it. The words "kitchen" and "cooking" don't exist in her vocabulary these days. She replaced them with "restaurant" and "eating out" as soon as I left home.'

Somehow they survived and managed to stop customers becoming too disgruntled with the long wait for food by bribing them with glasses of ice-cold rosé. It was gone three o'clock when James turned the sign and locked the door.

'What a day. A taste of things to come?' he asked.

'If it is, we need more staff and we need them quickly,' Tansy said, passing him his lunch. 'I'm knackered and there's still this evening to look forward to.' She took a plate of salad and joined James and Rosie at the kitchen table.

'But what if it's a one-off?' Rosie said. 'I can't afford to employ anyone else if it's not busy all the time. And if this food-poisoning episode gets out we mightn't have any customers.'

Quickly she told them both what the health inspector had said. 'Have to wait and see what happens there but I need to buy a new fridge, though, and quickly.'

Tansy shrugged. 'Reckon whatever happens you're going to have to take a chance on employing someone else, especially during the day. There's no way we can keep up this morning's pace, six days a week.'

'Seven from June,' Rosie said. 'You don't think it was worse because of me not being here first thing to organise things and all the other interruptions?'

'It didn't help, but there were a lot more people about today,' Tansy said.

The three of them took their time over lunch and Rosie was grateful when both Tansy and James opted to give up their afternoon break and stayed to help prep for the evening menu.

Thankfully the evening, although busy with a satis-factory number of customers, didn't have the frantic immediacy of the day. People were happy to sit and enjoy a leisurely meal.

James turned the sign around at nine o'clock. By nine-thirty, Tansy and James had left and Rosie was alone in the kitchen wondering what to do about Olivia's non-appearance. When her mobile beeped she grabbed it, praying it was Olivia.

But it was a text from Charlie: 'Back in France Mon. Pick u up 4 dinner @ 8 p.m.'

Rosie sighed and began tapping out her reply: 'Sorry no can do. Please st...'

A loud knocking at the kitchen door made her jump. Closing her phone she cautiously opened the door. A white luxury sports car was reversing out of the car park and Olivia was standing in front of her, a leather holdall at her feet.

'Hello, darling. I've got the right place then,' Olivia said.

'You didn't come in that?' Rosie said, pointing after the car as it filtered out into the traffic. 'No, of course not.'

'Oh, but I did,' Olivia said. 'Any food going? I'm starving. A glass of wine would be welcome, too.'

Taking a bottle of rosé out of the fridge, Rosie said, 'Ham sandwich or omelette?'

'Sandwich, please.' Olivia glanced at Rosie. 'I need to talk to you. It's important.'

'You're not ill, are you?' Rosie asked anxiously, handing her mother a glass of wine.

Olivia shook her head. 'No, darling, but I do have to tell you something you need to know about before you hear it from someone else,' Olivia said. 'Can we sit out on the terrace?

'Sure, go ahead. I'll be a couple of minutes. Take the wine with you,' Rosie said, watching her mother make her way through the restaurant. If she didn't know better she'd say her mother, usually the high priestess of calmness, was definitely on edge tonight.

***

Thoughtfully, Rosie spread butter on a couple of slices of bread. Olivia never had been a great one for making idle talk so, if she wasn't ill, what on earth was all this about? Was this something going to be about her long-absent father? Had he been in touch after years of silence?

Only eight when her parents split up and ten when the divorce was finalised, her father had barely figured in Rosie's life since then. At first there had been weekend visits and even an annual holiday together, but when she was a teenager he'd disappeared off to America and she hadn't seen him since. Despite him promising he'd show her the sights of New York and San Francisco, he never had.

She'd ceased a long time ago to miss his presence in her life. Occasionally he'd flit through her mind on the edge of some long-forgotten memory but that was about it.

Mentally, Rosie tried to work out how long it had been since they'd even spoken to one another. She'd been seventeen – so, a lifetime ago. Had Olivia heard from him in that time? Would she have told Rosie if she had?

Throughout her childhood she and Olivia hadn't exactly clung together for moral support, but both adult and child had wanted to protect the other from more hurt. Consequently they'd enjoyed a closer relationship than many of her friends did with their mothers.

Taking a couple of ham slices from the fridge, Rosie remembered how close she and Olivia had been, still were in many ways. It was just that these days their lives didn't revolve around each other to the same extent.

Rosie going to college had been the turning point for living separate lives and developing a more normal mother–daughter relationship. Hell, they even rowed sometimes now, something that would have been unheard of back in the days when Olivia struggled as a single mother to put food on the table and clothes on both their backs.

Quickly finishing making the sandwich, Rosie hurried after Olivia.

'This is a great location,' Olivia said. 'How's the café going?'

'Fine,' Rosie said. 'Apart from a food-poisoning accusation, which I'll tell you about later. But first you need to tell me what this is all about. Are you sure you're not ill? You're very thin.'

'I've been following the 5.2 diet for a couple of weeks,' Olivia said.

'So what is it? Has "he who shall not be mentioned" been in touch and upset you?'

'Good God, no. Haven't heard from him in years. We're definitely off his radar these days, thank God.'

'What the hell is it then?'

Olivia selected a sandwich before glancing up at her. 'The thing is, I've met someone whom I like a lot.'

'Oh, is that all?' Rosie said, relieved. 'That's great, Mum. I'm really pleased for you. What's his name?'

'Zander'

'Different,' Rosie said.

'He's Italian. He's also very kind, very sweet and says he loves me.'

'Was that him playing taxi?'

'Olivia nodded. 'Yes. He sends his apologies for not stopping. He needed to get back to Monaco. Breakfast business meeting tomorrow. He'll be back here next week to collect me.' She twirled the wine around in her glass before looking up at Rosie.

'I'd like you to meet him before...' She hesitated and then added, 'Before I move in with him in Monaco.'

'Blimey, Mum. It must be serious. How long have you known him? Where did you meet him?' Rosie struggled to take in the news of Olivia giving up her independent life to move in with a man.

'One of Rosemary's dinner parties three months ago. She sends her love, by the way.'

'Thanks,' Rosie said. Rosemary was her godmother and her mother's oldest friend. For years she'd been trying to find Olivia a husband. Had she finally succeeded?

'I'm not thinking of marrying him, so don't worry about that,' Olivia said, breaking into her thoughts.

'Mum, if you've met someone you love, marry him.'

Olivia shook her head. 'I'm not sure Zander's the marrying type.'

Rosie laughed and shook her head. 'This isn't the way it's meant to be. I'm the child. I should be the one talking to you about me moving in with someone.'

'Are you? Is it Charlie? It's about time you settled down,' Olivia said eagerly.

'No, I'm not planning on moving in with Charlie or anyone else.' As Rosie bent down to stroke Lucky sitting at her feet, Seb strolled across the beach and up to the terrace carrying a plate and a bottle.

'Hi, mind if I join you?' Seb asked. 'I've got some leftover salmon canapés that it would be a shame to waste.'

'Seb, this is Olivia, my mother. Mum – Seb. He owns the hotel next door.'

'Heard you had a spot of bother this morning,' Seb said, looking at Rosie. 'Got any names yet? Details of what they ate?'

Rosie looked at him. 'How did you…?'

'James.'

'I hope he's not busy spreading the news all over town,' Rosie said. 'Publicity like that I do not need. I'll have to have a word with him tomorrow.'

'I already did on your behalf,' Seb said.

'Thank you,' Rosie said. 'Monsieur Douce was very nice about it all but told me to expect a lawyer's letter. And I've got to get a new fridge. Must admit, the one here is pretty ancient.'

'How's business otherwise?'

'Today has been quite a day,' Rosie said. 'Tansy is nagging me to get more staff but I'm not sure I can afford to yet.'

'It would be a mistake not to,' Seb said. 'It's going to get busier every day from now on as summer heats up. You're going to need all the staff you can get.'

Rosie sighed. 'I'm not sure I can even afford one more person right now. Ideally, I could do with someone happy to come in at a moment's notice at odd times when needed. Asking for the impossible, I know. People want regular hours and money.'

'Try this number,' Seb said, scribbling on a piece of paper. 'Alicia. She works for me occasionally and might be the answer for you, too.' He handed Rosie the piece of paper as he stood up. 'See you tomorrow. Nice to meet you, Olivia.'

Olivia smiled. 'You, too.' As Seb left, she turned to Rosie. 'He's nice. You'd make a good pair – you look good together.'

'Mum! Stop it. One minute you're pushing Charlie at me – the next Seb, who incidentally is one of the best chefs down here and just a friend. Anyway, the only relationship I've got time for this year is with the Café Fleur.'

Chapter Fourteen

Erica stood rubbing the small of her back, achey and tired but happy, as she surveyed the shop critically. Three days it had taken her but now every shelf, cupboard, window ledge and the small amount of tiled floor space left was gleaming.

The stainless-steel bar holding the collection of vintage clothes was reflected in the glass doors of the old dresser where the second-hand books were kept. New kitchen paraphernalia stood on shelves mixed in with antique brass scales, Provençal plates, cuisine plaques, laguiole cutlery, with its signature tiny bee on the handles, and ancient kilner jars. Aprons and tablecloths patterned with olives, glasses of wine and cicadas hung from either end of the shelves.

Reproductions of jazz age posters and cards were arranged on the eighteenth-century wooden bureau she'd lovingly polished with beeswax. Tins of the same beeswax stood in a neat pile along with bottles of organic olive oil by the till, ready for impulse buying.

In among the orderly layout there were equally carefully arranged higgedly-piggedly corners too. Erica knew people liked to feel they were discovering something special or even unique. Pictures and frames leaning nonchalantly against the wall; wooden boxes of miscellaneous things; a pile of old embroidered linen;

tapestry cushions on old, wrought-iron patio chairs. It invited people to have a rummage; to discover their own treasure.

Standing there looking around, Erica sniffed and relaxed. The shop both looked and smelt wonderful. The perfume from the bunches of lavender hanging from the ceiling, the beeswax polish and the citronella candles had all blended together to give the place its own distinctive smell.

The only thing missing was Pascal sitting on the wheel-back chair by the counter, toasting her with a cup of coffee and saying, 'Here's to the new season.' Although if she stared at the chair hard enough she could almost imagine him there.

She sighed. She missed him so much. He'd been so proud of the way she'd brought her dream of The Cupboard Under the Stairs alive. In the early days, he'd been with her every step of the way, urging her on. Carrying on without him in her life had seemed impossible at one stage, but for Cammie's sake she'd had to try and keep her dream alive.

She turned as the shop doorbell tinkled and smiled in welcome at GeeGee.

'You timed that well,' she said. 'I've just finished and was about to have a coffee.'

'Thanks. I've brought you a couple of villa brochures,' GeeGee said. 'One I'm hoping you'll really go for. Where's Cammie?'

'Swimming and tea at Madeleine's. I've got to pick her up later,' Erica said, holding out her hand for the brochures. Flipping through them she knew instantly which one GeeGee meant.

Stone-built, with a traditional terracotta roof and the obligatory bougainvillea climbing over three quarters of the walls, the villa looked wonderful. The pictures of the inside showed a spacious layout decorated in creams and whites with occasional splashes of Provençal blue and yellow.

The immaculate lawns and flower beds surrounding it were equally stunning. 'Does it come with its own gardener?' Erica said. 'Gosh, it's got an infinity pool. I'd definitely have to employ a pool boy for that!' She glanced up at GeeGee. 'I know I said I could do expensive but this looks like it's off the scale? Where is it?'

'Owners are looking for a quick sale so the price can be negotiated. The only problem is it's slightly further out than you wanted. It's actually on the Cap.'

Regretfully, Erica put the brochures down on the table. 'I'm not sure I'm a Cap d'Antibes person, as lovely as that particular house is. It's so exclusive up there. Maybe somewhere a bit more down to earth?'

'Go through the brochures later and see if there's anything you fancy,' GeeGee said. 'I'm on my way to measure up your place and take some photos ready for doing the brochure.'

'Cammie and I will be home in about an hour,' Erica said.

'I'll probably have left by then. I've got to go back out and meet someone on the beach.'

Erica raised her eyebrows. 'Friend or client?'

There was the merest hesitation before GeeGee answered, 'Friend,' and opened the shop door. 'See you later then.'

'Okay – but don't think you're going to get away with not telling me who you're meeting!' Erica called out as GeeGee positively ran out of the shop.

***

Arriving early for her meeting on the beach, GeeGee opened her laptop and tried to settle to doing some work while she waited for her old friend Bruno to show.

Tossing and turning the other night, worrying about money and how her life was going nowhere, Bruno had popped into her mind. Strictly speaking, Bruno had been Jay's friend but, since Jay had left, their paths rarely crossed and she'd missed hearing Bruno's often inappropriate take on things.

Running his own successful holiday letting agency, maybe he could use some part-time help. Something she could fit in around seeing clients. Well, no harm in asking, she'd figured, and had rung him the next morning.

Now, as she saw him striding across the beach towards her, she crossed her fingers and prayed he'd be able to help her.

Living with Erica and Cammie was working out well. Erica insisted on feeding her every evening, saying, 'I've got to feed Cammie and me anyway, one extra is nothing,' but refusing to take any money. 'All in good time,' was her current mantra. But GeeGee was determined to pay her way – sooner rather than later.

'Long time, no see,' Bruno said, leaning in to kiss her cheek. 'Can't stay long, I'm afraid. I've got to get to the airport in half an hour.'

GeeGee smiled. No change there then. Bruno was always in a hurry.

'I need to up my income between house sales and wondered whether you needed any part-time help? I'm free every evening and all day Sundays. Office work? Cleaning? Anything.' God, she didn't sound as desperate as she was, did she?

Bruno regarded her thoughtfully before shaking his head. 'Patsy and I manage the office work between us. We've just taken on two new cleaners – if they don't work out, there may be something there. You still got a car?'

GeeGee nodded. 'Expensive necessity for the day job.'

'How d'you fancy doing a few evening airport runs then? Owners and their guests. We manage fifty properties now and it's a bloody nightmare when several parties arrive on the same flight and want collecting. Weekends are particularly difficult. I'm back and forth like the proverbial.'

'Sounds interesting,' GeeGee said.

'One way of putting it,' Bruno said, 'but airport tedium will soon set in, I can promise you, when flights are delayed.' He glanced at her.

'You don't have a dog, do you? Last woman I employed insisted the clients loved having a dog in the car to greet them. Maybe some of them did but mostly they didn't.'

'No, I don't have a dog,' GeeGee said.

'Okay. Get your car valeted – needs to be immaculate. I've got two lots of clients coming in at the same time Saturday night so I'll be at the airport, too, and can show you the ropes. Terminal Two at seven-thirty. I'll meet you in Arrivals.'

'Um, hate to ask, but what do I get paid? And how?' GeeGee said.

When Bruno named the price, she gulped. 'Really? I had no idea it would be that amount.'

'Clients know the door-to-door service is an extra they have to pay for at the time. You have to pay your petrol and parking out of it.'

Bruno stood up. 'Gotta go. See you Saturday then. Ciao.'

'Ciao... and thanks, Bruno.'

Watching him take the short cut through the hotel car park, GeeGee felt her spirits lift. Just a couple of weekend airport runs at the price Bruno had told her would help her finances considerably. She wondered how many Bruno meant by a few.

Chapter Fifteen

Olivia's mobile rang as Rosie unlocked the apartment door early Monday evening after they'd spent a couple of hours exploring Cannes. Leaving Olivia to answer it, Rosie went into the kitchen and surveyed the contents of the fridge. Two eggs, a bottle of chardonnay, a limp lettuce, half a tub of fromage frais. Not inspiring.

The leaflet she'd pinned to the back of the kitchen door caught her attention: 'Chinese Takeaway.' Supper solved. She'd order them both a Chinese. Rosie fished in her bag for her own mobile as the apartment intercom went.

'You ready, Rosie?' Charlie's voice boomed into the kitchen. 'Or shall I come up and wait?'

'Ready?'

'We've got a dinner date.'

Rosie sighed. 'You invited. I declined.'

'No, you didn't.'

'I sent you a text saying no…' Rosie's voice trailed away as she remembered starting the text but not finishing it, when Olivia arrived Friday evening. 'Well, I meant to,' she sighed. 'You'd better come up.'

She'd explain to Charlie face to face that she had no intention of having dinner with him and then he could be on his way while she and Olivia enjoyed their supper and the rest of their evening. She pressed the button and minutes later Charlie bounded into the apartment.

'I'm not having dinner with you, Charlie,' Rosie said. 'I'm tired. I'm going to order a Chinese and Mum and I plan a quiet evening.'

'Actually, darling,' Olivia said, reappearing from the bedroom. 'That was Zander. He's unexpectedly free this evening so he's picking me up for dinner in five minutes.'

'Well, that's sorted then,' Charlie said. 'Go and change.'

Rosie looked at him. 'Charlie, I do not want to come out with you this evening – or any evening, in fact. Understood?'

Charlie looked at her for several seconds before saying, 'Okay. We'll eat in. What's on the Chinese menu?'

'Charlie!' There was no way she was going to spend the evening alone in the apartment with him. 'Just go.'

Charlie shook his head. 'I want to talk to you, Rosie. So we can either stay here or we can go out and have dinner. You decide.'

'I'll wait for Zander downstairs,' Olivia said. 'I'll probably be late so don't wait up for me, darling.' With a quick spray of Dior and a wave of her hand she opened the door.

'Give my regards to Zander,' Charlie said.

'Will do,' and Olivia was gone.

'You know Zander?' Rosie asked.

'We've met a couple of times. Must say I'm surprised at Olivia being his current squeeze.'

'Why?'

Charlie shrugged. 'Wouldn't have thought she was his type. You haven't met him yet then?'

'No,' Rosie said, wondering what Charlie was not telling her. The thought of her mother being anyone's current squeeze was disturbing.

'Rosie, please go and get ready.'

'Charlie...'

'Rosie, we're both hungry. There's no food here, so let's just go and get some together. There's an Italian bistro in the next street. We can go there.'

'Okay, I'll come for a bowl of pasta and then I'm coming home – alone,' Rosie said. At least this way she'd get Charlie out of the apartment. And maybe she'd get him to say more about Zander.

But Charlie clearly didn't want to talk about him and shrugged off her 'So what does Zander do?' question as they waited for their food to arrive with one word: 'Businessman.'

He raised his glass. 'Santé.'

Rosie picked up her own glass of chilled Prosecco. 'Santé. I hope your emergency in the UK wasn't too bad a one.'

Charlie looked at her and sighed before picking up his own glass. 'The emergency was a friend who was in a state of shock and needed a helping hand.'

Rosie waited for him to elaborate but when he didn't she asked, 'So what are we going to talk about?'

'Firstly, I need your help,' Charlie said quietly. 'Suggesting James asked you for a job wasn't just me selfishly wanting to know what you were up to. It's also a case of needing you to keep an eye on James without him suspecting, which is why he believes he's there to report back to me about you.'

'And does he?'

'Report back? Well, I gather you're getting busier and need more staff. Oh, and you've already poisoned somebody.' Charlie forked up some pasta. 'Need any help with that, by the way? Firm's new lawyer is a hot shot.'

'I'm still waiting to hear precise details,' Rosie said. 'I keep going over and over the dishes we served that Saturday evening and wondering if anyone else was ill but didn't make an official complaint.' Rosie sighed. 'I guess I'll just have to wait and see what these people are claiming. Anyway, James. He's a good worker and I like him. Why do you want me to spy on him?'

'Dad seems to think he's mixing with the wrong crowd down here. Wants an eye kept on him.'

'In that case – why not give him the chef's job on *A Sure Thing* like he wanted? He'd be too busy then to get in trouble,' Rosie said.

Providing food from the tiny galley onboard the yacht had been hard, continuous work, usually in the sweltering heat of summer, leaving her exhausted by the end of the season. 'No time to go ashore,' she added.

Charlie poured more wine into their glasses. 'He does genuinely need more experience before he takes on that responsibility.'

'So what d'you want me to do?'

'Keep him as busy as possible and let me know if… Oh, hell, Rosie, I don't know. Basically, keep an eye on him and let me know if something seems awry. I never realised having a kid brother could be so worrying.'

'Okay. Against my better judgement, I'll keep an eye on him,' Rosie said. 'But I honestly don't think you need to worry. James is a sensible boy.'

'Thanks. Now we've got that out of the way, let's talk about us.'

'Charlie! There is no us.'

'But there could be, Rosie – and I want there to be,' Charlie said, taking a hold of her hand across the table. 'That night we had dinner in The Recluse, I tried to tell you how I felt about you now that we've met again, but you refused to listen.'

Rosie pulled her hand away. 'Charlie, stop it. There is no point.'

'We were good together in the old days. We could be again. I've changed, Rosie. You have to believe me.'

'Charlie, you may have changed but you let me down big time at college. Remember? When I fell pregnant and really needed your support, you walked away. Which means I can never ever totally trust you again.'

'I know I behaved abominably all those years ago at college but I would never behave like that now. Please put it down to the arrogance of youth, Rosie... and forgive me?' Charlie pleaded. 'Give me a second chance?'

Rosie hesitated. Would she be making one of the biggest mistakes of her life by not forgiving Charlie and rekindling their youthful friendship? He was right – they had been good together back in the day. She'd even been silly enough to think Charlie could be her Mr Right and they would be spending the rest of their lives together, before it had all gone wrong.

Charlie's reaction to the news of her pregnancy had been one of sheer panic. But she'd consoled herself with the thought that it was just the shock. The unexpectedness of it. Once he'd got used to the idea, everything would be fine. Only it wasn't, the relief when she'd miscarried at eleven weeks evident even as he tried to console her.

If she was honest, she had to admit he had changed – inevitably he'd matured and grown up – but there was something else different about him, too.

'You were my first love and I want you back in my life,' Charlie said now, taking her hand again and stroking it. 'You've never told me what happened after we broke up and... I left to go travelling.'

The thought, 'No and you never even tried to find me and ask,' swirled into Rosie's head. You just vanished and got on with your own life and conveniently forgot all about me, until fifteen years later when William bought *A Sure Thing* and we met up again.

'Back in your life? Charlie, that is not going to happen,' Rosie said, trying to pull her hand back and failing.

'It could if only you'd accept my apology and forgive me. Rosie, please give me the chance to prove to you that I'm a different person to the boy who let you down.'

Rosie sighed. Charlie had always been obstinate. They could be here all night unless she agreed to be friends again. 'Okay. It's a bit late, but apology accepted.'

'So we can start again? Forgive and forget?'

'Forgiving is the easy part, Charlie. Forgetting even after all this time is more difficult,' Rosie said. 'But yes, we can be friends again.' Rosie held up her hand as Charlie went to protest, as she'd known he would, at the thought of being just friends.

'Friendship is all that's on offer, Charlie. Take it or leave it.' Rosie stood up. 'Right, now we've sorted that out, I'm going home.'

Charlie insisted on walking Rosie back to her apartment. When she pleaded a headache and also pointed out that Olivia would be back soon, to Rosie's relief he reluctantly left. She could only hope that he wasn't going to keep badgering her for more than friendship. Because that was somewhere she had no intention of going. Surely she'd now made that plain enough.

* * *

Rosie mooched around the flat for a few moments not sure what to do – sleeping on the put-u-up meant she couldn't get undressed and go to bed before Olivia came home in case she brought Zander up. No way did Rosie want to be wearing pyjamas when she met the new man in her mother's life.

Pouring herself a glass of wine she sat and waited, pushing away thoughts of what might have been with Charlie and trying to stay awake enough to work on the restaurant menu diary. She'd decided to keep a record of her daily menus even though it made her feel a bit like one of those Victorian hostesses who'd kept a record of both food and guests at dinner parties to avoid serving the same dish to the same people twice.

For the Café Fleur, though, keeping a daily food menu of what she'd made, and more importantly what had proved to be popular, would be invaluable in working out what gave her the best returns. She smothered a yawn. God, where was Olivia?

Looking at the entries in the diary so far, Rosie could see that lasagne and tiramisu were by far the most popular. There was a scribbled 'pizzas' in the suggestion column. Rosie sighed.

Pizza had been requested a lot this week. People seemed to expect to find them on a beach-café menu but she hated making them as much as she hated eating them. She was determined to keep them off the menu for as long as she could. Besides, there were a lot of pizza places around – too much competition. She had more than enough competition to cope with right next door, in the shape of Seb, without adding to it.

Absently she typed Sebastian Groc into the search bar on the laptop. Within seconds the screen was filled with images: Seb in his chef whites; Seb laughing sexily; Seb looking immaculate at a Monaco charity fundraising do. There was a brief bio under that one: Celebrity chef Seb Groc, who has earned not one, but two, Michelin stars for The Recluse, announced his resignation from the restaurant recently, saying it was time to do his own thing. We wish him well in his new venture.

Rosie scrolled down the page to find more images of Seb – several with different glamorous blondes on his arm. Seb was clearly very popular and not just for his food. Thoughtfully, Rosie clicked the web page closed, resisting the urge to click on the *Wikipedia* page for his biographical details. She didn't need to know the ins and outs of Seb's private life. It wasn't as if they were ever going to be more than competitors over a decent lunchtime menu.

It was nearly one o'clock before Lucky-dog's warning growl told her Olivia was coming up the stairs.

When the door opened and Olivia appeared it was all Rosie could do to stop herself demanding, 'And what time d'you call this?'

Which was just as well, as standing directly behind Olivia, nuzzling her neck as she tried not to giggle, was a man. And not just any man.

'Darling – we hoped you'd still be up. Rosie, meet Zander. Zander, this is my daughter, Rosie. Do close your mouth – you look like one of those fairground-amusement contraptions that spit out prizes.'

Rosie obediently snapped her mouth closed. Fairground-amusement contraption? When had her fairground-hating mother last seen one of those? Right at that moment, anyway, she couldn't spit anything out – she was dumbstruck.

She knew now exactly what Charlie had meant with his remark about Olivia being Zander's current squeeze.

'Rosie, I am so pleased to meet you.' Zander took her hand as he gazed into her eyes. 'Your mama, she never stops talking about you.'

Oh. Not good. A real Italian smoothie.

'She's barely mentioned you to me,' Rosie muttered for want of anything else to say, and clenched her mouth into the form of a smile. If she wasn't careful the sentence, 'And I don't believe for one moment that your intentions towards my mother are honourable,' would spring ready-formed from her lips.

'Rosie, would you mind awfully if I left tonight?' Olivia asked.

'What, right now?'

Zander put his arm around Olivia's shoulders. 'Olivia, she has told you, she comes to live with me, yes? For me, next week is very busy and I cannot collect her – so I take her now.'

'You could catch a train tomorrow, Mum... after we've talked?'

Olivia shook her head. 'So much easier if I go with Zander now. I'll just get my things.'

'Well, if you've made your mind up,' Rosie said. 'Want a coffee before you go?' If she could delay them, maybe Olivia would change her mind and stay.

But no, coffee was declined and within five minutes Rosie was waving the two of them goodbye.

'I'll ring you tomorrow,' Olivia said as they left. 'We'll have a natter then.'

Apparently Olivia was going to be living in Zander's penthouse overlooking Monaco harbour, so he'd clearly got a bob or two.

'You're welcome to come and see us any time,' Zander had said but, even as she'd muttered a polite 'Thank you,' Rosie knew she was going to be too busy for the next few weeks to take up that particular invitation.

Closing the apartment door behind them, a stunned Rosie climbed into bed and tried to sleep. After all those years of not having a regular boyfriend, of professing not to even want one, Olivia had disappeared off to Monaco to live with a guy who looked like a young Franco Nero – right down to the mesmerising blue eyes.

Rosie sighed. What was it with mothers? Did they get to a certain age and think, 'Hey, how can I really embarrass my kids? I know – I'll be a cougar!' She could only hope that Olivia knew what she was doing and wasn't making the biggest mistake ever.

Snuggling into her duvet, Rosie sent a silent promise out into the universe. If Zander hurt her mother, she, Rosie, would personally kill him.

Okay, kill was too strong a word, but he'd certainly need medical attention when she'd finished with him.

Chapter Sixteen

Rosie wiped the tears away with the back of her hand. This was ridiculous.

'Are you all right?' Tansy asked on arriving for work the next morning.

Rosie sniffed. 'I'm fine. It's just these damn onions. You'd think by now they'd have developed a non-crying onion.'

It had absolutely nothing whatsoever to do with the letter currently stuffed into her apron pocket. No way was she going to admit it was anything but the onions.

Tansy looked at her but accepted the explanation. 'James not in yet?' she asked.

'He's upstairs, checking out the studio. He's asked to rent it for the rest of the summer – or until he can find somewhere else. Apparently his place is being sold and he has to get out. I haven't agreed yet, though. What d'you think?'

'It could work. Especially if you let him have it in lieu of wages. You wouldn't have to shell out so much money every week then.'

'The thing is, it's barely habitable up there so I can't charge him much. Can't have his friends tramping through the restaurant to visit him either.'

'Hey, we're getting so busy his social life will be as limited as ours,' Tansy said.

'True. Can I leave you to finish off the veg? I have to go across to the hotel for something. I'll only be about ten minutes. Okay?' Rosie ignored the unspoken question from Tansy and left her to it.

She and Seb had somehow slipped into the habit of meeting on the beach at the end of the evening and sharing a glass of wine before Seb walked Rosie and Lucky-dog home. It had started one evening when Seb had spied her walking Lucky-dog on the beach before she headed home and he'd sat on the rocks with wine, waiting for her to return.

The evenings Seb didn't appear, either because she'd finished too early for him or he was busy in the restaurant, Rosie missed him. Today, though, she couldn't wait until this evening to talk to him. She needed to see him now.

Seb was checking off a wine delivery as Rosie pushed open the kitchen door. 'Coffee?'

Rosie shook her head. 'No, thanks. I want to ask your advice. But if you're busy, I'll come back.'

Seb put his clipboard down. 'I can finish this later. What's up?'

Rosie pulled the crumpled letter out of her pocket and handed it to him. 'This came Recorded Delivery this morning. My French is pretty good these days but I just wanted you to confirm I'd understood it correctly.'

Seb whistled as he quickly scanned the letter. 'My clients are asking for compensation in regard to the food poisoning they contracted at your establishment. This is to include: refund of their extra hotel costs, the cost of cancelled and deferred air flights and also compensation with regard to the general distress they have suffered. In our opinion a court would impose a settlement figure of around fifty thousand euros, excluding costs. To avoid this going to court, our clients are prepared to settle for forty thousand euros.'

'That's one hell of a lot of euros,' he said, handing the letter back to Rosie.

'What do I do? I haven't got that kind of money,' Rosie said, feeling the tears starting to rise up again and biting her lip.

'You've got to fight it, obviously,' Seb said.

'But that's going to take more money that I haven't got. And if it gets out I've already poisoned people, nobody's going to come to Café Fleur anyway.' Rosie sighed. 'Charlie did say his new lawyer was top notch and suggested I could use him but I can't afford legal fees. No, I'll have to close the café down and plead poverty. Will that work in France?'

Seb shook his head. 'Doubt it.'

'I'll have to run away then,' Rosie said. 'One way or another it's going to ruin me.'

'Rosie, you have to fight it. You can't just give up,' Seb said. 'I'll help you. First you need to find out the names of these people – nationality, too, if you can. And then you need to know exactly what they ate. Write back and ask questions. That won't cost you anything. If nothing else it will delay things for a few weeks and give you a chance to get established and earn some money.'

'Not likely to earn forty thousand euros,' Rosie said. 'I'll be lucky to earn enough to pay the bills this first year. I never dreamt people could demand that kind of money.'

'Me, I think it's a try-on,' Seb said. 'A scam. That's why you need to find out who these people are. Nothing is going to happen quickly – this is France, remember.'

'Great. A summer with this hanging over me,' Rosie sighed.

'Push it to the back of your mind,' Seb said. 'Just concentrate on making Café Fleur work. And come to a party in Cannes with me this weekend. The film festival started yesterday so it'll be a good one.'

'Thanks for the invite, but no thanks,' Rosie said. 'I wouldn't be great company.'

'Sunday night. Posh frock. Pick you up at ten,' Seb said. 'No argument.'

Chapter Seventeen

Erica smoothed the duvet cover into place and took a final look around the guest bedroom. Towels in the en-suite, flowers on the dressing table and the latest Donna Leon paperback (Amelia's favourite author) on the bedside table.

Now to get on with supper. Amelia was due to arrive any time soon and Cammie was already hyper with excitement. She adored Amelia's visits and was always asking when she was coming down again. She'd always loved visiting Grandma Amelia and Granddad Jean-Pierre up in the mountains but hadn't once asked to go since Pascal died.

Erica bit her lip. Pascal had been close to his parents and they had spent many weekends with them, driving up on a Saturday evening, coming home Monday afternoon. When Cammie started school they'd had to shorten their visits and leave Sunday evening. They hadn't been up to visit Amelia and Jean-Pierre once this year.

From the way Amelia was beginning to talk on the phone about visits, Erica knew she'd soon start to apply pressure. Would probably bring the subject up this weekend. She'd just have to beg Amelia for patience. She personally wasn't ready for what would be an emotional visit and the logistics of getting Cammie there with her phobia about cars would be difficult.

Pulling the bedroom door to, Erica went downstairs and joined Cammie and GeeGee who were setting the table for supper. She got busy preparing the salad before the doorbell pinged.

'Granny Amelia's here,' Cammie shouted and ran to let her in.

After a flurry of hugs and kisses, Cammie dragged Amelia off to her room to show her the beach project.

As they disappeared upstairs GeeGee said, 'I have to go out this evening so you and Amelia can have a good catch-up.'

'You don't have to go out,' Erica said. 'If you're just being considerate.'

GeeGee shook her head. 'I have to meet someone.'

Erica raised her eyebrows. 'Who is it this time?'

GeeGee laughed and shook her head.

'Promise I'll tell you later if it works out.'

It was gone nine o'clock before supper was finished and Amelia was reading Cammie her bedtime story while Erica tidied up. When Amelia reappeared, Erica said, 'Go on up to the terrace. I'll bring the rest of the rosé up.'

Amelia was standing taking in the view and took the glass of wine Erica handed her with a sigh, before saying quietly, 'Camilla tells me you're selling this house and she's getting a dog when you move?'

Erica bit her lip. Damn. She should have realised Cammie would tell her grandmother about moving house and getting a dog at the first opportunity. It was all she talked about these days.

'Long way to go yet,' she said now. 'The house isn't officially on the market. And then we have to find somewhere we like.'

'D'you remember the Bertrands?' Amelia said. 'Their place in the village is up for sale. It would be ideal for you. Camilla says she misses seeing us.'

Erica sipped her wine. Thanks, Cammie. That little gem would add fuel to Amelia's emotional blackmail.

'Lovely house but there's a slight problem. Two actually. I have Cammie's school and the shop to think about,' she said. 'The school has been brilliant with Cammie since Pascal. They've been so understanding. She's starting to shake off the melancholy although the refusing to set foot in a car still has to be dealt with. I don't want to jeopardise things and set her back by totally changing her environment.'

'Camilla would soon settle at the local school – the one Pascal went to. They'd look after her, too. As for the shop – you could sell it. You don't need to work, anyway,' Amelia said, dismissing Erica's words with a wave of her hand.

'Maybe not, but I can't sit around doing nothing for the rest of my life,' Erica said, taking a deep breath and trying to keep calm. Amelia meant well and clearly didn't realise how much the shop meant to her.

'We'd love to have you living closer. Families should be together. It's been a long time since you came up.'

'I'm sorry about that,' Erica said. 'I've missed spending the weekends up with you, too.' She hesitated before adding, 'It's just that at the moment I can't bear the thought of being with you and the family without Pascal there.'

There was a brief silence before Amelia said, 'I can understand that.' She looked at Erica sadly. 'It's our Ruby anniversary soon. Jean-Pierre wants to invite a few friends. Not exactly a party but it won't be just family. Would that be easier? Could you bear to come up for that?' she added gently. 'It's on a Sunday so the shop won't be open. We can discuss things more then. Could even get the Bertrands to let you look around the house properly.'

'I don't know. It might be easier with other people around but...' Erica's voice trailed away and she took a deep breath. 'One thing is definite, though. I don't want to look around the Bertrands' villa. It would be lovely to be nearer you but I have no intention of selling the shop. Besides, both Cammie and I like living down here on the coast. So please, forget the idea of the Bertrands selling me their place.'

Erica took a sip of her wine before saying, 'I do promise we will try to come for your anniversary party.' She might struggle to get through a celebration of a long and happy marriage, when she'd be denied the chance of achieving the same with Pascal, but deep down she knew she had to be there for Cammie's sake.

Chapter Eighteen

Sunday night and Rosie went home too tired to really think about putting on a a posh frock ready to party with Seb. 'If I fall asleep on him, he'll only have himself to blame,' she muttered as she struggled to do the back zip up on her dress.

'Seb, I warn you, I'm dead on my feet,' she said when Seb arrived to collect her.

'You'll wake up when we get there. You can always have a snooze on the way. Nice dress.'

'Not OTT, is it?' Rosie asked. The sparkly flapper-style dress was the nearest thing to the 'posh frock' Seb had told her to wear that she currently possessed.

'Not by Cannes standards,' Seb said, opening the door of his Porsche Carrera.

'Nice car – even by Cannes standards,' Rosie said, sliding in. How she was going to get out again without flashing her knickers crossed her mind.

Approaching Cannes along the bord de mer, luxury, chauffeur-driven limousines with glamorous occupants were nose to tail. As they sat in a traffic jam near the Palais des Festivals, Seb glanced across at her.

'Have you talked to your mother yet?'

'No,' Rosie sighed. 'I think she's avoiding me as much as I am her. I know we can't avoid each other – or the subject – for ever. But right now, I don't know what to say.'

'Wish her well, maybe?' Seb said. 'Zander's a bit of a playboy but basically he's an okay guy.'

'He might be an "Okay guy",' Rosie said, 'but he's ten years younger than my mum.'

Seb shrugged. 'If they make each other happy, so what?'

'I suppose you're right,' Rosie sighed. 'It's just that I can't get my head around my mother being a cougar in the eyes of the world.'

'There are worse things to be called,' Seb said.

Music was blaring from a grande belle époque villa when Seb turned into a driveway a few moments later. Rosie, remembering to turn her body so her legs exited neatly, congratulated herself when she managed to get out of the car without giving the attendant valet a flash. Leaving the Porsche for the valet to park, Seb took her hand and they walked up the steps and under the portico entrance.

Glasses of champagne were being passed around and Rosie and Seb clinked glasses before they both took a sip. Rosie froze as she tasted her drink.

'What's the matter?' Seb asked.

'It's got bits in it,' Rosie whispered. 'What do I do?'

'Drink it. It's only tiny flakes of gold. All the rage down here this year,' Seb said.

'But...' Rosie said.

'It won't hurt you,' Seb said. 'Come on. Let's take in the view from the terrace.'

Rosie, following him, took another sip of the champagne, wondering if she could somehow filter the gold bits through her teeth and save them. Gold was at an all-time-high price, she knew. How many glasses of champagne would it take to give her a decent amount? Surely it couldn't take that many? If she did have to pay the food poisoning people off, it could be a lifesaver.

Taking another gulp of her champagne, Rosie pushed the bits she could feel in her mouth against her back teeth and gum with her tongue and prayed they'd stay there until she could harvest them.

***

The large terrace had an 180-degree view over the Bay of Cannes. With its discreet lighting, bougainvillea climbing up the golden stone walls, and night-scented jasmine covering the pergola at the head of a flight of steps that led down to the Olympic-size, horizon swimming pool in the grounds below, it could have been the setting for a scene out of the latest Hugh Grant romcom.

'Merde,' Seb muttered. 'Forgot Pierre would be bringing Veronique.'

Rosie followed his gaze and saw an anorexic woman clinging to the arm of a much older man.

'You don't like her?'

'She's a nightmare – loud, vulgar and full of herself. And now she's married to Pierre she thinks she merits the same VIP attention as him.'

'Who is he?'

'Ex-French diplomat. Nice guy. Why he had to go and marry that woman – should have kept her as his cinq-à-sept secret.'

Rosie, who'd never understood the French acceptance of extra-marital affairs, said, 'Shouldn't have had a mistress in the first place!' She glanced curiously at Seb. 'So "cinq à sept" is still accepted here?'

'Of course. Even expected in certain circles,' Seb said. 'Come on, let's dance.' And taking her by the hand, he led Rosie back into the ballroom of the mansion where the disco was.

'Not going to introduce me to Veronique then?' Rosie asked.

'I've no doubt you'll meet her later. She won't be able to contain her curiosity about you,' Seb said.

Seb was right: an hour later, as Rosie begged for a rest from dancing, Veronique appeared at their side.

'Seb, darling. It's been ages. How are you?'

'Veronique,' Seb said, submitting to cheek kisses. 'Fine. And you? Where's Pierre?'

'Been nobbled by an American who wants to talk business.' Veronique turned to Rosie. 'Hi. And you are?'

'Rosie of Café Fleur next door to me,' Seb said, his arm around Rosie's shoulders.

'Ah, so you're the mad Englishwoman who's taken it on. I wish you well with that place but personally can't see it working.'

Before Rosie could reply, Seb said, 'She's doing a great job of turning the place around.'

Veronique pulled a face. 'Really? I'd heard she was already in trouble.' She shrugged. 'Whatever you say.' Veronique turned her back on Rosie. 'How's Isabella these days, Seb? See much of her now you're not in Monaco?'

'Enough,' Seb said. 'Come on, Rosie, let's dance. See you around, Veronique.' And taking Rosie by the hand, Seb practically dragged her in the direction of the dance floor.

Rosie, dying to ask 'Who's Isabella?', found herself caught up in an energetic rock number and had no breath to talk .

It was gone two o'clock when Seb looked at Rosie. 'Shall we call it a night?'

Rosie nodded tiredly. 'Please. You okay to drive?'

Seb shook his head. 'No. We'll grab a taxi back. I'll pick the car up tomorrow.'

Traffic was quiet and the taxi soon had them back at the hotel. Rosie looked at Seb.

'Thanks for taking me – I enjoyed it. I'll see you tomorrow – I mean later!'

'Hang on. I thought we'd share a nightcap before I walk you home,' Seb said.

'You don't have to walk me home,' Rosie protested.

Seb raised his eyebrows at her and said, 'I'll get the drinks.'

Rosie waited on the beach while Seb went into the hotel. The cool air down by the sea was refreshing and she breathed in the salty tang. It was a beautiful night; although there was too much light pollution to see the stars, the moon was clearly visible. Watching Seb walk back to the hotel, Rosie smiled. The fact she'd enjoyed this evening so much was down to him. He had a definite way of making you feel special, that was for sure.

She glanced across to where Café Fleur was in darkness save for a dim light behind the curtain of the studio. James was home then. Slipping off her shoes, Rosie walked slowly along the shoreline towards Seb's habitual rock, enjoying the feel of the cold water lapping over her bare feet. She sighed happily. Life would currently be better than good if it weren't for the food-poisoning threat hanging over her.

'Feels good?'

Rosie nodded, taking the glass of orange-coloured liquid and ice and looking at Seb.

'Cointreau. Santé.'

Rosie took a sip of her liqueur. 'Thanks for singing my praises to Veronique, by the way. D'you really think I'm doing a great job? Have you changed your mind about my cooking?'

Seb shook his head. 'I had to shut her up somehow,' he said. 'Your cooking's all right, I suppose.'

Rosie, about to protest, saw his lips twitch and asked instead, 'I wonder what she meant by saying I was in trouble already? I thought we'd managed to contain the food poisoning accusation after we'd told James not to talk about it. I suppose the damage was done before.' Rosie sighed.

Seb shrugged. 'You know what it's like down here for gossip. Veronique's probably got a friend working at the Mairie where the complaint would have been lodged originally.'

'But that means the details could be common knowledge,' Rosie said.

'Don't worry about it. It's not affected business, has it?'

'Not sure. We've been really busy with lunches recently. Evenings started off good but are a bit on the quiet side now, though,' Rosie said. 'Whereas you, you always have a full car park in the evening.'

'I've already got my reputation. People know me,' Seb said. 'So it's easier.'

'I'm beginning to wonder whether it's worth staying open past six o'clock,' Rosie said. 'But I do need to get the Café Fleur name out there in time for the locals to know about me for winter.'

'You're planning on staying open all year then?'

'I need an income from something,' Rosie shrugged. 'I'm hoping the locals will have taken me to their hearts by then. And there's sure to be a few tourists around, too. Let's face it, winters down here are mild and people still come to the beach. It's got to be worth a try.' She didn't add that the food poisoning episode should be settled one way or the other by then.

'So, who's Isabella, by the way?'

'Someone who lives in Monaco,' Seb said. 'You'll meet her one day soon.'

Rosie waited for him to say more but when he didn't she drained her glass and said, 'I need to go home, Seb.'

'Let's go. Don't forget your shoes.'

Walking back to the apartment with Seb's arm companionably around her shoulders, Rosie struggled to keep the yawns at bay. At the door to the villa, Seb hugged her briefly and placed a light kiss on her forehead.

'In you go then. Sweet dreams. See you in a few hours.' As he turned to go, he added, 'I'm glad you enjoyed the party – and the champagne. Incidentally, I'm not a big fan of gold teeth!' And then he was gone.

Rosie raced upstairs straight into the bathroom and stared intensely at her teeth, before triumphantly removing three flecks of gold with her finger and carefully placing them on a piece of tissue.

Chapter Nineteen

Rosie was enjoying the luxury of a sleep-in the morning after the party, knowing that Tansy was in charge of the weekly prep at the restaurant, when her mobile rang.

'Are you coming in soon?' Tansy asked. 'Only there's a man here asking for you.'

'It'll only be a rep,' Rosie said sleepily. 'Can you deal with it? Just don't order anything too expensive! Otherwise tell him to come back later. I'll be there in about an hour.'

'Okay. See you.'

Rosie glanced at her watch: nearly eleven o'clock. Another five minutes and she'd have a shower and go to the beach. She was going to miss the slower pace of Monday mornings when the restaurant was open seven days a week. It was only a matter of days before that happened and the summer season totally took over her life.

Both Tansy and James were in the restaurant when Rosie got there.

'You cope with that rep all right?' Rosie asked, helping herself to a coffee.

'Turns out he wasn't a rep,' Tansy said. 'Said it was a personal matter.'

'Did you get his name?'

Tansy shook her head. 'Wouldn't leave it. Said he'd call back some other time.'

'Weird.' Rosie frowned. The only thing she could think of was it being something to do with the food poisoning thing – in which case she was glad she hadn't been there. 'Did he look like a lawyer?'

Tansy shook her head. 'If you mean was he wearing a suit and carrying a briefcase – no. Just the usual South of France uniform: Ray-bans, polo shirt, shorts and deck shoes. Oh, he had longish hair tied back in a ponytail.'

'And as there's always an arsehole under a ponytail, we'll take it he wasn't a lawyer then!' Rosie said, laughing. 'Oh well, if it's important he'll be back.'

'How was the party last night?' Tansy asked. 'You and Seb have a good time? See any celebs?'

'It was good,' Rosie said. 'If there were any celebs there, I didn't recognise them. I did meet this local woman called Veronique, though, who seems to think Café Fleur is doomed already.'

The café phone rang just then.

'That's probably Olivia,' Tansy said. 'Sorry – forgot to tell you, she phoned here earlier. Seems to think you've been avoiding her – which you have!'

Rosie sighed before lifting the receiver. 'Hi, Mum. How are you?'

A minute later, Rosie found herself agreeing to go to Monaco for supper.

'Zander's in Italy until later so we can have a good chat. Clear the air? I know you're worried about me. If you get here early enough we could even do a spot of retail therapy? My treat before you say you can't afford anything.'

'I'll see you later, Mum – about seven,' and Rosie closed her phone.

'That's my quiet evening in sabotaged then,' she said. 'Right, let's get on.'

It was late afternoon when Rosie fed Lucky and gave her a quick walk, before racing home and settling her in the apartment and running to the station to catch the train.

Rosie loved the ride along the coast to Monaco. Working on the yachts she'd seen it from offshore so often she'd barely glanced out of the galley window towards the end. Now she enjoyed looking at the Med from the other side as the train hurtled past villas and huge apartment blocks and she caught glimpses of the luxury yachts out at sea that had once been a familiar part of her life.

Strange to think Olivia was now becoming a part of this different world – if only temporarily. Surely her relationship with Zander wouldn't last? And then Rosie would be left to pick up the pieces.

As the train lurched into the long tunnel at Cap d'Ai that would take her into Monaco/Monte Carlo station, Rosie resolved to talk to Olivia about the fact she was setting herself up for disappointment/heartbreak by living with Zander. They'd have to have a proper mother–daughter talk – ironically the wrong way round.

Half an hour later, as they sat drinking coffee on the Café de Paris terrace watching the world go by, Rosie broached the subject.

'Mum, about you and Zander.'

'What about me and Zander?' Olivia said. 'I'm happier than I've been in years. I think I make him happy, too. You have a problem with that?'

Rosie shook her head. 'I'm glad you're happy, obviously, but…' She hesitated.

'You're worried about Zander's reputation? About the age gap?'

'Yes to both,' Rosie said. 'But mainly I worry that you'll end up hurt.'

'Possibly. But I'm not that naive, I know the score. Meantime, I'm enjoying life with a man I am exceedingly fond of. I only wish you were currently as lucky. Heard from Charlie lately?'

'We're not talking about me,' Rosie said. 'But no, thank goodness.' She could live without Charlie trying to involve her in his life again.

Olivia glanced at her before saying quietly, 'I've spent a great deal of my adult life alone. I don't want you to do the same.'

'Me neither,' Rosie said, equally quietly. 'But I'm not going to take up with just anyone to avoid that.'

'That's been my reasoning all these years,' Olivia said. 'So trust me. It's a bit late, but now I've met him, Zander isn't just anyone to me. He's special. I had high hopes of Charlie being special for you.' Olivia glanced at Rosie. 'He's a good guy.'

'He may be a good guy,' Rosie said quietly. 'But he's got too much money and a possessive, controlling streak. Besides, right now, I have to concentrate on the Café Fleur.'

Olivia laughed. 'Darling, you can never have too much money.'

Rosie shrugged. 'Maybe not, but you can be too possessive. Anyway, Charlie moves in a different circle to me. It's not one I feel comfortable in.' She jumped as a loud bang rang out when a lorry dropped its load of Armco safety barriers in the road.

'You'll have a good view of the Grand Prix from Zander's apartment,' she said.

Olivia shook her head. 'We won't be here. Zander's taking me to Italy that weekend to get away from all the hype and noise.'

'He doesn't like Formula One?' Rosie said. 'I would have thought he'd be involved in the socialising, if nothing else.'

'Oh, I think he likes it but says TV gives a better coverage and he can watch in Italy. Besides, he's got a good price for renting the apartment out. He says we'll definitely be back in time to go to a celebration party on the Sunday evening, though,' Olivia added, finishing her coffee. 'Which reminds me. I need a dress. Let's go.'

Two hours later, when Olivia had found not only a dress but also shoes, and Rosie had declined the offer of a new outfit, they made their way back to the apartment overlooking the old port.

Rosie stood on the balcony wondering what it would be like to have the money to live in Monaco permanently. 'D'you like living here?' she asked as Olivia joined her on the balcony and handed her a glass of rosé.

'Most of the time,' Olivia replied. 'There's just something about this place that makes it special. Although sometimes I do feel I'm living in a dream. I know people perceive it as pretentious and way too glamorous to be true but there are lesser mortals like me living here, too. Imagine, though, what it must have been like in the days of Princess Grace, before almost all the grande belle époque villas vanished.'

She turned as the apartment door slammed. 'Zander's home.'

Rosie turned away as Olivia and Zander embraced and kissed. Honestly, her mother was behaving like a lovestruck teenager!

Zander insisted on taking them out for supper and then, despite Rosie's protests, said, 'And after we walk you to the station, Olivia and I, we have to meet someone at the Casino later, so I'm sorry, I can't drive you home.'

Later, as the train rattled along the coast, Rosie realised she'd enjoyed the evening. She could also see the attraction Zander had for Olivia. She'd never seen her happier – so she had to be pleased for her, didn't she? Besides, what business was it of hers anyway?

She wouldn't stand for Olivia interfering in her love life so how could she even think about interfering in hers? Olivia had been on her own now for so long Rosie didn't really understand why she'd had this sudden need to move in with someone. She'd always had a busy social life, never mentioned being lonely. Maybe Zander really was special to her?

Rosie frowned as she came to a decision. Whatever Olivia and Zander had going on, it was none of her business and was best ignored until it petered out. Which Rosie was convinced it would eventually. She'd just have to make sure Olivia knew she'd be there for her if and when needed.

Chapter Twenty

It was the last weekend of the film festival and Café Fleur had been mega busy. It was gone seven o'clock Sunday evening before an exhausted Rosie said goodnight to James, leaving him to lock the restaurant door behind her, and made her way home with Lucky. Her mobile rang as she opened the door. Olivia.

'Hi, Mum. How was Italy?'

'Put Channel Three on the TV, *now*,' Olivia said, ignoring the question. 'It's the presentation of the awards at the festival.'

'Why? You know I'm not into all that. And I'm so tired all I want to do is collapse.'

'Just do it,' Olivia insisted. 'And hurry. Otherwise you'll miss it.'

Puzzled, Rosie did as she was told. She was just in time to see a man waving his trophy in the air and leave the stage before the camera swung back to the presenter.

'Mum! Is that who I think it was?'

'Yes. Although he's going by the name Tiki Gilvear these days. Tiki! I ask you, what sort of name is that? Apparently, he's fêted everywhere in America as a brilliant scriptwriter after he penned some blockbuster movie.'

'He's got a ponytail,' Rosie said.

'And doesn't that look ridiculous on a man of his age,' her mother practically snorted down the phone.

'He was always good at making a fool of himself without realising it. Oh, I've got to go. Zander is waiting. I'll ring you in the morning and we'll talk more then. Bye.'

Rosie switched the phone off and sat down numbly in front of the television, her mind barely registering the scenes flashing before her eyes. Until, that is, the camera scanned the auditorium and she caught another fleeting glimpse of a smiling Tiki Gilvear.

Now she had the unwelcome answer to who'd been asking for her at the restaurant: Tiki Gilvear. He could have left that name with Tansy – it wouldn't have meant anything to her. Thank goodness she hadn't been there and he hadn't bothered to come back. At least she'd been spared the embarrassment of a face-to-face meeting and telling him to get lost.

Absently, Rosie stroked Lucky. Why had Tiki Gilvear come to the Café Fleur to see her in the first place? Why hadn't he bothered to make a second attempt to contact her? Not that she had any desire to see him. There was nothing left to say to each other. Thankfully, with the festival finishing this evening, he'd be off back to America in the morning and his life of fame over there.

***

Monday morning at work, Rosie was still trying to put Sunday evening's TV scenes out of her mind. Sleep had evaded her for most of the night and there were huge bags under her eyes.

'I've got some industrial-strength concealer in my bag if you want some?' Tansy said.

'I look that bad?'

Tansy nodded. 'Afraid so. What's up?'

Rosie shook her head. 'I just couldn't sleep for some reason.' No point in telling Tansy that learning the identity of the ponytailed stranger had thrown her. She'd only want to know who he was and start to question why he'd turned up now, and Rosie had done enough speculating about that herself during the last few hours.

Rosie moved towards the coffee machine. 'Coffee will help. James been down yet?'

'I sent him off to get some cream and to order the weekend crabs. He should be back soon.'

Rosie flicked through the reservations book. 'We're in for a week of busy lunchtimes by the look of this. We're going to need Alicia every day. I just hope she's available and Seb hasn't already booked her.'

'Talking about me? Morning girls. You all right, Rosie?' Seb asked, giving her a concerned look as he walked into the kitchen.

'I'm fine, thanks,' Rosie replied, wishing she'd taken Tansy up on the concealer. 'Actually, we were hoping Alicia would be available every day this week and not already working for you. What are you doing here anyway? Haven't you got a hotel to run?'

The words came out sharper then she intended and she gave Seb a half-smile by way of apology.

'Take no notice of her,' Tansy said. 'She's had a hard night. Didn't get much sleep.'

Rosie closed her eyes in exasperation at the way Tansy had phrased the words. She dreaded to think what Seb would make of them.

'What she means is, I didn't sleep very well last night and I'm tired.'

'You need some fresh air. Come on. It'll do you good. Clear your head,' Seb said opening the door. 'Besides,

I need to talk to you,' he added as Rosie went to protest she didn't have the time.

'Fifteen minutes,' she said to Tansy. 'Could you phone Alicia for me, please? Tell her we need as many hours as she can give us this week.'

The sun had yet to come around the headland and there were few people about so the beach still had that deserted, beginning-of-the-day air about it.

Seb, with his customary indifference to wet feet and shoes, happily squelched along in his dock-siders, where the waves lapped the shore, while Rosie did her best to stay upside of the tide line.

'Ugh. I don't know how you can do that. Why don't you just go barefoot?' she asked. 'Your feet are going to be so cold and clammy by the time we get back.'

Seb glanced down indifferently. 'I'll change when I get back. What's wrong? I know you like to paddle.'

'Of course I do – but properly, with bare feet,' Rosie said. 'I can't stand wearing wet and cold shoes or socks.'

Smiling, Seb shook his head at her before pulling a toothpick out of his pocket and starting to chew on it.

'Are you out of cigarettes and desperate?' Rosie said.

Seb shook his head. 'Thought I ought to make a real effort this summer to stop. Chewing on one of these cinnamon-flavoured things is supposed to help.'

'And does it?'

'Not so far, no.'

Rosie laughed. 'Good luck, anyway. So, what did you want to talk to me about?'

'I need you to come to a party in Monaco with me next Sunday afternoon,' Seb said.

'Need?'

'Mm. My ex-partner is going to be there and I don't fancy going on my own.'

'Ex-partner as in ex-girlfriend?'

'Yes.'

'But if I come with you, won't she assume that I'm now your girlfriend?'

Seb nodded. 'That's what I'm hoping.'

'But I'm not.'

'You could be. Just for Sunday, if you like.'

Rosie stopped and looked at Seb. 'Why would you want…? What's her name?'

'Zoe.'

'Why d'you want Zoe to think I'm your girlfriend, when I'm not?'

Seb sighed. 'It's complicated but, basically, I need her to know that we're finished – a fact she's patently refusing to believe. I'm hoping that if she actually sees me with someone else, it will sink in that we are truly history and we can go back to being civilised friends.'

'Why did you break up, anyway? And how long ago? Did your gambling habit have anything to do with it?' Rosie asked, deciding she needed more information before committing herself to being paraded before an ex as the current girlfriend.

'It's a long story. She involved me in something and then decided I was superfluous to requirements and told me to get lost. My gambling habit was not involved but my personal morals were.'

'How long ago did this happen?'

'Six years,' Seb answered flatly. 'We had a big argument, but on principle I refused to get lost as she'd demanded.'

'Is that why she thinks you're still hung up on her?' Rosie asked.

'I was determined to remain civilised and friends. It is better that way.' Seb shrugged his shoulders. 'But Zoe, she took it as a sign that I couldn't let her go when she wanted to move on. Now, though, she has decided she made a mistake and wants me back in her life. She can't accept that I'm serious when I say I don't want to be in her life that way.'

Rosie sidestepped a larger than usual wave before asking, 'So, during these six years, Zoe has never met a girlfriend of yours to convince her you're over the affair?'

'I worked unsociable hours at The Recluse and I was always alone when I saw Zoe. It is only now, with the hotel, I can have private time when I want. Within reason.'

'But there must be someone else you could take – Isabella, for instance,' Rosie said, remembering Veronique's question at the party.

Seb smiled. 'It's Isabella's party – that's how I know Zoe will be there. Please come with me, Rosie. I promise you'll have fun.'

'Okay,' Rosie said, 'I'll come with you.' At least she'd get to meet this Isabella woman. Pretending to be Seb's girlfriend might be fun, too.

'Thank you,' Seb said, catching hold of her hand and swinging her around to face him. 'And now, Rosie, tell me why did you not sleep last night?'

Rosie hesitated. Should she tell Seb about Tiki Gilvear? On the one hand it was nobody else's business, but she could do with discussing it with somebody.

'Are you still worried about Olivia and Zander?' Seb said as she hesitated.

'No, its not them. I've decided their affair will just have to burn itself out. It's something else.' Rosie stopped, a horrified expression on her face as she looked downwards.

'Seb Groc, *how could you*?' With Seb still holding her hand, she was standing not only below the tideline but in the sea.

'I've got wet feet!'

Seb burst out laughing.

'It's not funny.' Wrenching her hand out of Seb's and moving on to dry sand, Rosie bent down and took her shoes off. 'That's it. Talk over. I'm going back to the café.'

Chapter Twenty-One

GeeGee was tired but happy. For the first time in months, she actually had some spare cash in her purse thanks to Bruno. This last weekend she'd been back and forth to the airport no less than ten times picking up his clients.

It had taken a couple of trips before the sense of being the new girl on the block had left her. By then all the tips Bruno had given her that first evening had become second nature: try and find a parking space on an easily accessible floor – otherwise, near the lift – 'Don't want the clients having to walk too far,' he'd said. Get an official sign from the desk to write names on; pay the parking fee before you get to the exit. Above all, smile – 'People will forgive you a lot if you smile,' he'd said.

Last night had been the first real test of her ability to smile on the job. The flight, due to arrive at 11.05 p.m., was 'en retard' when she walked into the Arrivals hall. Nobody on the information desk could give her even an estimated time of arrival.

Bruno had warned her late-night flights were a real pain but it was always best to hang around the airport in case things suddenly improved, so she bought herself a cup of coffee and a magazine and settled in for the wait. Three coffees and three hours later the flight landed.

Five hours sleep, a hot, reviving shower, and she was sitting at her desk in the agency the next morning failing to laugh at a joke Hugo clearly felt was in line for Joke of the Year.

'Had a sense of humour bypass today, have we?' Hugo said. 'You'd better get yourself sorted before your ten o'clock appointment,' he added before turning away. 'Or I might just have to take over.'

GeeGee resisted the urge to shout after him, 'That joke was racist and so not funny. And steal my clients again – I'll show you how funny I can be.' She knew from previous set-tos with him that it didn't pay to provoke Hugo.

She took her ten o'clock clients for their second viewing of an apartment in a modern block on the bord de mer and managed to keep a professional smile fixed in place when they said they'd like to buy it. They'd never have guessed she was 'this close' to punching the air with delight. She just knew things were on the turn for her. To celebrate, she took them to Café Fleur for coffees and to start the paperwork.

After they'd left she sent Erica a text: 'Fancy lunch on the beach? Bring Cammie. I'm paying.' Time to treat her favourite people.

Waiting for them to arrive, GeeGee checked her emails before closing down the laptop and ordering a glass of rosé the next time James passed on his way to the kitchen. Doing a spot of people-watching, sitting by the sea on a sunny day with a glass of wine, was something she didn't do very often but today she'd enjoy it.

A cluster of luxury yachts were moored out in the bay around the l'ile de Lerins, a helicopter buzzing around the largest one. Fascinated, she watched as it slowly descended onto its landing pad.

After Dan had signed for apartment 4c, she'd looked up the yacht he was crew on. Owned by a Russian, it was definitely a serious contender for Mega-Yacht of the Year and was one of the few that carried a helicopter. Maybe that was the yacht he worked on anchored out by the islands and Dan was one of the crew on the deck greeting the helicopter's passenger as they stepped onboard.

Sipping her rosé, GeeGee wondered if Dan would remember his offer of coffee when his purchase of apartment 4c completed. She'd definitely take him up on it if he did, but he'd probably forgotten even saying it.

A few customers were having an early lunch and GeeGee recognised a couple of locals. She smiled. Word was beginning to spread about the Café Fleur and she was pleased for Rosie's sake.

She frowned as a man on a nearby table began gesticulating at James angrily. Briefly, she wondered what that was all about but Erica and Cammie arrived at that moment and by the time they'd sorted themselves out and ordered lunch, the man was standing up to leave.

* * *

The Tuesday lunchtime rush was in full swing when James, coming into the kitchen with new meal orders, said, 'Compliments to the chef from some guy on table twelve. Wants you to join him for a liqueur.'

'You know I don't drink with the customers, James. I'm way too busy today, anyway. Thank him and politely decline on my behalf, will you? Is he a regular?'

James shook his head. 'No.' He picked up the desserts for table nine and went back to the terrace to deliver the message. Two minutes later he was back. 'Guy says he's not paying his bill until you've been out to see him. Think he means it.'

Rosie sighed. That's all she needed. A perverse customer. What was it with the guy?

'What's he like, James?' Tansy said. 'You never know, Rosie, he could be a millionaire after your body as well as your tarte tatin.'

'About sixty, designer clothes, Cartier watch, well spoken – oh, and he's got a ponytail,' James said.

Rosie froze.

'Sounds like the guy who was here before,' Tansy said. 'You know, the one who...?'

'I know the one,' Rosie said. 'James, I'm sorry to use you as a go-between but would you please go tell Mr Tiki Gilvear that he is not wanted here and the management have requested he leaves immediately. Threaten him with security, if you have to. There is no charge for his meal.'

'Is this Tiki Gilvear, as in the film producer who's just won the Palme d'Or at Cannes?' Tansy asked, looking at her shocked.

'Just do it, James,' Rosie said, ignoring her. 'Now.' She moved across to the side kitchen window from where she could see one or two of the tables at that side of the terrace. She saw GeeGee, at her usual table, busy tapping away on her laptop, look up as James went to the next table and delivered Rosie's message to the man sitting there.

Even after twenty-five years and the addition of a ponytail, Rosie would have recognised the man sitting on the terrace as her father.

He was clearly not taking the order to leave without protest and customers were openly watching the scene with interest. Rosie bit her lip. How the hell was she going to make him leave if he refused? The security she'd told James to threaten him with didn't exist. Could she phone Seb and ask him to come over? He'd be busy with lunches, too.

She watched as James briefly left him to fetch a piece of paper from the restaurant bar, which he handed to Tiki, who then dismissed him with a wave of his hand. James stayed out on the terrace clearing tables, talking to other customers, while waiting for Tiki to finish writing.

Rosie willed him to hurry up and leave. At last he put his pen down, folded the paper and beckoned James over. James took the paper and then stood to one side as Tiki left the terrace. It was only when she felt herself sigh and relax her shoulders that Rosie realised she'd been holding her breath, willing Tiki to go.

'Are you going to tell us what this is all about?' Tansy said. 'Or is it some big secret?'

'In a minute. Thanks, James.' Absently, Rosie took the piece of paper. She continued to watch Tiki Gilvear walk away from Café Fleur – she needed to know he'd gone.

When a young, blonde woman ran up to join him and they hugged, Rosie muttered, 'Well, of course, he'd have to have a bimbo in tow.'

As Tiki and the blonde disappeared from view, Rosie finally looked at the piece of paper she was holding:

Dear Rosie,

I am sorry you declined to talk to me today. I have to leave for London this evening for a few days but I will be back at the weekend for a holiday for a few weeks. I am staying at the Beach Hotel and I would be grateful if you could see your way to meeting me as I wish to discuss a matter of some importance to me with you. T.

P.S. Thanks for lunch – it was delicious. My turn next time.

Rosie looked up to see both Tansy and James watching her. She sighed. 'Okay. I'll put you both out of your misery. But this is strictly between ourselves – okay? Tell no one. Tiki Gilvear – or, to give him his real name, Terry Hewitt – is my long-absent father. And he is totally wrong if he thinks for one minute I am interested in meeting up with him or hearing anything he has to say.'

As for having lunch with him… No way. She screwed the note into a ball before throwing it in the kitchen waste bin before glaring at both Tansy and James. 'We've got customers waiting. Move!'

Rosie was still in a foul mood later that afternoon when Charlie turned up unannounced.

'What d'you want?' she demanded, not caring how rude she sounded.

'Nothing in particular,' Charlie said. 'Thought I'd just pop in and see how you were doing. Have dinner with me tonight?'

'No, thanks, I'm busy.'

Charlie was silent for all of two seconds.

'You seeing much of Seb?'

Rosie glared at him. 'None of your business if I am.'

'You know's he a gambler?'

'So?' Rosie said. 'None of my business – or yours – what he gets up to in his spare time.'

Charlie shrugged. 'Just want you to know what you're getting into.'

Rosie resisted the urge to tell Charlie that she wasn't getting into anything. That she and Seb were friends, that was all. The least said to Charlie about anything in her life, the better.

'Goodbye, Charlie.'

Infuriatingly, Charlie stayed put and watched as Rosie started to do the regular weekly bar stocktake. More house rosé needed, more champagne wanted in the wine fridge. By the time she got onto the bar snacks inventory his looming, silent presence was really irritating her.

'Heard you went to a party with him the other night. You could come to a party with me.' That did it.

'Charlie, listen to me. We keep having the same conversation. We're friends and that is all we'll ever be – despite you and my mother wishing for more. I am not going out with you again however many times you ask me. Watch my lips: I. Am. Not. Interested. Okay? Go and find someone who is. How about Sarah?'

'Olivia thinks you should come out with me?' Charlie said.

Rosie sighed. Damn. If she wasn't careful the two of them would be in cahoots plotting her downfall. Mentioning Sarah had been deliberate on her part, hoping Charlie would pick up on the name, but he'd ignored the mention of her totally.

'Charlie, please go. I've got lots of work to do. As from this weekend the restaurant will be open seven days a week so I need to at least try and get organised.'

Charlie looked at his Rolex. 'Shit. Got to go anyway. Got a meeting with Dad. I'll see you.'

Unfortunately, Rosie didn't doubt it and watched him leave, wondering how long it would be before he was back.

Later that evening, back at the flat, a tired and exhausted Rosie made herself a sandwich and poured herself a large glass of cold rosé before phoning Olivia. She needed to talk to someone who would understand.

'Terry turned up at the restaurant lunchtime,' Rosie said. 'He seems determined to talk to me before he goes back to the States. Any suggestions as to how I get rid of him?'

'How long is he going to be around?' Olivia asked.

'He's in London for a couple of days but then he's coming back for a holiday. I just know meeting him would be a complete waste of time. What on earth would I say to him after all these years?'

There was a short silence at the end of the phone, before Olivia said, 'Would it help if I came with you for moral support?'

'Remembering the way you two used to lay into each other, I don't think that's a good idea,' Rosie said. 'I'm too tired to think straight right now. At least I've got a few days' reprieve while he's away. I'll talk to you soon. Love you,' and she hung up.

Pouring herself a second glass of wine as a nightcap, Rosie couldn't help being pleased that the festival was over and the droves of showbiz types had all but disappeared, back to wherever they hung out. There were always celebs around down on the Côte d'Azur but not en masse like at festival time when every other person was 'something' in films.

If only Terry was leaving, too. By rights he should be flying back to the States clutching his Cannes trophy to work on his next blockbuster. He definitely shouldn't be staying at Seb's for the next few weeks hoping to see her. Especially when there was no chance of that happening. After all these years she had nothing to say to him – and zero interest in any excuses he might conjure up to explain away his behaviour all those years ago.

Chapter Twenty-Two

Seb walked into the kitchen Sunday afternoon as Rosie and Tansy cleared up after a busy lunchtime.

'My girlfriend ready for Monaco then?'

'Girlfriend?' Tansy said, looking from one to the other and back to Rosie. 'Is there something you meant to tell me?'

'Seb. I'd totally forgotten about this afternoon,' Rosie said, ignoring Tansy. She'd explain later about being Seb's make-believe girlfriend. 'Have I got time to go home and change?'

'Sure. Nothing too sexy, though!'

Rosie looked at him.

'I want Zoe to get the message I'm happy with an ordinary girl,' Seb said. 'As opposed to a sexy Barbie doll,' he added with a smile.

'Gee, thanks. I'll come just as I am then, shall I?' Rosie said.

'Perhaps take your apron off,' Seb said, grinning at her.

'Know the expression "digging a hole", Seb?' Tansy said. 'I'd say you're about to disappear in one up to your neck!'

'Rosie knows what I mean,' Seb said. 'And what I want. Don't you?'

Rosie shrugged. 'I suppose so. Let's just hope Zoe gets the message.'

Back at the apartment, where Seb gave her five minutes to change and settle Lucky while he waited downstairs, she flung on a pair of clean jeans and pink T-shirt. Reaching for a pair of trainers, she stopped.

What the hell. She didn't have to look that ordinary. It was Monaco they were going to, after all, and surely Seb would appreciate her making an effort even if she *was* only his make-believe girlfriend. She took her favourite pale-blue sundress with spaghetti straps out of the closet, pulled it over her head and slipped her feet into her wedged espadrilles. That was better. She did at least feel feminine if not sexy. Besides, who knew who she might meet at this party?

Fleetingly, she wondered if she was doing the right thing agreeing to go to Monaco with Seb today. Curiosity to see both Zoe and Isabella had been the main reason for her agreeing to be his pretend girlfriend for a couple of hours, but suddenly she found herself wondering what she was letting herself in for. Too late to back out now, though.

Slipping into the passenger seat as Seb held the car door open for her, Rosie smothered a yawn. It had been a hard week. She could do with staying home and collapsing with a glass of wine rather than having to put on a show for Seb's ex.

The Porsche was speeding through one of the numerous tunnels on the Monaco road when Seb, glancing sideways at Rosie, said, 'Tiki Gilvear's back at the hotel. I gather you know him?'

'He's a friend of Olivia from a long time ago,' Rosie muttered.

'He did mention he was hoping to catch up with Olivia,' Seb said, accelerating and overtaking a lorry. 'And... other friends.'

Rosie glanced at him suspiciously. Had Terry been talking about her to Seb? She sincerely hoped not. It was none of his business. 'How long is he staying?'

Seb shrugged. 'Open-ended. Says it depends on something he needs to sort and he's not leaving until it's resolved. Could be a couple of weeks or a couple of months.'

Rosie's heart sank. A couple of months! Did that 'not leaving until it's resolved' refer to seeing her? Be more than a couple of months in that case. She'd have to ring Olivia and warn her.

'Rosie...' Seb hesitated before continuing. 'I really appreciate this afternoon. Let me return the favour. If there is anything you need to talk about – I make a very good listener. I might even be able to help.' He glanced across at her.

Rosie shook her head. 'There's nothing to talk about but thanks for the offer.' She stared out at the passing countryside. She'd been tempted before to talk it over with Seb, but would it help? In a way it would be good to talk to someone impartially. Someone who could help get her thoughts straight. Work out the best way to proceed.

Would talking to Olivia help? Probably not. She'd been far too affected over the years to view the subject of her ex-husband dispassionately. But it was nobody's business other than Olivia's and hers, so best to keep it that way.

She'd have to make damn sure she wasn't available when Terry came calling at the café again, as she was now sure he would at some stage. She'd put James and Alicia in the restaurant, find another person to man the takeaway, and then she could stay in the kitchen with Tansy.

'I need a couple more staff,' she said now, glancing at Seb. 'I don't suppose you happen to know anyone?'

Seb sighed. 'Like Alicia, you mean? Afraid not. Try putting a notice on the door. This time of year the students are starting to be around looking for work. Maybe James knows someone?'

'I'll ask him,' Rosie said.'How long are you planning to stay at this party?'

'Depends,' Seb said.

'On?'

'Zoe, mainly.' Seb shifted gear and steered the car into the right-hand lane ready to take the sharp bend down onto the Cap d'Ail road when the lights changed. 'We'll be there soon and find out how welcome we are!'

Rosie digested this silently. Didn't sound as though this party was going to be all fun and games. She looked at her watch. Coming up to six. On reflection it was a funny time for a party. Thoughtfully she glanced across at Seb.

'Is it a real party? With food and everything? Or just aperitifs?'

Seb laughed. 'Oh, it'll be a real party. Not sure the food will be to your taste but there will be some.'

Seb pulled up outside an apartment block. One of the most exclusive and expensive blocks in Monaco. Thank God, she'd dressed up a bit.

'The party's here?' Rosie asked.

Seb shrugged. 'Zoe's had an apartment here for years. Come on, let's go find the party girl.' He picked up a package from the back seat before locking the car.

As the uniformed concierge acknowledged their presence they made for the elevator at the far end of the marbled floor foyer.

'You didn't tell me it was actually Zoe's party.'

'It's not. It's Isabella's.' Seb pressed the elevator button for the tenth floor and thirty seconds later the doors opened directly onto Zoe's apartment – and the noise of a children's party in full flow hit them.

Seb had his arm around Rosie's shoulders as they stepped out of the lift. 'Come on, girlfriend, it's showtime,' he muttered.

'Why didn't you tell me it was a children's birthday party?' Rosie hissed. 'I would have brought a present.'

'Not necessary,' Seb said. 'This is from both of us.' He was scanning the crowd of children playing an energetic game of musical chairs.

'Seb, darling. You're finally here.' No cheeky air kisses from this thin as a cocktail stick and twice as brittle woman; it was a full-on snog. When she finally let Seb go, she turned a puzzled look on Rosie.

'Who's this?'

'My girlfriend. Rosie, meet Zoe, my ex girlfriend,' Seb said, placing a heavy emphasis on the word ex.

Rosie flashed a brilliant smile at Zoe.

Zoe pouted. 'But I thought we were going to try to...'

'Daddy!' A small girl hurled herself at Seb and shrieked with delight as he picked her up and swung her high.

'Isabella!'

Rosie swallowed hard in surprise. Daddy? Why hadn't Seb warned her Isabella was his daughter? Looking from Seb to Zoe, realisation dawned. They'd been more than friends. Isabella was their daughter. And Zoe wanted them back together again as a family. Thanks a bunch, Seb, for putting me in the middle!

Isabella dragged Seb off to meet her friends, leaving Rosie momentarily stranded. Zoe looked at her and gave a short laugh.

'He didn't tell you Isabella was his – *our* – daughter, did he?' she said. 'Better ask him what else he hasn't told you. How long have you been his girlfriend, anyway?'

'Not long,' Rosie said, watching Seb with Isabella and her friends. He clearly adored the child. What had he said? Something about Zoe calling his personal morals into question? Had Zoe thrown the jibe when he'd declined to be a full-time father to Isabella?

'There's food and drink in the anteroom for the adults,' Zoe said with a wave of her hand. 'Help yourself. The party bags are in there, too, if you want to start filling them. We need twenty.'

The last sentence sounded suspiciously like an order, which Rosie decided to ignore as she helped herself to a glass of wine and some smoked-salmon blinis.

The anteroom opened out onto a balcony overlooking a square with a fountain and a small lawn. As Rosie wandered out with her drink and food, two women regarded her with interest.

'Hi. You with Seb Groc?' one of them drawled.

Rosie nodded. 'Yes.'

'You'd better watch your back with Zoe,' the other woman warned. 'She doesn't take competition kindly.'

Rosie shrugged. 'She doesn't bother me.' If she was Seb's girlfriend for real there would clearly be a problem, but as she was only acting the part for the day she could afford to ignore Zoe.

Rather than stay out on the balcony with the two women, Rosie returned to the anteroom to finish her wine and food. The party bags were still lying there waiting to be filled.

Curiously, Rosie looked to see what they were going to contain. There were the usual sweets and colouring books, packets of girly designer pink tights, packages of luxury bath gels and soap and a pile of boxes containing child-size gold bracelets with a heart fastening. Zoe must have spent a fortune on this lot, Rosie thought. Especially on the bracelets in their velvet boxes from the jeweller by the Casino.

Still, it was all probably par for the course in Monaco. Briefly Rosie toyed with the idea of starting to fill the party bags but quickly dismissed the thought. She wouldn't do Zoe's bidding on principle.

Out in the sitting room, Seb was engrossed in organising the children in a game of noisy musical bumps. How long did he plan on staying? He certainly seemed to be enjoying himself. She smiled as he hugged Isabella to him as the game came to an end and whispered in her ear.

Perhaps she'd go and join in the fun. Anything was better than loitering in the anteroom and feeling uncomfortable. Seb saw her as soon as she stepped back out into the main room and swiftly involved her in the 'What's the time, Mr Wolf?' game he was organising.

Fifteen minutes later, loud shrieks heralded the arrival of the professional entertainer Zoe had hired to finish the party. As the children clustered around him, Seb made his way over to Rosie.'

'I'm ready to go,' he said. 'I've said goodbye to Isabella.'

'What about Zoe?'

'We'll do that together,' Seb said, taking hold of her hand. 'Come on.'

'But I told Isabella you'd stay and put her to bed like a normal daddy,' Zoe protested when Seb said they were leaving.

'Isabella knows I've got to get back to the hotel,' Seb said.

Zoe glanced in Rosie's direction. 'And she hasn't filled the party bags.'

'Do them yourself,' Seb snapped, and holding Rosie tightly by the hand he made for the lift.

Standing next to Seb as the lift whooshed them down to the ground floor, Rosie glanced at him. 'You owe me. You promised me I'd have fun. You lied. Tell me something: how did you get involved with a bitch like Zoe in the first place?'

'You didn't take to her then?' Seb asked, a tight smile on his lips.

Rosie shook her head. 'Not one little bit. I liked Isabella, though.'

'I hoped you would.'

'Why didn't you tell me Isabella was your daughter?'

Seb shrugged. 'Didn't want you pre-judging me before we came.'

Rosie was about to say something when the lift stopped and the doors opened.

'Come on, let's get the car and go back to our own places,' Seb said.

'I can see why you and Zoe didn't stay together,' Rosie said. 'But Isabella deserves to have you in her life more than the occasional Sunday. I'm sure you do your best to see her but so many men think their presence isn't necessary in their children's lives – until it's too late.' She sighed.

'Well, at least you give me some credit and didn't tar me with the Tiki Gilvear brush,' Seb said and winced. 'Merde!'

The silence in the car was long and loud as Seb took the road up out of Monaco towards the autoroute. Rosie, too furious to speak, realising Seb knew all about her rift with Tiki, sat there trying to control her temper.

As Seb drove up to and through the toll booth onto the A8, she finally said, 'You've been talking to him?'

'Insisted I had dinner with him and Saskia the other evening.'

'Is Saskia the young blonde bimbo I've seen him with?'

Seb nodded. 'Yes. He wanted to sound me out – see if we were friends, see if I could persuade you to at least meet with him.'

'No chance.'

'He also wanted Olivia's current address.'

'I hope to hell you didn't give it to him,' Rosie said. 'You're in trouble if you did. Mum's threatened to kill him more than once in the past. She'd probably kill you, too, for telling him.'

Seb shook his head. 'No, I didn't. But he knows about her and Zander, so it's only a matter of time before he finds it.' He hesitated. 'He seems to genuinely want to make amends. I quite like the guy.'

'Shows how much you know about him. But then you single fathers would stick together.'

Rosie registered a sharp intake of breath from Seb, before she found herself thrown back against her seat as Seb stamped his foot hard down on the accelerator and the car surged forward into the fast lane.

Turning her head to protest at the sudden speed, the look on Seb's face stopped her from saying a word.

She didn't say anything either as they sped past their slip-road exit. Part of her wished she was at the wheel, in control and able to vent her own feelings by stamping on the accelerator.

They were halfway to Saint-Tropez before Seb finally slowed down.

'You're lucky there aren't any gendarmes around this evening,' Rosie said. 'Now, will you please take me home?'

'Sure,' Seb said. 'Rosie, I know you don't want to talk to me about Tiki Gilvear but I am truly nothing like him. I think it would help you to talk about it.'

'No, thanks,' Rosie said. 'It's private and none of your business.' Just when she'd begun to realise how much she liked Seb and even to fantasise secretly about the possibility of them having a summer romance, this had to happen. She ignored Seb's sigh of frustration. It wasn't her fault. It was Terry who'd involved him in their family feud, not her.

Chapter Twenty-Three

Rosie rang Olivia as soon as she got back to her apartment. She had to warn her that the holiday Terry was planning was for an indefinite period of time and that he was possibly planning to contact her.

'If he turns up at the apartment you might have a hard job not seeing him.'

'Zander will get rid of him for me,' Olivia said. 'I'm more worried about you. Especially as he's staying at Seb's.'

'I can't believe after all this time – it's nearly twenty-five years, for God's sake, since I've seen him – he wants to speak to me. Can't help wondering why.'

'Somehow I doubt his guilty conscience has kicked in,' Olivia said. 'There was usually an ulterior motive behind everything he did.'

'D'you think now he's made his fortune in the States he wants to give us some?' Rosie said, quickly throttling the treacherous thought of how useful some extra cash would be. 'Make up for all the years he ignored us?'

'I wouldn't hold your breath,' Olivia said. 'Terry always kept a tight hold on his wallet.'

God, what a Sunday this was turning out to be. Olivia's remark about Terry and his wallet had reminded her how it wasn't just his wallet Terry had always kept a tight hold on – he was also capable of keeping his emotions on a tight rein. The last time she'd contacted him she'd learnt that the hard way.

Worried and desperate enough to ring and ask for his help she'd sneaked a look at Olivia's address book and written down the latest telephone number for him she could find. Somewhere in California.

Even now, all this time later, the way he'd failed her still hurt. She still remembered the conversation. How one-sided it had been. How he'd listened to her tear-laden ramblings before sighing and saying, 'I'm truly sorry to hear what you've told me but I'm too far away to help. Besides, right now, I've got enough problems of my own. I'm sorry – you and Olivia will have to cope on your own.'

She'd never told Olivia about that phone call and she'd never contacted him since. As far as she was concerned her father had died at the end of that conversation. The letters that had arrived in the following months had gone straight in the bin, unopened. The message must have finally got through in the end because it was years now since she'd received either Christmas or birthday cards from him.

As for Seb, Rosie knew she owed him an apology for being so snarky with him after Monaco. But he should have warned her about Zoe and Isabella. It wasn't fair the way he'd thrown her in at the deep end with Zoe.

Talk about the ex from hell. Rosie didn't think Zoe had believed for one nanosecond that she really was Seb's new girlfriend. Rosie took a long drink. It was a good job she wasn't really. Imagine having to live with Zoe refusing to relinquish her hold over Seb and using Isabella as a bargaining tool. Life would be hellish.

Still, she couldn't help feeling a bit sorry for Seb, although it was his own fault for becoming involved with the scary bitch in the first place.

***

'So, how many houses are we looking at this morning?' Erica asked as she got into GeeGee's car. 'Remember, I've only got two hours before I have to be back at the shop.' She couldn't leave the part-time assistant on her own for longer.

'Two, definitely, maybe a third, but we can leave that one for another day if we're pushed for time,' GeeGee said, easing the car into the traffic on the bord de mer, concentrating on getting into the right lane for the lights. 'Must admit I wasn't expecting this amount of traffic this morning.'

'Perhaps we should have walked,' Erica said.

GeeGee shook her head. 'Nope. I've got an airport run to do for Bruno straight after.'

'During the day? I thought you were the fill-in driver for evenings on weekdays?'

'I am but today is manic with people leaving at the same time so I said I'd do a twelve o'clock departure run for him.'

'I know you want the money but don't overdo things, will you? Three nights this week it's been gone one o'clock before you've got home.'

GeeGee shrugged. 'It won't last for ever and right now I need the money.'

Five minutes later, GeeGee turned off the main road into an impasse and pulled up in front of some dark-green gates. The pressing of the intercom button set off a bout of frenzied barking in the villa. Erica looked at GeeGee, eyebrows raised. 'Is it safe?'

'The dogs are fine but beware of their owner, Delilah – she's got a bite all of her own.'

Before Erica could comment, the gates swung open and a woman appeared, struggling as she tried to hold back three large dogs.

'Dogs are harmless. Shut the gate and I'll release them. Once they've had a sniff they'll wander off and leave us in peace.'

Erica bent down to stroke a black bundle of fur as it inspected her feet and legs. 'You smell nice,' she said.

'Cerise insists on rubbing herself against and sleeping on the rosemary bush at every opportunity,' Delilah said, looking at Erica. 'Are you genuinely looking to buy? If you're not you can leave now before you waste any more of my time.'

'I'm looking to buy,' Erica confirmed. 'Whether your house is what I'm looking for remains to be seen. Could be you're wasting my time.' She glanced across at GeeGee, the question 'Is this woman for real?' implicit in her look.

'Perhaps we could go inside now the dogs have finished their sniffing?'

Delilah turned without a word and led the way indoors. Inside, there was furniture everywhere, making it difficult to move around or see things properly. Antique stuff alongside modern stuff and Billy bookcases. A curious mixture. Erica kept her face neutral and stayed silent as she manoeuvred her way through the sitting room, the tiny kitchen, three overcrowded bedrooms and finally out through the French doors onto the terrace by the pool.

The garden was a surprise. A beautiful oasis of lavender, lantana bushes, lemon trees, oleander and several rose bushes. It smelled heavenly. Two large pottery elephants stood at the the head of the pool steps. Delilah clearly took more pride in her garden than her house.

Erica turned her back on the pool and looked at the villa. Was this the house for her and Cammie? Cleared of all the furniture, the rooms, apart from the kitchen, would be a good size. In her mind's eye she could see her own furniture in situ and the place gleaming.

Questions were beginning to form in her mind. Questions that she would ask GeeGee once they'd left. She was blowed if she was going to show any interest in the place to Delilah.

Erica glanced at her watch. 'Thank you. We've another house to view this morning so we'll get out of your way.' She left GeeGee to say goodbye and made her way back out to the front garden before Delilah could react.

As the electric gates clanged close behind them, Erica said, 'Well, that was interesting. Have to say she brought the worse out in me. D'you get many clients like her?'

GeeGee shook her head. 'No, thank goodness. Did you like the villa, anyway?'

Erica sighed. 'Yes and no. I'm not sure it's big enough for me – the kitchen definitely isn't. D'you know why she's selling?'

'Downsizing to an apartment apparently.'

'She'll have to get rid of some of that furniture. You could barely move in there.'

'Let's go see the next house,' GeeGee said. 'Maybe you'll like that one better.'

The owner at the next house was charm itself, offering them coffee and cake when they arrived and answering all Erica's questions with a smile. It was a lovely villa but, as Erica said to GeeGee when they left, 'Having the dual carriageway at the end of the garden makes it a no-no for me. I'm sorry.'

Chapter Twenty-Four

GeeGee took Erica back to The Cupboard Under The Stairs, before driving down into the Old Town and picking up the couple for the airport.

After dropping them at the 'kiss and fly' space outside the Departures hall, GeeGee began to make her way out of the airport. She was still on the outer limits when her phone rang. She pulled over. Bruno.

'Are you by any chance still at the airport?' he asked.

'Just about to exit Terminal 2,' GeeGee said. 'Why?'

'Could you please get to Terminal 1 for the London arrival due in ten minutes? Something's come up here and I can't make it.'

'Sure. Name? And where do I take them?'

Bruno's sigh of relief was audible down the phone. 'Bring them to the Auberge and I'll meet you there. I'll pick up the tab on this one, GeeGee, next time I see you.'

'Okay,' GeeGee said, surprised. 'So who...?

'It's my brother and his wife,' Bruno said. 'I think you met them last year so you won't have a problem recognising them.'

'I'll see you within the hour,' GeeGee said.

By the time she'd parked and made her way to the Arrivals hall the flight had landed and passengers were beginning to drift into the baggage-collection area. Standing, looking through the large glass doors, GeeGee spotted Adam, Bruno's brother, with his wife, Lucy, coming through, chatting animatedly to a man that looked remarkably like... Jay!

She moved back away from the glass doors, trying to compose her thoughts. What the hell was he doing here? Surely Bruno would have told her if he'd known he was coming with Adam? Hopefully it was a coincidence that he was on the same flight as Adam and once he'd reclaimed his baggage he'd disappear to find his own transport.

Thankfully, Adam and Lucy cleared Customs quickly and came through the doors on their own. GeeGee went forward to greet them.

'Hi. Bruno has been held up so, as I was out here anyway, he's asked me to take you back to the Auberge.' If she could get them out onto the concourse quickly enough and on their way to the car, she could avoid an embarrassing situation with Jay.

'Hi, GeeGee. Nice to see you again.' Lucy hesitated, before adding, 'I hope it's not going to be a problem but we met up with Jay on the flight and, expecting Bruno to meet us, we've offered him a lift into town... knowing Bruno would want us to.' She smiled uncomfortably at GeeGee.

GeeGee took a deep breath. Okay, this was her personal nightmare from hell, but short of creating a scene in public, there was nothing else she could do except go along with it.

'Where is he?'

'Coming through Customs any minute,' Adam said. 'Ah, here he is.'

GeeGee managed to sidestep the kiss on the cheek Jay leant in to give her and responded to his, 'Hi, it's great to see you,' with a barely audible 'Hi' back. Jay didn't seem to notice, though.

'The car's quite close,' GeeGee said. 'Follow me.'

Thankfully, Lucy insisted on taking the front passenger seat, leaving the two men to talk in the back. The journey along the bord de mer seemed never-ending to GeeGee. She just wanted Jay out of her car.

'So, how's things these days?' Lucy asked her as they approached Cagnes-sur-Mer.

'Oh, you know, the same as always,' GeeGee said, conscious that Jay was probably ear-wigging in the back.

'How long are you down for?' she asked. The question she couldn't, and wouldn't, ask was how long did Jay plan on staying? Was he back for good? Or just a holiday?

'A couple of weeks – or until Bruno and Patsy get fed up with us.'

Drawing up outside the Auberge, GeeGee breathed a sigh of relief on seeing Bruno standing there waiting. As everyone got out and took their cases out of the boot, Bruno came up to her open driver's window.

'I'm really sorry about...' he said, jerking his head in the direction of Jay. 'I'd never have asked if I'd known.'

'It's not your fault,' GeeGee said. 'Have they got everything? I'll see you, Bruno.' And she drove off quickly before Jay could say anything to her.

One of her mum's favourite sayings had been, 'Life is full of surprises – pleasant or otherwise.' Jay turning up back down here was sure as hell a surprise in the 'otherwise' category. But she couldn't help wondering: Why the hell had he come back?

Chapter Twenty-Five

Glorious weather meant that the restaurant was busy with lunches every day the following week, leaving Rosie with no time to worry about Seb or Terry Hewitt. She pinned a STAFF WANTED notice to the shutters and prayed someone suitable would turn up soon.

Seb had been right about lots of students being around looking for work, but few of them had the necessary documents to work in France. Rosie sighed as she turned yet another hopeful down. No way was she going to fall foul of the French authorities by employing anyone on the black.

When Yannick, an ernest-looking French boy with glasses, who looked in need of a proper meal, appeared one afternoon, clutching all his necessary paperwork, she gave him a day's trial – and then employed him.

But it was Gina, taken on two days later as a waitress and takeaway assistant, who made Tansy raise her eyebrows.

'Bit posh, that one. I doubt she'll last five minutes,' she said. 'Bet she's got a trust fund.'

'She'd hardly want to work in a café then, would she?' Rosie said. 'Give the girl a chance. She's got the right papers to work in France and we do need the help.'

While lunchtimes were manic, weekday evenings on the beach continued to be quieter than she'd anticipated.

Rosie realised, looking at the accounts one afternoon, that she was losing money staying open after six o'clock. People clearly didn't come back to the beach after spending all day there. Talking it over with Tansy, she decided that, apart from Fridays and Saturdays, and the occasional 'Jazz on the Beach' evening, she'd close at six o'clock. So much for trying to gain a reputation to attract out-of-season customers later in the year.

Seb was still clearly upset with her as he hadn't called in since that Sunday in Monaco. Rosie managed to shrug indifferently when Tansy asked where he was.

'I think he's got a few personal problems,' she said.

'I miss him popping in,' Tansy said, expertly piping meringues onto a tray. 'I think you should go across and see him. You were always good onboard at helping solve the crew's personal problems.'

'Don't think I can help Seb in this case,' Rosie said. 'Besides, you know who is still there. I don't want to risk bumping into him.'

Terry had walked past the restaurant a couple of times in the week and she'd stayed in the kitchen out of sight of customers. She knew, though, she owed Seb an apology for last Sunday. Besides, he might know if Terry was planning on checking out soon, having failed to meet up with her.

'I might go over later tonight,' she said. 'I do need to talk to Seb.' If she left it till after nine, dinners in the hotel restaurant should be finished and people would have started to leave for the evening's entertainment in the local casinos and nightclubs. Including Terry.

It was almost ten o'clock when Rosie pushed open the door at the hotel's side entrance and spotted Seb in his 'inner sanctum' – the cubbyhole on the other side of the kitchen where he planned menus and did the books.

The sous-chefs were doing what prep they could for the morning breakfasts, while other staff were busy cleaning the kitchen. A cleaner mopped the floors.

'Is it safe to come in? Or are you too busy to talk?'

Seb looked up from the accounts book he was studying. 'No room in here,' he said. 'We'll go up to my apartment.'

'I don't want to stop you when you're obviously busy. I've only come to apologise for last Sunday,' Rosie said. 'I'm sorry I was so snarky.' There, she'd done it. Now she could leave.

'If you're afraid of bumping into a certain person, he's not here.'

'He's left?' Rosie smiled. That would be good news.

Seb shook his head. 'No, he's gone to Monaco for the evening.'

'Monaco?' Rosie said. 'He hasn't gone to see Olivia?' She didn't think much of his chances if he had.

'Said he was going to the Casino and then the Sporting Club. Maybe he'll bump into Zander and Olivia there.' Seb shrugged. 'So it's safe enough for you to come through and have a drink. Please, Rosie...' This as she shook her head. 'I need to talk to you. I also owe you an apology.'

Conscious of the interested looks the kitchen staff were giving them, Rosie gave in. 'Okay.'

'Have you eaten?'

Rosie shook her head. She'd completely forgotten about food this evening. 'No.'

'Neither have I. I'll have something sent up.' He scribbled a note and handed it to one of the staff. 'Ten minutes, please. My apartment.'

Taking her by the hand, Seb led her to a cupboard and opened the door. Rosie looked at him and giggled.

'It's like Narnia only with a lift, not a wardrobe!' As Seb gave her a puzzled look, she said, 'I'll explain another time. Childhood memory.' Surely her favourite childhood book had made it across the channel?

Two minutes later and they stepped out into Seb's penthouse apartment.

'Wow,' Rosie said as Seb opened a pair of French doors onto a roof-top terrace hidden from general view. 'You're full of surprises.'

Grecian urns filled with lavender and night-scented jasmine were placed randomly around the black-and-white, terrazzo-tiled marble flooring. A wrought-iron round table and two chairs were perfectly positioned by the rail for watching the sunset over the distant Esterel mountains.

'What a wonderful secret place,' Rosie said. 'I had no idea this was up here.' She wandered over to the balcony and gazed down onto the beach while Seb fetched a bottle of champagne and two glasses from the small, galley-type, outdoor kitchen discreetly hidden from view by three strategically placed pots containing palm trees. 'You can spy on everyone from here.'

'I rarely have time to come up here when there are people about. It's great up here at midnight, though – relaxing,' Seb said, pouring the champagne.' Good view for the fireworks festival, too.'

'You could sleep out here in August,' Rosie said, 'under the stars.'

'Too many mosquitoes around,' Seb said, handing her a glass. 'Don't worry – there are no bits in this one! Santé.'

Rosie smiled. 'Santé.'

A buzzer sounded. 'Supper,' Seb said, walking back into the apartment and opening the door. Rosie watched as he pushed the small room-service trolley out onto the terrace and lifted the covers.

'Try these first,' he said, 'while the batter is crisp.'

'Mmmm,' Rosie said appreciatively, taking a bite. 'I've had – and made – courgette flowers before but this is... aubergine. I might pinch this idea!' She grinned at him.

Seb gave her a stern look.

'What's the terrine?'

'Monkfish.' Seb cut a slice and handed her a plate and fork.

'This is seriously good,' She said moments later as she scooped up the last bite. 'Ever thought of being a chef?'

As Seb topped up their glasses, she looked around the terrace. 'Isabella's?' she asked, seeing a scooter tucked out of sight by the galley.

'Yes. She uses the terrace like a race track. Rosie, about Zoe,' Seb said. 'I'm sorry she was such a bitch to you. I knew she wouldn't be pleased with me but didn't think she'd be so rude to you.'

'That's a jealous woman for you,' Rosie said. 'If I was really your girlfriend then it would be a problem, but I'm not, so it isn't.' She sipped her wine. 'I still can't imagine you two as a couple.'

Seb shrugged. 'It was an on-off thing – until she became pregnant. When it was definitely off.'

'Babies do change things,' Rosie said. 'Especially if one of the parents doesn't want it.'

'You mean, especially if one of the couple decides the other has fulfilled their usefulness and wants out of the relationship.'

Rosie looked at him. 'You mean you ended it when Zoe became pregnant?'

'No. I was about to end it when Zoe beat me to it,' Seb said. 'Without telling me she was pregnant.'

Rosie looked at him. 'But you said she'd questioned your morals. I assumed you'd walked out on her because of Isabella.'

'You're jumping to conclusions again, Rosie. You really must break the habit.' Seb shook his head. 'Zoe wanted a baby but not a husband. She decided I had the necessary attributes for fathering her child, stopped taking her pills and got pregnant.' He studied his glass of wine before looking up at Rosie.

'She used me to get a baby. I didn't find out it was mine until she was about to give birth. Which was when my uptight, old-fashioned morals were thrown into question. I was supposed to walk away. Not want the responsibility.'

'Like many so-called normal men would,' Rosie murmured.

Seb downed the rest of his wine before pulling a packet of toothpicks out of his pocket.

'Still not smoking? Well done.'

Seb shrugged. 'Thanks. Anyway, when I learnt Zoe didn't want me involved I was furious. Isabella was as much my child as hers – she couldn't deprive me of knowing her. But apparently she could, even though my name is on the birth certificate.'

'What made her change her mind?'

'Oh, that's a fairly recent thing!' Seb said. 'Initially she was furious with me when I wouldn't disappear out of their lives. She did deign to agree to letting me see Isabella once a month – if she didn't cancel. Which she did frequently.' Seb took a draw of his cigarette.

'But then the novelty of being a single mother wore off. A couple of years ago she decided perhaps she'd made a mistake. I had my uses, after all, so it was time for us to embrace life as a family – for Isabella's sake, she said. Suddenly I was given full access any time I wanted. Which is wonderful. But I can't accept the strings she's now started to pull.'

'She wants the two of you to get back together, doesn't she?' Rosie asked quietly.

Seb nodded. 'Says Isabella deserves a proper family – and a brother or a sister. I love Isabella and I'd lay my life down for her, but Zoe…' He shrugged. 'I was never in love with her and I don't believe she ever loved me. The more I tell her I'll do anything for Isabella but I don't want to be with her, playing happy families, the more determined she becomes that I can't possibly mean it. Which was why I thought if you came with me on Sunday she'd see I'd moved on from her and get the message.'

Seb glanced across at Rosie. 'I'm sorry. I shall have to think of another way.'

'I think whatever you do you're going to have problems for a very long time with Zoe,' Rosie said. 'I hope Isabella isn't affected too much.'

'I'll do my damnedest to make sure she isn't,' Seb said. 'Isabella isn't the problem – Zoe is.'

Rosie finished the last of her wine. 'I'd better get going. Thanks for supper.'

'I'll walk you home,' Seb said.

'I need to collect Lucky from the restaurant first,' Rosie said. No point in arguing with Seb. He'd simply shrug his shoulders at her in his usual infuriating way and do it anyway.

Walking away from the Café Fleur, Lucky on her lead, a voice said, 'Evening, Seb, Rosie.'

Rosie caught her breath and quickened her step, refusing to acknowledge that she'd even heard the greeting.

'Evening, Tiki. Good time in Monaco?' Seb called out. 'See you in the bar later?'

'Do you have to collaborate with the enemy?' Rosie asked, all the sympathetic thoughts regarding Seb's problem with Zoe disappearing in an instant.

'Your enemy – my guest,' Seb said. 'I'm rarely rude to guests – only if they deserve it. Joining them in the bar for an evening drink is part of being a good host.'

Rosie shrugged. 'Just don't discuss me or Olivia with him.'

'You have my word.' Seb leant in to give her a friendly goodnight kiss on the cheek, before saying, 'Night, Rosie. See you tomorrow. And Rosie... thanks.'

Chapter Twenty-Six

While the others got on with the routine daily chores, Rosie gave Tansy's wedding cakes their final brandy soaking. Now they just had to sit for a few weeks before the marzipan and icing needed doing.

Rosie glanced around. Tansy was humming softly to herself as she sorted stuff in the fridge. James and Yannick were talking football in the restaurant as they sorted bottles and glasses. Gina was outside giving the terrace a sweep and wiping down the picnic tables.

Having extra staff had made a huge difference although Rosie couldn't help fretting about how much money she now payed out in wages. It was worth it to be less stressed. She'd just have to hope the sun kept shining and Café Fleur stayed busy.

Gina and Yannick had both fitted in well. Rosie smiled to herself thinking about them and the way Yannick coloured up like a tomato whenever he had to speak to her. Probably something to do with the low-cut tops she favoured.

As Rosie was putting the cakes away in their air-tight tins, Alicia came over. 'I could do the cake decorating for you if you like? I love doing things like that. It's a bit of a hobby of mine.'

'You're a star,' Rosie said. 'I can't tell you how much I was dreading doing the icing. I'll pay you, of course – or rather, Tansy will.'

Next job on her agenda was to find some musicians for Café Fleur's first ever Fête de la Musique. Rosie was conscious she'd really left it a bit late.

The pianist from the party – gosh, that night seemed such a long time ago – was already booked but had given her the telephone number of a couple of mates who played guitar and sax. She prayed that they would be good – and free to come.

It was sure to be a late night. All the Fêtes de la Musique that Rosie had ever been to had carried on well past midnight. Hopefully, it would attract some new customers. As long as it wasn't Terry Hewitt and his young blonde.

Rosie had watched them walk past the restaurant a couple of times. The blonde had even bought ice creams from the takeaway. She knew Olivia and Zander had been at the Sporting Club in Monaco one evening when they'd walked in. Olivia had told her they'd left immediately before Terry had a chance to spot them.

And Seb had told her yesterday that Terry had booked his best suite for another three weeks.

'It's good for my business you two not talking,' he'd said. 'Keep it up and he might stay all summer.' Rosie shivered. What a terrible thought.

She couldn't help wondering what Terry thought he was up to – the message must be loud and clear. Neither she nor Olivia had any intention of talking to him, so why couldn't he just get on the next flight out of Nice and go home? People must be clamouring for him after his big Cannes win.

Olivia, meanwhile, seemed to be enjoying living a glamorous life with Zander whisking her here, there and everywhere. Off to Corsica for a week before heading down to St Tropez for a holiday on some yacht owned by a multimillionaire friend of Zander. At least the chances of her bumping into Terry with all this jetting around was less likely.

Tansy handed her a cup of coffee. 'What are you thinking? You've been standing there in a trance for about five minutes.'

Rosie took a sip of the coffee.

'Oh, this and that. Mainly the Fête de la Musique. Hoping it will be a good night.'

No need to mention her worries about Terry. He was bound to leave soon. He couldn't be on holiday for ever. He had to go home some time.

***

Fête de la Musique day and the restaurant was busy with lunches. The French doors leading onto the terrace were folded back and all the tables on the terrace were occupied. Rosie, working behind the bar, hummed softly to herself as Hervé the guitar player strummed his way through a variety of songs. The atmosphere in the restaurant itself was lively, with happy customers tapping their feet to the music and clapping as Hervé finished a melody.

GeeGee, Erica and Cammie came down during Cammie's lunch hour. When Cammie got up and began to dance by herself, Rosie smiled. GeeGee had briefly filled her in about how losing her father had affected Cammie when Rosie had mentioned how quiet the little girl always was. To see Cammie dancing so happily was lovely and Rosie clapped her enthusiastically when Cammie stopped in front of her and did a wobbly curtsy.

'That was lovely, Cammie,' she said. 'Run and ask Mummy if I can give you an ice cream as a reward.'

Watching her daughter dance, Erica had to swallow hard to stop herself crying. Cammie had always loved to dance and Pascal had encouraged her. Had joined her many times, doing silly movements that made her laugh. It had been a long time since Cammie had jigged around so unselfconsciously. The doctor who had gently said they would both need time had been right. Life was making small healing advances through their sorrow.

Seeing Saskia walk in and sit at a table unnerved Rosie somewhat. Fleetingly she thought about asking her to leave but decided against it. If her father's bimbo wanted to eat in the restaurant that was okay; she could handle that. At least he wasn't with her.

Rosie acknowledged Saskia's presence with a nod and sent James over with a menu. Dealing with the bill of another customer, she saw James taking a small carafe of the chilled house rosé from the fridge and placing it on Saskia's table.

'I'll take the order into the kitchen,' she said, holding out her hand. 'She's waiting for someone to join her? Okay. You stay out here and I'll send Yannick out to help you.'

'Salad niçoise,' she called out back in the kitchen. 'Table five. Yannick, go through and help James, please. I'll take over in here for a bit.' No way was she going to be forced into a face-to-face confrontation with Terry in the restaurant if that was who Saskia was waiting for. Which it was.

'Tiki Gilvear's arrived. D'you want me to tell him to leave? If not, he'd like a salad niçoise, too, with chips on the side,' James said. 'He says he expects to pay this time.'

'He hasn't asked to see me?' Rosie said.

James shook his head. 'No.'

'I'll prepare his salad,' Rosie said, reaching for a plate. Treat him as just another customer. Stay in the kitchen and everything will be fine.

A party of six took the last table in the restaurant and as soon as people left a terrace table their places were taken by new people off the beach wanting to eat. In the flurry of preparing and cooking meals, Rosie lost track of time, and looked at her watch in surprise when James said something about it being four o'clock and time to turn the sign around.

'I'll do it,' she said. 'You grab a bite to eat and then help Gina on the takeaway.' She was in the restaurant before she realised her mistake. Terry and Saskia were still there. Damn and double damn. They should have left ages ago.

Ignoring them, she made for the French doors and systematically began to close them before turning the sign to CLOSED on the last pair. Inside her head, she repeated the mantra 'they'll be gone, they'll be gone, they'll be gone when I turn round' – but they weren't.

In fact, Terry was watching her while Saskia finished the large knickerbocker glory Rosie remembered making some ten minutes ago, having no idea it was destined for their table.

'Rosie, please may we talk?'

Terry's oh so English voice that Rosie remembered had acquired something of a mid-Atlantic twang, which sounded strange to her ears.

She shook her head. 'I have no interest in talking to you. We have nothing to say to each other.'

'Not true, Rosie. We have lots to say to each other.'

'It's years too late.'

'It's never too...'

'Yes, it is,' Rosie interrupted. 'For you and me, it *is* too late. So, just get off my back. I'm not interested in you or anything you have to say.'

Terry seemed to visibly shrink before her eyes as he heard her words. Rosie looked away. There was absolutely nothing he could say that would make her change her mind.

'Are you sure there's nothing I can say to persuade you? There's so much I'd like to tell you, to talk to you about.'

'Nothing,' Rosie said. 'I hope you and your bimbo enjoyed your meal.'

'Hey, I'm not a bimbo,' Saskia said, looking up from scraping the last of the ice cream out of the dish.

Rosie looked at her. 'You're blonde, cute, young and with him.' Rosie jerked her head in Terry's direction. 'So in my book that qualifies you as an old man's bimbo.'

Rosie's hand shook as she picked up their empty glasses before walking away. 'I'll send somebody through with your bill. Please pay it and then leave. Forever.'

Chapter Twenty-Seven

It was late afternoon when GeeGee returned to the beach after doing a couple of house viewings with a new client. The evening session of Fête de la Musique was still hours away but the beach was crowded with sun worshippers and families. The takeaway was busy with people coming off the beach for ice creams and drinks but several of the terrace tables were free, including her favourite one, tucked away in the back corner of the terrace.

Making her way towards it she ordered her usual coffee from Rosie before sitting at the table, grateful for the shade of the parasol protecting it from the sun. Placing her laptop in front of her she waited for her coffee – and Jay.

Erica had been furious on her behalf when she'd told her at lunchtime about Jay's reappearance. And the fact that he wanted to see her 'to talk'.

'He ups and leaves with the lame excuse he needs to find himself and now he wants to talk? Honestly, GeeGee, I hope you told him no.'

One look at GeeGee's face and she'd sighed. 'You agreed to see him, didn't you? Why?'

GeeGee had struggled to explain her reasons then, and right now she still wasn't sure why exactly she was sitting here waiting for Jay to show.

'Something to do with getting closure over that part of my life maybe?' she'd told Erica in the end.

After the initial shock over his unexpected appearance at the airport and her anger at the situation she'd found herself in, she'd calmed down and tried to view things rationally. Was he here because he wanted them to get back together? If he did – was that something she wanted? There had been no fluttering heart when she'd seen him, so she guessed that answered that particular question. She was over him. So why agree to see him?

When Jay had texted her asking to meet and talk, she'd thought about refusing, saying there was no point, but in the end had decided it would be better to be civilised and stay friends. Besides, she'd like to ask him why he'd gone without given her a reason. Sending an email twenty-four hours later apologising and saying he needed 'space to find himself' was not good enough.

Wanting closure was probably nearer the truth than she'd realised when she'd given that as the reason to Erica. She did need to know what had gone wrong – from his point of view, because she hadn't been aware of anything being wrong until he upped and left. The question she wanted answered was quite a simple one: 'Why?'

If he came out with that old cliche – 'It wasn't you, it was me' – she'd smile, agree and restrain herself from saying something sarcastic or even slapping him. Of course it was bloody well him – he was the one who'd walked! And now he was back – walking towards her.

Watching him as he strode confidently across the beach, her brain reregistered his sexy looks. Two women waiting in the queue at the takeaway were giving him covert, apprising looks, disappointment flitting across their faces as they saw him approach GeeGee's table.

This time, GeeGee didn't avert her cheek as he leant in to kiss her. 'It's really good to see you,' Jay said, sitting down opposite her. 'How's things?'

'Great,' GeeGee said. 'Couldn't be better.' No way was she going to admit anything else to him. Besides, things *were* good and getting better.

'You?'

Before he could answer, Rosie appeared with a bottle of Prosecco nestling in an ice bucket and a plate of canapés.

'Thanks,' Jay said as she placed everything on the table. 'You don't mind, do you? I ordered this once I knew you were coming.'

GeeGee shook her head. 'Just the one glass for me – I'm driving, but food will be good.' Taking the glass he poured for her she said, 'Are you celebrating something?'

'Santé,' Jay said as they clinked glasses. 'I'll tell you later. For now let's celebrate me being back and the two of us sitting here together again. We completed lots of deals here, didn't we?' he added, looking around.

GeeGee nodded, deciding to ignore the phrase 'together again'. 'We did. How long are you back for?' Thoughtfully, she took a bite of salmon and cream cheese blini and wondered where the conversation was headed.

Jay took a long drink of his Prosecco before looking at her. 'I'm back. Full stop.'

Stunned, GeeGee looked at him. 'For good? But I thought you were enjoying life in London. What happened? You get bored?' If the last question sounded bitchy she didn't care. Was he expecting them to get back together as if nothing had happened?

'It was good and I learnt a lot. I also worked out the things in life that matter to me.'

'You did what you wanted then – you found yourself,' GeeGee said, trying to keep a note of antagonism out of her voice. 'But doesn't the new you want to make the most of it in London?'

'Decided I'd rather live on the Côte d'Azur,' Jay said. 'More sunshine for a start.' He offered GeeGee the bottle before topping up his own glass when she placed her hand over her own. 'Besides, you're here.' As he grinned at her, GeeGee saw the old Jay she'd thought had loved her.

'Stop right there,' GeeGee said. 'You dumped me, remember?'

Jay looked at her silently but GeeGee stared him down, determined to try and make him... she wasn't sure what. Apologise? Say it was a mistake? Grovel?

As the silence lengthened between them, GeeGee sipped her drink. This was silly. She didn't want to play games with Jay. She wanted him to hurry up and get this conversation over with. She sighed.

'You said you wanted to talk, so could you get on with it? Please don't tell me, though, that you want us to get back together.' There. She couldn't put it any plainer than that, could she?

'No, this isn't about us getting back together,' Jay said. 'Although I have missed you, so maybe...?'

GeeGee shook her head vehemently. 'No chance.'

'Shame. Well, my good news is I'm taking over the agency from Hugo as of next week. I wanted to give you the heads-up about the current contracts for desk rents being revised and upped from the first of September. You might want to look for a desk in another agency if you have a problem with the idea of paying me rent.'

GeeGee listened to his calm voice delivering his news and shattering her world once again. Her ex-boyfriend was now going to be her boss and charge her for the privilege.

Hugo had already increased rents at the beginning of the summer, assuring everyone that would be it until next year. GeeGee felt sick. More money to find.

'How much is the increase?'

'Ten per cent.'

'That's plain greedy on your part.'

Jay shrugged. 'Have to make a start somewhere to cover the costs of buying the agency. You can put your own rates up.'

GeeGee picked up her bag and her laptop before standing up. 'I take it I have a desk at the agency until September?'

Jay nodded.

'Good. I'll email you officially relinquishing it from then.' Resisting the urge to throw her glass of Prosecco over him, GeeGee turned and walked away.

Her hand was shaking so much when she reached her car she could barely steady the key enough to fit it in the lock. An hour ago and she'd been congratulating herself on getting her life sorted and here she was being thrown back to square one come September. It was a different square one, though.

She took a deep, deep breath. Jay had disrupted her life when he left her last year and now he was back and about to do it again. Only this time she was fighting fit and it wouldn't be the knockout blow it had been last time. This time she had options. Didn't she?

Chapter Twenty-Eight

Hervé returned with the saxophone player for the evening session and soon there was an enthusiastic and happy crowd on the beach around the restaurant. Serving food from the takeaway, plus customers in the restaurant, it was extra busy, which suited Rosie just fine. No time to brood over things.

The earlier meeting with Terry and Saskia had left her feeling edgy and unsettled. Being busy stopped her thinking about the encounter too much. But it all came back with a thud near midnight when Seb accompanied Terry and Saskia down to the beach and they sat together at one of the terrace tables.

James took the glasses and the champagne they'd ordered over and carefully popped the cork before filling the glasses and placing the bottle in the ice bucket. Rosie watched as he wrote down their food order. Wordlessly, she took it from him and started to prepare the several plates of nibbles ordered.

What the hell did Seb think he was doing coming here all pally with Terry? It was only hours ago she'd told Terry to leave. Why did he think he would be welcome again? Was he banking on Rosie not making a scene in front of her customers? Well, he was right in that respect but that didn't stop her from having words with Seb when he came across to say 'Hi' and to ask for a second bottle of champagne.

'I could refuse to serve you another one,' Rosie said. 'Then you and your "friends" could leave.' She glared at him, glad there was a momentary lull in people queuing for drinks. 'Take them back to your place.'

'Rosie, it's business,' Seb said. 'He's a customer of mine who asked me to join him for a drink during the Fête de la Musique. I tried to tempt him with Cannes and the Croisette but he insisted we came here.'

'Did he tell you I told him to leave this afternoon? Forever. Why doesn't he just *go* home?'

'If you mean back to the States – he's not going. His plans have changed since London. He's relocating to Europe. In fact, he's asked me to help find him a house. I've introduced him to GeeGee and she's shown him one villa in particular that he really likes.'

'What? He intends to live around here?'

Seb shrugged. 'Wants somewhere on the coast. But keep it to yourself. He doesn't want word to get out yet that he's not returning to LA.'

Rosie sighed. 'Why this particular piece of Europe? Why can't he go to Italy? Or Spain? Anywhere – just not near me!'

Why, after all these years, did they both have to end up on the same bit of Europe? It was far too late to start playing happy families.

'Why won't you at least talk to him?'

'Because I have nothing to say to him. At least nothing he would want to hear.' Rosie picked up a cloth and vigorously began to wipe the counter down.

'You could listen to him. He might have something important to tell you.'

'I'm not interested in anything he might have to say. It's years too late for that.'

Rosie threw the cloth into the sink underneath the counter and glanced across to where the musicians were playing. Earlier they had encouraged a couple of their friends to sing along with a medley of songs from the 1920s. Now they were playing a selection of Charles Aznavour hits.

'What's he doing? He had better not be coming over here,' she said, watching as Terry left his seat and made his way towards the musicians.

'Think he's asking for a special request,' Seb said. 'What music does he like?'

Rosie stared at him. 'How the hell should I know?'

'He's your father. You must know something about his likes and dislikes.'

'None of your business, but seeing as he left Olivia and me when I was eight, I have absolutely no idea of his musical tastes – or his tastes in anything else, for that matter... *except*, he clearly likes bimbos.'

'Okay.' Seb held his hands up in surrender. 'I'm sorry.'

Rosie looked past him and saw Tiki taking to the microphone. 'Oh, my God. He's going to sing.'

'Can he s–'

The glint in Rosie's eyes stopped him in mid-question. Seb turned to watch as Terry began to sing the Charles Aznavour song 'Yesterday When I Was Young'.

'At least he's in tune,' Rosie muttered.

'I've heard worse,' Seb said. 'Think he's singing it to you.'

'Embarrassing,' Rosie said, realising Seb was right. Terry was sending glances her way, trying to catch her gaze. Steadfastly she looked anywhere but in his direction.

Minutes later, breathing a sigh of relief that the song was at last coming to an end, she made the mistake of looking at Terry directly. As he sang the words, '... the time has come for me to pay for yesterday when I was young,' he looked across at her, and caught her gaze.

'If he thinks that little performance is going to change my mind, he's wrong,' Rosie said. No way was she going to admit to being shaken by what appeared to be genuine emotion.

'Right, I've got work to do.' She went to move back into the kitchen. Seb put out a hand and stopped her.

'Rosie, listen to me – you have to talk to him.'

She shook her head but something in the tone of his voice made her look at him. 'Why? I can't think of one single reason why I should do that.'

Seb hesitated before saying, 'He's ill. And Saskia's not his bimbo. She's your sister.'

Chapter Twenty-Nine

As late as it was, but knowing she wouldn't sleep if she went back to the apartment, Rosie took Lucky for a run on the beach and then sat on the rocks. Thrilled as she had been with the success of Café Fleur's first Fête de la Musique celebrations, all the stuffing had been knocked out of her with Seb's announcement about Terry. She'd been there for about ten minutes trying to think things through when Seb arrived.

'I thought I'd find you here. Want some company?'

Rosie shrugged. 'If you like. I warn you, though, I'm not in the mood to say nice things.'

'I've told you before I'm a good listener. I might even be able to help – alternative view and all that.'

'I suppose Terry asked you to tell me he's ill? Well, it won't work. I won't be blackmailed into feeling sympathetic towards him and behaving differently,' Rosie said, picking up a pebble and trying to send it skimming across the sea. It plopped into the water a mere metre from the shore line and disappeared from view. 'Because that's what he's trying to do by telling you to tell me he's ill. Pure blackmail.' Another stone followed the first.

Seb sighed. 'No, it's not blackmail. He'd asked me not to tell you. I broke his confidence when I told you.'

'So why did you?'

Seb was silent for several seconds. 'Because I wanted to help you make the right decision.'

'You mean give in and talk to him.'

'You might regret it later if you don't.'

'The thing is, I don't really care if he's ill. I know that's wrong but I can't help it.'

Rosie knew from the look on Seb's face he was shocked at her statement. But it was the truth as far as she was concerned. She sighed.

'We've been estranged for more than half my life. Terry let Olivia and me down big time and then blew any possibility of a close father-daughter relationship for ever when I was seventeen – and that was nine years after he deserted Olivia and me.'

Frustratedly, Rosie picked up a handful of pebbles and threw them into the water one by one. Plop. Plop. Plop. Stones barely hitting the top of the water before disappearing.

'Sure, I'll feel sad like I do when anyone I know dies, and I'll probably have a pang of loss when Terry eventually goes but...' Rosie shook her head. 'It won't be a pang of loss for a loved one. There is no love connection between Terry and me and please don't mention that old cliché about blood being thicker than water. I no longer believe it.' Had never believed it, if the truth be told.

'As for Saskia, I've been an only child all my life. I don't need a sister now.' Particularly not a sister who had clearly had the sort of home life with a loving father she'd been denied.

'Maybe she needs you,' Seb said quietly. He was silent for a few seconds before continuing. 'Not having some sort of reconciliation with Tiki, though, might just be one of those things you regret afterwards for the rest of your life.'

'I'm sure I'll learn to live with it if that happens.'

'You're only thinking about how you feel. I think Tiki is hurting badly inside and wants to tell you he's sorry in person. It's your decision but I think other people might take the view you're selfish in denying an ill man the opportunity to clear his conscience.'

'Other people can think what they like,' Rosie said. 'He might be my father but I owe him nothing. The fact he may – "may" – have a guilty conscience over the way he treated Olivia and me is tough luck. Personally, I doubt it – as Mum says, there was usually an ulterior motive behind everything he did.'

'I wish you could feel generous enough to forget his past mistakes and talk to him,' Seb said quietly.

Rosie tried again to skim stone after stone across the water – all sank with predictable failure a yard from the rocks. If only her anger and bitterness would sink with them.

'And I wish you'd butt out and mind your own business.'

Seb held up his hands. 'Sorry. Only trying to help.'

A long silence sprang up between them before Rosie glanced at Seb. 'You truly think I should see him, don't you?'

Seb nodded but didn't speak.

Rosie sighed. What the hell was she supposed to say, to do? Talk about being emotionally blackmailed into seeing Terry.

Why was he so intent on talking to her at this late stage anyway? Seb didn't know the history behind their estrangement, but deep down Rosie had to acknowledge that he was probably right. She should meet him.

Rosie wished Olivia was around to give her a hug. That was another thing – she'd have to talk to her soon, to tell her about Terry being ill and staying permanently on the Riviera.

Rosie's last stone skimmed across the water twice, as if encouraging her to do what she acknowledged deep down was the right thing to do. To be generous, as Seb had put it, and go and see her father. But not yet. No way could she could face it at the moment.

She needed time to adjust, to think about what to say to him. How to make it plain that after all these years, even if she did agree to talk to him, there was no place for him in her life afterwards.

'Come on, Lucky, time to go home.' Rosie bent down and clipped on the dog's lead.

Seb walked alongside her back to the café where Rosie turned to him. 'Don't bother to offer to see me home. I need some space to think – without any pressure from you.'

Silently, Seb took a step back and watched Rosie walk away, before following her at a discreet distance and watching her reach home safely.

Chapter Thirty

Sunday morning and Erica, with an excited Cammie alongside her, was sitting on Le Petit Train as it made its way out of Nice. Views of the outlying industrial zones soon changed to views of riverbeds and the steep-sided mountain valleys of the Var as the train made its way up into the hills.

Stations, tiny and seemingly from a bygone age, were either stopped at or slowly chugged through, giving tantalising glimpses of the villages they served. Cammie was entranced with everything she saw. The last time they'd done this journey by train, she'd been a tiny baby. Pascal had always preferred to drive the sixty kilometres to his parents place. Driving hadn't been an option today and Erica was enjoying seeing views previously denied her from the passenger seat of the car.

As the train pulled out of Puget-Théniers, Erica began to gather their things and handed Cammie her pink rucksack to slip over her shoulders.

'A few more minutes and we'll be in Entrevaux,' she said. 'Look, there's the citadel on top of its mountain.'

'Can we climb up to it?' Cammie said.

'Probably not this visit,' Erica said. 'There won't be time today and we have to go home on the first train tomorrow morning. But next time, I promise.'

Jean-Pierre, waiting for them on the platform as they stepped off the train, picked up Cammie and swung her around. 'Bonjour, ma petite,' he said, giving her a hug as he set her back down giggling, before turning to greet Erica with cheek kisses and a bear-like hug.

'I'm so pleased you've come today,' he said. 'Amelia is quite made up. She's back at the house,' he added, as Erica looked around for her. 'She's a bit stressed over tonight's party. Says she has one or two things she's forgotten to do.' He sighed. 'Danielle and co. have arrived so that should help calm her.'

A five-minute walk along a quiet track and they were at the house on the hill overlooking the ancient town where Amelia and Jean-Pierre had lived all their married lives. Where Pascal and Danielle had grown up. Where memories of Pascal were everywhere. Photos on the piano in the sitting room; exam certificates framed and hung on the staircase; his skis hanging in the boot room along with his mountain bike propped against the wall.

Amelia gave them both a hug and a kiss. 'I'm so pleased you've come. It means so much to me and Jean-Pierre to have you both here, even though...' Her voice trailed away.

Tears were clearly not far away and Erica opened her weekend bag quickly.

'Cammie and I have brought you both something,' she said. 'This needs to go in the fridge.' She placed a bottle of pink champagne on the kitchen table. 'Cammie has made you a special card,' she added placing it alongside the champagne.

'And we hope you both like this,' she said as she handed Amelia a box wrapped in red-and-silver paper. 'Happy Ruby Anniversary.'

Amelia gasped as she saw the vintage red Cranberry Glass decanter and two glasses nestling in the box.

'They're beautiful,' she said, holding the decanter up to the light. 'Thank you. We'll treasure them.'

'Right,' Jean-Pierre said, 'I've booked a table for a family lunch at our favourite restaurant in the Old Town. We have half an hour to get there.'

'Come on, Cammie, let's get you out of your jeans and into your pretty frock,' Erica said, hoping that her own outfit in her weekend bag wasn't too creased and in need of an iron. 'Usual rooms?' she said, picking up her rucksack.

Amelia nodded. 'All ready and waiting. I'll come up with you.'

Erica smothered a sigh. This was going to be hard, sleeping alone for the first time in the room she and Pascal had always shared when they visited. The room that had been his growing up and still contained lots of his things because Amelia had always resisted clearing them out and turning it into a bona fide guest room, insisting it would always be Pascal's room.

'I hope you'll be comfortable in here, Erica,' Amelia said, opening the bedroom door. 'I've given it a bit of a makeover.'

Erica stood and gazed around. The room had been completely transformed. Freshly painted white walls, new curtains and carpet, and a new, shabby-chic chest of drawers standing in the corner. Erica bit her lip as she looked at the only reminder that this had once been Pascal's room: a silver-framed photograph of him holding Cammie as a baby and smiling broadly at the camera had been placed on the bedside table.

'I thought my new guest room deserved a happy picture from the past,' Amelia said quietly, looking across at the photo.

Wordlessly, Erica turned and hugged Amelia, knowing how much courage it had taken for her to change things and move forward in a life where her son would never need the room again.

***

Erica had always thought walking across the drawbridge and through the gatehouse of the old portcullis guarding the entrance to the medieval town akin to taking a step back in time. Today was no exception. The tall, ancient houses, the narrow streets, the air heavy with history, all threatened to push Erica's imagination into overdrive and back to the fifteenth century.

Pascal had often teased her about her vivid imagination, but even he had admitted once to finding the atmosphere in the old, fortified town to be somehow crackling with the memory of ghostly, sinister, ancient events.

'Not a place you'd want to be alone in on All Saints Night,' he'd told her.

Following Jean-Pierre, as he led the way to the restaurant, Erica held Cammie's hand and kept her mind firmly in the twenty-first century.

The atmosphere in today's Entrevaux, with the sun shining, trees in full leaf, hanging baskets filling the air with a delicate perfume and the laughter of happy people, was truly centuries away from its brutal past.

Seated next to Danielle for the meal, she tried to relax. It was the first real family 'do' since Pascal had died and it was strange not to have him at her side in the midst of his family. Listening to their rapid French as they reminisced about the last forty years, Erica tried not to feel like an interloper.

She'd been part of this family for nearly ten years now and had been made to feel welcome from day one, but today, as Danielle reminisced with her parents about her childhood with Pascal, Erica tried hard not to feel left out. She'd heard some of the stories before, of course, but one or two new ones surfaced during the course of lunch.

Erica knew that, with only ten months between them, Danielle and Pascal had been inseparable while growing up. A closeness that had endured into adulthood. Being close, though, hadn't stopped them from squabbling or getting each other into trouble from time to time.

'I was the one who invariably got blamed for most things,' Danielle said as the desserts arrived. 'Pascal said it was my right as his big sister to take the blame although, as teenagers, I have to admit, it wasn't unknown for him to cover for me.' She shrugged and looked at Erica. 'I guess you could say we always had each other's backs. I miss him.'

'Me, too,' Erica said, glancing across the table to where Cammie was sitting with her cousins, hoping she wasn't being upset by all the talk of Pascal. Seeing her giggling at something Carla was saying, Erica relaxed. Cammie was clearly having her own fun. So good to see her laughing with her cousins.

Amelia followed her glance. 'Perhaps Cammie could come and stay in the school holidays. Spend time with us on her own.' She smiled hopefully at Erica. 'We'd love to have her and promise we'd take great care of her. I'm sure she'd love it.'

Erica returned the smile. 'Maybe,' she said, fighting the immediate negative reaction that sprang into her mind. Cammie might love it but could she let go of the one constant in her life? Even for a few days?

After lunch, everyone returned to the house and, while Cammie joined the cousins to watch a DVD in the sitting room, a thoughtful Erica went to the kitchen to help Amelia and Danielle organise the final details for the evening's party.

'It's such a shame you have to go back so early tomorrow,' Amelia said, slicing a quiche into bite-sized pieces. 'I wish you could both stay longer.'

'GeeGee kindly offered to open up and man the shop for me for a couple of hours in the morning, but she has her own commitments,' Erica said, smothering a sigh.

It was going to be a long evening if Amelia kept harping back to the 'wish we saw more of you' conversation.

Chapter Thirty-One

Sitting out under the stars on the roof terrace while Erica was away, GeeGee thought about the future. It was all very well vowing to herself that this time she wouldn't let Jay's actions scupper her life because she had options, but what exactly were her options?

Along with a bottle of rosé, her notebook was on the table beside her, ready for the ideas that would kickstart her future. So far she'd drunk half the bottle of wine, and not a single idea had popped into her head. Instead she'd gone round and round in circles.

Give up selling houses? A job she really enjoyed and one she'd struggled to qualify for since she'd lived in France? Increase her airport runs? They'd certainly made a difference to her finances. Bruno had said he was overloaded, that he might welcome her doing more. Get a part-time job – even ask Erica if she needed any more part-time help in The Cupboard Under the Stairs.

No, she couldn't ask that. Erica would feel under pressure to say yes and she was already indebted to her for a roof over her head. But she could tell Rosie, if she ever needed a temporary pair of hands at Café Fleur for a couple of hours, to give her a call.

GeeGee topped up her glass again. It was all a bit, well, bitty. Maybe she should concentrate on one job, the one with the best chance of bringing her in the most money, which had to be selling property. Her desk at the agency was safe for a few weeks, by which time she'd need to have organised something else for her public profile. So she needed to come up with an idea and implement it before then.

Did she need a bricks-and-mortar shop window? Could she work from home – wherever home was by the end of summer? How many clients had actually walked into the office? Any who did were invariably snaffled by Hugo, and Jay was sure to do the same. Most of her clients came by word-of-mouth recommendations – both the buyers and the sellers. People were happily telling their friends about her. Could she build on that quickly enough?

She put her glass down and opened her laptop. Idly she clicked on and started to browse her website. Looking at the pages containing the letters of grateful thanks from clients she'd helped find their dream home or holiday apartment, an idea floated into her brain. Could she offer home management services?

GeeGee smacked her forehead as the thought streaked through her brain. How stupid was she? Why had she never thought of this before? Sell houses, manage the properties she sold that were often rented out, and do airport runs to help the inevitable cash-flow problems. Three businesses linked by a common theme.

All she really needed office-wise was her laptop and a printer. An online business didn't need a bricks and mortar address. Her website was up and running. She was already registered in the French system as self-employed so that wouldn't be a problem. The money she saved from not having to pay for an agency desk could be spent on advertising her services and updating the website.

Okay, it seemed a simple enough plan that might work, although there were sure to be unseen problems cropping up. Financially, things would be tight but a couple of her current clients were on the verge of completing on holiday apartments. She'd make sure to tell them about her new management services.

Her fingers flew over the keys as she made a note of things to do, arranged in order of importance. She finally had a life plan instead of stumbling from crisis to crisis. Now all she had to do was make sure it worked.

Chapter Thirty-Two

Late afternoon and Rosie was playing with Lucky on the café terrace before going home when she saw Seb and Isabella coming towards her. Damn. She'd been avoiding Seb since Fête de la Musique night, despite knowing she'd been in the wrong, stalking off like she had.

Since then she'd done a lot of thinking about both Seb and Terry. And while she was still not ready to do the grown-up thing and meet up with Terry, she'd acknowledged to herself that everything Seb had said was right. And that she owed him an apology.

'Hi, Isabella,' Rosie said, bending down to receive the little girl's 'hello' kiss on the cheek. 'It's nice to see you again.'

'Can I throw the ball for your dog?'

'Sure – Lucky-dog would like that.'

As Isabella started to throw the ball for Lucky, Rosie looked at Seb.

'Once again, I owe you an apology,' she said quietly. 'I'm sorry – for telling you to butt out and also for storming off. Forgive me?'

Seb shrugged. 'You were upset – and I'd probably react in the same way if you started telling me how to deal with Zoe.'

Rosie smiled. 'I wouldn't dare!'

'I'm taking Isabella back to Monaco later. D'you fancy coming with us? There's a new bistro on the beach in Juan-les-Pins – we could have supper there on the way back?' Seb looked at her hopefully.

'For me to check out the competition?' Rosie teased. 'Sounds good – but I'd rather not meet up with Zoe at the apartment.'

Seb shrugged. 'No problem. I'll drop you off by the Café de Paris and you can have a coffee while I take Isabella home.'

'Okay. What time?'

'Sevenish?' His mobile bleeped with an incoming text message. 'Excuse me.'

Rosie watched Isabella playing down by the water with an excited Lucky, while Seb scrolled through to the message.

'Merde! Bloody woman!'

'It has to be a message from Zoe?' Rosie said, turning to look at him.

Seb sighed. 'The woman's a bloody nightmare. Rosie…' He paused. 'Change of plan. Is it possible you can do me a huge favour and look after Isabella for me for a couple of hours? I have to go and talk to Zoe – and I'd rather Isabella wasn't in the next room because I think I might just kill her mother.'

'Sure, you can drop both of us on the quay at Monaco and we'll have a wander around until it's safe for you to take her home. No?' she said, as Seb shook his head at her.

'No. I've been told to keep Isabella here with me because Zoe has decided to take off for six months!'

'What! When?'

'Leaving tomorrow!'

'Does Isabella know?'

'That's another thing – I have to tell her that her mother has run out on her. Thank God, the summer school vacation is coming up – getting her to school in Monaco every morning would have been a nightmare.'

He looked across to Isabella who was now sitting on the beach, her feet in the water and her arm around Lucky-dog, watching the waves. 'I've got a hotel to run – how the hell is looking after a six-year-old going to fit in with that?'

'You'll sort something out,' Rosie said. 'And I'll help. Starting now. Come on, let's go talk to Isabella and then you can get off to Monaco.'

She whistled for Lucky and both Isabella and the dog ran up the beach towards them.

'Isabella, darling, I have to go and talk to Mummy. You stay with Rosie until I return, okay?'

'Does that mean I'm not going home tonight?'

'You're staying with me for a couple of weeks,' Seb said. 'We'll talk about it when I get back.'

'Okay. Can I have a swing before you go?'

'Sure.' And Seb picked her up and swung her round and round before hugging her tightly and gently setting her back down and dropping a kiss on her head.

'I'll see you both in a bit. Thanks, Rosie.' Before she realised his intention, he'd kissed her, too. Not on the head. On the lips. Briefly, but still on the lips. What the hell did he mean by that?

With Lucky-dog to play with, Isabella was happy on the beach for a while when Seb left, before running up to Rosie.

'I think Lucky-dog is hungry.'

Rosie glanced at her watch. 'Well, it is time for her meal.'

'Can I feed her?'

'Of course. Let's go up to the restaurant and find her some food. How about you? Are you hungry, too?'

Isabella nodded.

Back in the café, Isabella happily filled Lucky-dog's bowl with meat and biscuits, while Rosie rifled through the fridge in search of something quick a six-year-old girl might eat.

'You like pancakes?'

'I can eat lots and lots of pancakes,' Isabella assured her. 'At least five – 'specially if they've got maple syrup on them,' she added, looking at Rosie hopefully. 'Daddy makes good pancakes – Mummy doesn't, though.'

'Pancakes it is then,' Rosie said, taking eggs and milk out of the fridge. 'Are you going to help me toss them?'

Isabella giggled. 'I'm not very good at catching them when they come down. And, once... once, I tossed one right onto the light!'

'We'll have to be extra careful today then – no way can I reach the light in here,' Rosie said, looking up at the kitchen ceiling.

An hour later, when she and Isabella had lost count of the number of pancakes they'd both tossed and eaten and the maple syrup bottle was disturbingly empty, Rosie said, 'Right, I think it's time you showed me your room in Daddy's apartment and we got you into bed.'

Isabella insisted on holding Lucky's lead in one hand and Rosie's hand in the other as they walked the short distance from the café to the hotel's kitchen entrance. Rosie, having vetoed using the main entrance for fear of bumping into Terry, just hoped no one would see them taking the short-cut through the kitchen with the dog.

'Quickly,' she said, 'into the lift before anybody sees Lucky.'

Once upstairs in Seb's apartment, Isabella ran into her room, while Rosie opened the French doors and let Lucky out onto the terrace.

Isabella reappeared in her nightdress clutching a book. 'Daddy always reads me a story,' she said. 'Sometimes two.'

'We'll start with one,' Rosie said, taking the book. 'Cleaned your teeth? Hop into bed then.'

Settling down on the edge of the bed, Rosie opened the book, but before she could begin to read, Isabella said quietly, 'Mummy's going away, isn't she? That's why Daddy's gone to see her now. To say goodbye. Will she be coming back?'

Rosie shrugged helplessly. 'Oh, Isabella, I'm sure she'll be back – that is, if she really is going away.'

'I know she's going away,' Isabella said

'Did she tell you that?'

Isabella shook her head. 'No, but I heard her talking on the phone. And yesterday she kissed me goodbye when Daddy picked me up – she never does that.' Isabella's tear-filled blue eyes stared at Rosie, begging for reassurance.

'Oh, Isabella, darling,' Rosie said, giving the little girl a hug. 'Daddy will be back soon. Perhaps he'll be able to tell you more. I know one thing for sure – actually, I know two things: one, – he's not going anywhere and will always be here for you; and two, he'll be so pleased to have you stay with him. He loves you to bits.'

'But won't I get in the way? Mummy is always saying Daddy's too busy with the hotel to bother with me more than twice a month.'

Rosie took a deep breath. Honestly, what was Zoe thinking, telling lies like that to Isabella? 'No, you definitely won't be in the way. Now, which story would you like?'

'The first one, please,' and Isabella snuggled down under the sheets as Rosie began to read. It wasn't long before her eyelids were closing and she was asleep. Carefully, Rosie stood up and tucked her in before gently placing a kiss on her forehead.

It was nearly eleven o'clock before Seb returned to find Rosie asleep on one of the loungers on the terrace, Lucky curled at her feet.

'Hey, I'm so sorry,' he said, sitting on an adjacent lounger and handing her a glass of rosé as she sat up.

'How'd it go?' Rosie asked sleepily. 'Did you kill her and toss the body into the harbour?'

'It was touch and go but no, Zoe is still alive and off to Indonesia in the morning for six months. To find herself, would you believe?'

'Isabella knows she's going away,' Rosie said quietly. 'She also thinks you find her a nuisance and that's why she only sees you twice a month.'

'Zoe told her that?'

Rosie nodded.

'Merde. She's a lying bitch.'

Rosie sipped her drink. 'So Isabella lives with you for the next six months and then Zoe reappears and whisks her back to Monaco?'

'No,' Seb said, throwing some of his wine down his throat. 'I told Zoe she'll have a fight on her hands when she comes back. I'm not going to just hand Isabella back. As far as I'm concerned, my daughter stays with me from now on.'

Chapter Thirty-Three

Monday morning, after dropping Cammie off at school and making a grovelling apology for being late to her teacher, Erica went straight to The Cupboard Under the Stairs. The shop was empty as she pushed the door open and GeeGee looked up from her laptop as Erica walked in.

'Hope you've got the coffee on. Amelia sent you cake,' Erica said, her voice trailing away. 'God, you look terrible. Something happened while I've been away?'

'Just Jay – and I've been busy,' GeeGee said. 'I'll fill you in with all the details later. Cake sounds wonderful. How was the weekend?'

'It had its moments but on the whole it was good,' Erica said, walking over to the coffee machine. 'Cammie had a great time.' She poured two cups before turning back to GeeGee.

'So what's Jay done now?'

'Only taken over the agency.'

'What? He's back permanently?'

GeeGee nodded. Before she could say any more the shop door opened and three women walked in.

'Bonjour,' Erica called out, before adding quietly to GeeGee, 'We need to talk. I could do with some advice, too. Shall we have ice creams on the beach later? Cammie's going to Madeleine's for tea. A little treat to cheer ourselves up. We can talk then.'

'Sounds good. I've got another house for you to look at, too,' GeeGee said. 'I'll print the details out and bring them with me.' GeeGee closed her laptop down and picked up her bag. 'Which means going into the agency. I'll see you later.'

Erica was the first to arrive at Café Fleur later that afternoon and ordered two large bowls of ice cream with Chantilly cream and all the extras for when GeeGee arrived. 'The bigger the better,' she said.

Rosie laughed as she took the order. 'You two celebrating or drowning your sorrows about something?'

'We're going to have a girly couple of hours and indulge our inner child with a treat. GeeGee has had some bad news and I've...' Erica shrugged. 'Well, I've got a difficult family decision to make.'

'Join the club,' Rosie said.

'Come and join us if you've got time,' Erica said. 'We can brainstorm each other's problems.'

'Might do that for five minutes, if it's not too busy. Thanks. Here's GeeGee, so I'll get on with the ice creams,' Rosie said.

'Why are you grinning inanely?' Erica said as Gee Gee joined her. 'What's happened now? Please don't tell me it involves Jay.'

'It does sort of but only in the way it will piss him off mightily when I tell him,' GeeGee said. 'Here, these are the villa details for you,' she said, handing over a brochure. 'What d'you think?'

Erica sighed and put the brochure down on the table without looking at it. 'Honestly? I'm not sure I'm doing the right thing any more.'

'You've changed your mind about selling the house?'

'No. The problem is more what to do when it's sold. Where to live.'

'Ah... Amelia put the pressure on over the weekend?'

Erica nodded. 'Very subtly, but something Cammie said on the way home has also made me think. She had a lovely time playing with her cousins and wishes we lived nearer them.'

Worriedly, Erica ran her hand through her hair. 'Maybe I am being selfish staying down here? Maybe I should be thinking of moving closer to family for Cammie's sake.'

'Write a list of the pros and then do the same for the cons,' GeeGee said. 'And then work out which are the important ones. The things that really matter to you. That will help you decide.'

'I need to think about what Pascal would want me to do, too,' Erica said.

'And then you have to do what is best for you – he's no longer here,' GeeGee said gently. 'Oh, these look divine,' she continued, as Rosie came over carrying two huge dishes of ice cream.'

'You not joining us then?' Erica said.

'Sorry – simply not got the time. Enjoy!' Rosie said as she placed one in front of each of them.

For several minutes they were both silent as they ate spoonfuls of delicious ice cream.

'This was a good idea of yours,' GeeGee said.

'Are you going to spill the beans over what's made you so happy since this morning?' Erica said.

'Seb introduced me to one of his guests who was house hunting recently and I've only sold him that villa that has links to the roaring twenties – F. Scott Fitzgerald and that crowd. You know the one I mean? Along the coast a bit. Been empty for a couple of years but it's been totally renovated in the last six months.'

Erica nodded. 'I know the one.' She could see why GeeGee was so happy – her commission would be mega.

'It means I can tell Jay where to stick his agency desk at the end of summer – maybe even earlier,' GeeGee said, scooping the last of the chocolate sauce out of her dish. 'I can't wait. And, there's more!' She put her spoon down in the dish with a satisfied sigh. 'I'm going to up my Internet presence, expand into holiday management and do more airport runs.'

'Wow. That's brilliant news,' Erica said. 'I think we need a glass of Prosecco while you fill me in on all the details. I'll go and order a bottle.'

Walking over to the restaurant, Erica wished a large commission could sort out her moral dilemma. When she got home she'd do as GeeGee suggested and write a list of pros and cons. Coast or country? If nothing else, it might help to sort things out in her mind.

Rosie carried the Prosecco and its ice bucket back to the table and glanced at GeeGee. 'Congratulations are in order, I gather?'

'It's all a bit hush-hush at the moment but I'm about to earn the biggest commission of my life,' GeeGee said, accepting a glass. 'I owe Seb big time for introducing me to the client.'

Rosie paused as she poured a second glass and handed it to Erica. 'Is the buyer staying at the hotel then?' she asked.

'Like I said, it's all a bit hush-hush until the papers are signed, so I'd better not answer that question directly, but you could be right.' GeeGee gave an exaggerated smile at Rosie and raised her glass. 'Cheers.'

'Cheers,' Rosie said. 'Is it near here? The villa?'

'Just along the coast a kilometre or two, near Cannes,' GeeGee said. 'Handy for the film festival.'

Rosie felt her heart sink. Any hope that Terry would change his mind and return to America died with GeeGee's last remark. He had to be the buyer whose proposed house purchase was making GeeGee so happy – and her wretched.

Chapter Thirty-Four

Rosie and Tansy were working in companionable silence in the kitchen – Tansy preparing veg and Rosie making another batch of tiramsu.

'It's your birthday on Friday. Got anything planned?'

Rosie shook her head. 'No. To be honest, I'd forgotten about it, I've been so busy.' And irritated with the Terry business. Oh, heavens. Terry. He wouldn't use the occasion to try and embarrass her again into talking to him, would he? Not that he'd remembered her birthday once in the last eighteen years.

'Might share a bottle of champagne with you lot after work on Friday,' she said. 'Unless you're all too busy.'

'Never too busy for champagne,' Tansy said. 'Can Rob join us?'

Rosie nodded. 'I'll see if Seb and Isabella can come, too.' She'd leave inviting him as late as possible, though. She didn't want to risk him mentioning anything to Tiki.

'Olivia?' Tansy asked.

'Not sure she'll be back from Corsica. Think it'll just be the... seven of us,' she said, mentally counting. A couple of bottles of champagne and a few nibbles and that would be her thirty-fifth out of the way.

'What about Charlie?' Tansy said.

'What about him?'

'You inviting him?'

'No,' Rosie said before Tansy could say any more. She hadn't heard from Charlie for a couple of weeks and she planned to keep it that way.

'D'you want me to make you a cake?' Tansy asked.

Rosie shook her head. 'No, thanks. I'm not that bothered about cake.'

Olivia phoned Friday morning to wish her 'Happy Birthday' and to say she was back in Monaco and both she and Zander would be over that evening.

Rosie hesitated before telling her, 'Mum, Terry is still around.'

'You've invited him?'

'No, of course not, but he keeps pestering me to see him and listen to what he has to say. What if he decides to make a scene tonight? I don't want you upset or embarrassed.'

'I'm long past being upset by him,' Olivia said.

'Mum, can we talk privately when you get here?'

'Sure. See you later.'

The restaurant was busy with lunchtime trade when the first of the bouquets arrived. A glorious mix of carnations and roses with tiny white and pink gypsophila. Rosie's hands were trembling as she opened the gift-card envelope attached to the cellophane – if this was from Terry it was going straight in the bin:

'Bon Anniversaire. Love Seb and Isabella. xxxxxx'

Rosie smiled at the row of kisses on the card, pleased she could keep the flowers – they were really too beautiful to throw away.

GeeGee, coming into the restaurant for a cup of coffee, said, 'Wow! Wish someone would send me flowers like that. Special occasion?'

Rosie nodded. 'Actually, it's my birthday.'

'Happy Birthday.'

'You busy tonight?' Rosie said, impulsively. 'I'm having a few drinks here, nothing special. I'd love you to come if you're free. Erica and Cammie, too – Seb's Isabella will be here.'

'I'll be here,' GeeGee said. 'And I'll tell Erica.'

The second bouquet arrived an hour later: 'Happy Birthday. Love Mum and Zander.'

Charlie's bouquet arrived after lunch, with a simple 'Happy Birthday' on the card.

'We're going to run out of vases at this rate,' Tansy said as Rosie placed two more vases either end of the restaurant bar.

Rosie primed Tansy to look after Zander that evening, while she had a quick word with Olivia. 'Five – ten – minutes at the most,' she promised Tansy, grabbing a bottle and two glasses when they arrived. 'Mum, follow me.'

'What's this all about then?' Olivia asked quietly, as they perched on the rocks on the shoreline, well away from people. There was no way Rosie wanted their conversation overheard.

'I need to talk to you about Terry. Do you still have any feelings for him? Would you see him if it was you he wanted to see?' Rosie asked, pouring them both a glass of champagne.

Olivia was quiet for a moment. 'No, I wouldn't see him, and no, I don't have any real feelings for him now after all this time. I've changed and so, I should imagine, has Terry. But we do have a shared past, which includes you, so that can never be forgotten. Although he did forget you for a number of years. Any idea why he wants to talk to you after all this time?'

Rosie took a deep breath. 'He's told Seb he's ill and wants to put things right between us. And...' Rosie glanced at Olivia. 'The blonde bimbo is his daughter.' Telling Olivia that Saskia was Terry's daughter was far easier than saying the words 'she's my sister'.

Olivia was silent, watching the bubbles in her glass before looking at Rosie.

'Seb sure about the dramatic "I'm ill" bit? It's not just one of Terry's ulterior-motive ruses to get you to see him? Seeing him is not going to put anything right – you can't undo wrongs; you can only apologise for them and hope the apology is accepted. Do you want to see him? Accept his apology if that is what he offers?'

Rosie shrugged. 'Not really, but Seb thinks I should for my own peace of mind later.'

'Seb could have a point. Depends on how good you are at putting these things out of your mind,' Olivia said. 'If you feel guilty, too, about the way things are between you and Terry, then maybe you should. To give you closure – not him. You might also find you like having a sister.'

'I don't feel guilty,' Rosie exclaimed. 'Why should I? And I definitely don't need a sister.'

'Well, you maybe could have made more effort to keep in touch with him, although I think you were protecting my feelings – not wanting to hurt me?' Olivia took a sip of champagne.

'Partly that,' Rosie said. She hesitated, before adding, 'I did have a row with him and said I'd never speak to him again.' She took a sip of her champagne before saying slowly, 'It was when I was seventeen and you found that lump.'

Olivia gave her a quick look but stayed silent and waited.

'I was so scared you were going to die. I found a contact number in among your papers and rang him and asked him to come back. He refused to even discuss it. Said he had problems of his own that made it impossible. Told me we'd cope. I couldn't believe he was being so cruel. He didn't even say sorry.'

Olivia sighed. 'Oh, Rosie. He and I were long finished by then. He had no reason to come back because I had a health scare.'

'He should have come back for me,' Rosie said fiercely. 'I really needed him then. When he said he wouldn't I lost my temper and told him I never wanted to see or hear from him again for the rest of my life. And I hung up on him.'

'Maybe you are as much to blame for the years of silence as he is then?' Olivia said gently.

'No, I'm definitely not to blame,' Rosie protested 'It was totally his attitude at the time!'

Olivia raised an eyebrow. 'Sounds to me like you're still hanging on to some teenage angst. If you're worried about upsetting me – don't be. I'm past being upset by him.' She stood up. 'Maybe you should take this opportunity to speak to him, then he and Saskia can both go back to LA or wherever and disappear out of your life. I'm going to find Zander. And I think you should really join everyone – it is supposed to be your birthday party.'

Before Rosie could tell her that Terry was staying around, Olivia began to make her way back up the beach. 'Come on, Rosie. Let's party. Look, Seb and Isabella have arrived.'

Rosie sighed. She was still no nearer to deciding about whether to meet up with Terry after all these years or not. Talking to Olivia had failed to help. It was clear, though, that Olivia herself had pushed her long-ago relationship with Terry into touch. Having Zander seemed to have helped her to finally shut the door on that part of her life.

As she began to follow Olivia back up to the restaurant, Isabella ran up to her, clutching a glittery balloon. 'Happy Birthday, Rosie. This is for you.' Beaming, she held it out. 'Daddy's made you a cake and I helped to decorate it.'

'Thank you,' Rosie said, bending down and hugging the little girl. 'Let's go and cut you a slice, shall we?'

'Ooh, please, but we have to light the candle first and sing "Happy Birthday".' Isabella slipped her hand into Rosie's to walk along the beach. An action Rosie found unexpectedly emotional.

Seb was talking to Zander when they got back to the restaurant but immediately came over and kissed Rosie. 'Bon Anniversaire.'

'Thanks.'

'Tiki says "Happy Birthday" as well,' Seb added.

'He's not planning on coming over is he? Because if he is...' Rosie's voice trailed away.

'Relax. He's taken Saskia to Jimmy's in Cannes for the evening.'

'Hope she enjoys it,' Rosie muttered.

'Look at the cake, Rosie. That's the bit I iced,' Isabella said, pointing to some wobbly stars and rosettes. 'If you turn the candle, like this, it plays "Happy Birthday" to you.' She looked up at Rosie as the tinny notes played. 'Daddy said you wouldn't want lots of candles.'

'Daddy was quite right,' Rosie said, picking up a knife. 'This looks too good to cut but here goes.' And she plunged the knife into the cake as everyone sang 'Happy Birthday'.

It was a perfect evening for a birthday party on the beach and Rosie relaxed and began to thoroughly enjoy being spoilt. Olivia and Zander gave her an iPad – something she'd secretly coveted for a long time but hadn't been able to justify the expense of. Even Charlie turning up didn't spoil things and she graciously thanked him for the flowers before introducing him to GeeGee and Erica.

She even managed to have an extra quiet five minutes with Olivia before she and Zander left at the end of the evening, when she finally told her about Terry's house-hunting plans.

Olivia just shrugged and said, 'Makes no difference to me where he lives these days. Or with whom.'

Rosie wished she could feel the same nonchalance about the thought of living on the same stretch of coast as Terry and Saskia, but she couldn't. All she knew was the inevitable meeting was closing in on her.

Chapter Thirty-Five

Seven o'clock Tuesday evening and Rosie and Tansy were doing the final end-of-day clearing up before leaving, when the phone rang. Rosie had her arms full of bottles of wine for the fridge, so Tansy answered it.

'It's Seb. Wants to know if you can help him out this evening and babysit?'

'What time?'

'ASAP.'

Rosie nodded. 'Okay. Tell him I'll be there in ten minutes,' she said.

Seb had employed a part-time childminder to look after Isabella during the day and a couple of evenings while he was busy in the hotel but Rosie knew that the evenings were difficult. Now she was only opening on Friday and Saturday evenings, she'd offered to babysit if he got stuck. She liked Isabella so it was no hardship.

Not wanting to take Lucky through the hotel kitchens, which would be getting busy with prepping the evening meals, Rosie clipped the dog's lead on and made her way to the hotel's main entrance, praying that Terry wouldn't be around.

The floor-indicator light over the lift at the far side of the foyer showed it was on its way down, so Rosie waited. It would be quicker than the stairs and easier on her legs, which were tired after a busy day. What she really needed and wanted to do was spend a relaxing hour in a hot, sweet-smelling bath, with a good book and a glass of wine.

The lift doors opened and Saskia stepped out.

'Hi... Sis.' The drawling emphasis Saskia placed on the last word made Rosie squirm.

'Hi,' she muttered, stepping past her into the lift, raising her hand ready to press the button for the top floor once the lift doors closed. But Saskia had turned and placed her foot against the door.

'I've always wanted a sister and now I've got one. Shame you're such a selfish cow.'

Rosie opened her mouth to respond but Saskia didn't give her a chance.

'I can't understand why Dad feels the need to talk to you but he does. If you weren't such a self-centred bitch you'd meet him and listen to what he has to say. I guess, though, you're all "me me me", and stuff what other people need.' Saskia glared at Rosie.

'I certainly don't care what you think,' Rosie said, aware that people were giving the two of them curious glances, 'but, you should remember: there are always two ways to look at things. Maybe, just maybe, Terry has a guilty conscience. And for what it's worth, I'm not that thrilled to learn about you either. Personally, I've never wanted a sister and now I've met you that hasn't changed. Now please take your foot away from the door. I'm in a hurry.'

Rosie was shaking as she pressed the lift button and sighed with relief as the door closed and the lift began its upward journey. How dare Saskia call her a bitch for not talking to Terry. She wasn't a bitch. A bitch was someone like Zoe.

Seb opened the apartment door to her, dressed in his kitchen whites. 'Rosie, thanks so much... Hey, are you okay?'

Rosie nodded. 'Think so. Just had words with Saskia in the lift. Where's Isabella?'

'Waiting out on the terrace for you,' Seb said, giving her a concerned look. 'I've got to go, two short in the kitchen tonight – we'll talk when I get back. Shouldn't be too late. Help yourself to whatever you want – oh, and Isabella needs a bath and to be in bed by nine.' A swift kiss on the cheek and he was gone.

Out on the terrace, Isabella was riding her scooter and weaving around a complicated course she'd set up with boxes and a couple of chairs.

'That looks fun,' Rosie said, sinking down onto a sun lounger to watch her.

'I'm going faster and faster,' Isabella said. 'Daddy timed me earlier and I did it in less than a minute.'

Watching Isabella navigate around the obstacles, Rosie remembered another course. A course that had involved Terry, her and a horse. It was the last summer Terry had been around at home, so she must have been about eight.

Horse mad at that age, she'd begged and begged her parents for riding lessons and that year they'd given in and taken her to the local riding stables every Saturday. She'd loved every minute there and spent hours grooming Twinkle, the grey pony who was her special favourite. Her only ambition that summer was to be good enough to be selected for the Pony Club gymkhana team.

Terry, for some reason, took it upon himself to train her and one afternoon set up a couple of obstacles and small jumps for her and Twinkle to practise on. Rosie had trotted and cantered Twinkle around this makeshift course so often that they both knew it off by heart and Rosie had high hopes of being included in the team.

It was that summer, though, when everything in her life had fallen apart for the first time. She failed to make the team and after consoling her and telling her, 'There's always next year, Rosie,' Terry had gone away, leaving her bereft.

She could still remember the hollow feeling in the pit of her stomach, when Olivia told her, 'Daddy's gone away and he's probably not coming back.' Somehow, too, her interest in all things horsey had died that year.

Glancing at Isabella now, Rosie wondered if she'd felt the same hollow feeling when Zoe had left. However hard the remaining parent tried – and Olivia had given her all to Rosie like Seb was now endeavouring to do with Isabella – the hurt you'd been left with didn't go away for years. But Zoe was at least coming back in a few months' time.

After Isabella got bored with scootering, they curled up together and watched a couple of cartoons before Rosie said, 'I think it's time we got you ready for bed.'

Once Isabella was bathed and tucked up in bed, Rosie read to her until she fell asleep and then tidied the bathroom. Not strictly necessary, as Seb clearly had the hotel chambermaids come up to clean and tidy everything every day. The numerous towels were pristine and the bathroom cabinet well stocked. There was even a scented candle placed on the shelf at the end of the bath.

Looking at the large, fluffy bath sheets, the shampoos, the soaps, the body lotions, Rosie wondered who used the feminine ones. In the few months she'd known him, she'd never seen Seb with a woman other than Zoe and she doubted that Zoe had ever seen the inside of this bathroom.

Wistfully, she stroked the large, white bath sheet. She imagined pouring some of the expensive bubble bath into the tub full of hot water and sinking down into its relaxing depths. Wrapping yourself in such a soft-feeling towel afterwards would be wonderful.

She glanced at her watch. Was there time before Seb returned? Could she? Would Seb mind?

Rosie shook herself. She had a perfectly adequate bath back in her own apartment. Okay, it wasn't as luxurious as this one but she had a few drops left of an expensive bath essence Olivia had given her last Christmas. Her towels were as large, too. Not as soft because conditioner had been struck off her shopping list for a few months now for not being a strictly essential item. Besides, towels dried you better and quicker without conditioner.

Regretfully, Rosie closed the bathroom door and made her way out onto the terrace where Lucky-dog had curled up on one of the sunlounger cushions. Helping herself to a glass of water from the small kitchen out there, Rosie wandered over to the railings and surveyed the scene before her.

The sun, setting over the Esterels, was throwing eye-blinding streaks of fiery red and orange lights over the sky for miles around. A game of volleyball down on the beach had attracted a few spectators and a cheer rang out as someone scored. As two of the players high-fived each other, Rosie realised one of them was Saskia.

Her sister. Who thought she was a bitch. Correction. Her half-sister. So did that make her only half a bitch?

Rosie watched as Saskia leapt across the court to hit a ball high in the air. Cut-off ragged denim shorts emphasised her long legs and slim body as she ran barefoot along the sand. Judging from the shouts of encouragement from the other players, the teams were a mixture of teenage American girls and French boys.

Watching them, Rosie realised Saskia was younger than she'd initially thought. She could only be about sixteen or seventeen. Which meant she must have been born around the time Rosie's own life at that age had been massively disrupted and was threatening to take off in an unexpected and unwanted direction.

As the light faded, the game finished and the players began to make their way towards the Beach Hotel car park. A tall, dark-haired boy had his arm around Saskia's shoulders and was saying something that made her laugh as they walked.

Rosie jumped as Seb touched her on the shoulder. 'Oh, I didn't hear you coming. I was miles away.'

Seb glanced down at the beach. 'Watching Saskia?'

Rosie nodded. 'She called me a self-centred bitch earlier. D'you think I am?'

Seb shook his head. 'No, you're not a bitch.' He hesitated. 'You might be a little self-centred but...' He shrugged. 'We all react in our own way to events we regard as hostile or threatening. Any decision we make is always based on our own needs in the end.'

At least Seb didn't think she was a bitch – that was something. The self-centred jibe stung, though. The fact she didn't want or need Terry in her life after all this time didn't make her self-centred, did it? As for embracing Saskia as a sister – she just didn't need it. Ah, there was that word again. Need. Need. Need. Well, on a need-to-know basis, neither Terry nor Saskia figured very highly on her list.

'Isabella get off to bed okay?' Seb asked.

'No trouble.'

'I've bought some canapés up. A glass of wine to wash them down?'

'Thanks. Then I'd better go home.'

While Seb organised their impromptu supper, Rosie moved back from the railings and sat down on one of the wooden transat loungers. A small side table next to it held a pile of leaflets and some glossy house brochures she'd not noticed before. Idly, she picked one up and began to flick through.

The caption underneath the picture on the first brochure contained the letters 'POA'. Of course it would. Nobody who could afford a house like that would want the neighbours knowing how much they'd paid. Not that there appeared to be any neighbours within two hundred yards at least of these particular houses.

'Are you thinking of buying something?' Rosie asked as Seb returned with food, plates and wine.

Seb shook his head. 'Not me. These are all houses Tiki's looked at recently. GeeGee asked me to put them in reception in case any of my other guests are looking to buy.'

Rosie ignored the mention of Terry and picked up another brochure.

'Wow, this one is so amazing,' she said, holding out the page for Seb to see. 'Imagine living there.'

Situated on a headland, the pictures showed the villa with its grounds running down to the rocks that bordered the Mediterranean. There was even a small, private landing stage and a flight of steps leading up to the house.

The house, with its huge glass windows glittering in the evening sunlight in the photo, had, the text informed her, been built to capture the views and light from all directions.

'Back in the 1920s when it was built, it was one of *the* places along the coast,' Seb said, handing her a plate of canapés. 'I've heard there were some wild parties held there. Money no object.'

'I can believe it,' Rosie said. 'As a party venue it must be unbeatable. It's all art deco fixtures and fittings inside according to these photos.'

Seb nodded. 'Mostly – the bathrooms are still mainly marble with Aphrodite statues and free-standing baths. The kitchen's been updated and the indoor swimming pool has been renovated. Those pictures don't do it justice.'

Rosie glanced across at him. 'You've been inside? You lucky thing.'

'Tiki asked me to accompany him when he viewed it.' Seb hesitated before adding, 'It's going to be his new home in a few weeks. You can see inside it any time you like. You could even stay there, if you wanted to.'

Shocked, Rosie turned away from Seb and stared out unseeingly at the horizon. So this was the villa that GeeGee had been celebrating selling that day on the beach. With 'POA' again printed underneath the details of this house, no wonder she'd been so happy. Terry had to be seriously wealthy if he intended to make that particular villa his home.

Chapter Thirty-Six

With the Café Fleur being busy during the daytime and several evenings a week being spent looking after Isabella, there wasn't any time for Rosie to brood over things. And definitely no time for a meeting with Terry. That didn't stop her subconscious going into overdrive at night, though, as she tossed and turned in the heat under the inadequate ceiling fan over her bed.

The glossy pictures in the brochure were still flashing into Rosie's mind at odd times. The sheer opulence of the villa Terry had bought, so overwhelming when contrasted with the home she had grown up in with Olivia.

Before her father had dumped Olivia and her and run away to America, he'd always belittled money and materialistic things. 'Those things won't make you happy,' he'd say earnestly. 'Happiness comes from within.' What a hypocrite he'd turned into. She definitely didn't need – or want – a father like him back in her life.

Although, of course, he wasn't Terry Hewitt, Rosie's father, now – he was this different person, Tiki Gilvear. A stranger in more ways than one. Someone she wished had never made himself known to her, forcing her to make a decision about him. Re-evaluate things.

As for his new villa, it might epitomise the three things everyone associated with the Côte d'Azur: the glamour, the lifestyle and the money; but she could live without all three – although she could certainly do with the Café Fleur earning its keep!

If he really was ill, meeting him would be the kindest thing to do. Let him have his say and simply say goodbye. Refuse to be drawn into an argument over the past. And if it was just a ruse to get her to talk to him, well that would put an end to any reconciliation he might want.

Living here she could bump into him any time, any place. Better to get the hostilities out of the way to avoid any embarrassing public situations in the future. Although, if it was confession time, Rosie couldn't help feeling Terry would be better off seeing a priest.

Deep down she knew the decision to meet up with him at some stage before the end of the summer had already been made. But it was definitely going to be on her own terms. For starters it would have to be a private meeting – no Saskia present.

And that was another thing. Was Saskia planning to live in Europe, too? What about her mother? Where was she?

A sudden thought struck Rosie. Did Terry have a wife back in the States? Had he walked out on her like he had Olivia?

* * *

When Charlie phoned out of the blue and invited Rosie to a party onboard *A Sure Thing* Sunday evening, she tried hard to say no, thank you.

'We're really busy at the moment, Charlie, and I'm tired. I haven't got the energy for partying.' But Charlie wasn't having it.

'Please come. There's a couple of people I'd like you to meet and William said specifically to invite you. Said he misses you. Like I do,' Charlie added.

It was the mention of William that made her decide, against her better judgement, to go. She still had to meet his new wife and congratulate him on his marriage.

'Okay. Thanks.' She hesitated before adding, 'Can I bring a partner?'

'If you're thinking of bringing Seb – he's already invited,' Charlie said. 'See you Sunday then.' And he'd hung up.

Rosie sighed. She had been thinking of asking Seb to go with her – much like he'd asked her to go to Zoe's that Sunday. Just for support, of course; not to pretend he was more than a friend. Would have been good to have walked onboard as part of a couple rather than alone.

Seb was waiting for her when she walked over to the hotel that evening, having promised to look after Isabella for a couple of hours. She desperately wanted to talk to him about Terry and was hoping that Seb would have time to talk before he went down to the kitchens.

Before she could say anything, Seb took hold of her by the shoulders to give her his usual kiss on both cheeks before holding her away from him and looking at her.

'Gather you've got an invitation to the party on Sunday night. Shall we go together?'

'That would be... wonderful,' Rosie said, kissing him on the cheek in return and feeling her spirits lifting.

'Then, if you want, you can introduce me to people as your boyfriend. But only if you like,' he added quietly.

Rosie looked at him. 'Is this because of me pretending to be your girlfriend to get Zoe off your back?'

Seb shrugged. 'I thought it might help with Charlie. But I do like the idea of being introduced as your boyfriend – for real.' He pulled her gently towards him and hugged her before placing a gentle kiss on her forehead. 'Gotta go. Talk later.' And he was gone, leaving a stunned Rosie to go and find Isabella.

Once Isabella was in bed, Rosie helped herself to a glass of rosé from the fridge and wandered along the terrace before leaning on the wall and thinking about Seb's words. Words that she found herself strangely in sync with. She would, she realised, like to be able to call Seb her boyfriend.

Despite telling Olivia and anyone else who would listen that she didn't have the time, or the inclination, for a man in her life, Seb had crept up on her. Got through her armour without her realising.

He was no longer a person on the edge of her life; he'd become an integral part of it. Seeing him every day, babysitting Isabella several times a week, their lives had begun to merge together seamlessly without her noticing. In fact, Rosie realised with a shock, the thought of either of them not being in her life was unbearable. But could he possibly be as serious about her as she realised, with a jolt, she was about him? She needed to know that she wasn't just a summer fling for him before she made any attempt to analyse her own feelings about him.

Chapter Thirty-Seven

Erica turned the counter fan on to full blast and stood in front of it. Even if the air it wafted towards her was warm and failed to cool her, it was a relief to feel the draught of air. At least she had a glass of ice-cold apple juice to drink, with more in the fridge.

The Cupboard Under the Stairs had been busy all day but now, late afternoon, the shop was empty and Erica was able to catch up on some paperwork. Paperwork that included a scrappy piece of paper with the words 'Coast/Country' and 'Questions' written across the top.

She'd taken GeeGee's advice and tried to write things down objectively, but so far nothing had helped to make up her mind. There were so many unknowns hidden behind every question. It was like trying to second-guess whether it was going to rain and spoil the fireworks on 14 July. Only far more important and life-changing.

Top of the list was the question: sell the house or stay put? The answer here was easy – the house was already on the market. She and Cammie needed a new home for their new lives without Pascal.

The next question: where to buy? Coast or move to the country? Amelia had persuaded her to take a look at the Bertrands' house in the village before she left, but Erica hadn't been convinced it was for her and Cammie. It didn't sing out to her in a 'if you buy me you'll be happy here' way. She knew it was silly to expect a building to throw out welcoming vibes at her but she couldn't imagine living in that house or even up in the village if she was honest.

Her life revolved around Cammie and the shop down here – what would it revolve around in a village up in the back country? Cammie would go to school, make friends and have the cousins to play with. Whereas, she would have no purpose to her life. Amelia would no doubt get her involved in local things but she loved the shop and would miss the buzz it gave her.

Erica sighed. She needed to move on and selling the house was a part of that. GeeGee had said she was bringing a couple at the weekend for their first viewing, so things were beginning to happen there. Once sold, she could buy the kind of house she and Pascal had always dreamt of owning. The fact he wouldn't be there to share it with her made it bittersweet but she'd keep looking for the house of their dreams. Selling the house was one thing; selling the shop was something else. She couldn't envisage herself ever doing that.

Sipping her cold drink she realised decisions were being made. Keeping the shop meant she was definitely staying on the coast.

She turned to welcome a customer. 'Bonjour. Can I help you? Rosie,' she said surprised. 'How lovely to see you.'

'Hi. I can't think why but this is the first time I've been in here,' Rosie said looking around. 'It's amazing – a real treasure trove. I need to find a belated wedding present for my ex-boss.'

'Have a browse, see if there's anything that takes your fancy,' Erica said. 'Give me a shout if you need help.'

'It's so difficult finding something for a couple who already have everything,' Rosie said ten minutes later as she approached the counter, clutching a coffee-table-size book, *Belles Demeures en Riviera*. 'I know William loves learning about the history of the Côte d'Azur. I think he and Caroline will be fascinated by the black and white photographs in here. So many of these lovely villas have been pulled down.'

'It's a beautiful book,' Erica agreed. 'Do you want to write an inscription in it before I gift-wrap it?'

Rosie shook her head. 'No, thanks.' She picked a Congratulations card out of the rack. 'I'll write my message on this for you to slip inside.'

While Erica wrapped the book, Rosie fell in love with a silk scarf hanging on the vintage rail. Colourful peacocks and green leaves on a yellowy background.

'I'm going to treat myself to this,' she said, handing over her card. 'Your shop is far too tempting.'

After Rosie left, promising to return now she'd discovered the shop, Erica looked at her list again before screwing it up and throwing it into the wastepaper basket. The most important decision had been made. Stay on the coast. Fingers crossed everything else would fall into place behind it.

Chapter Thirty-Eight

Walking with Seb to the marina where *A Sure Thing* was moored Sunday evening, Rosie felt tired but happy. Seb was carrying the heavy book for her in one hand and holding her hand held tightly in the other.

The hot, sunny weather meant that Café Fleur was super busy every day and the weekly accounts were showing healthy signs of a small profit. The food poisoning accusation, though, was still a worry, with no details from the lawyer yet. Perhaps it had all been a mistake and she wouldn't hear any more about it?

She'd been thinking, too, about Terry and Saskia, ever since the thought that somewhere out there she might have a stepmother. Maybe Seb would know.

As they turned down onto the quay leading to the pontoons, she said, 'Has Terry ever mentioned his wife to you?'

'No.'

'How about Saskia? Does she talk about her mother?'

Seb shook his head. 'No. Why?'

'It occurred to me I must have a stepmother out there.'

'You can ask Tiki when you talk to him,' Seb said. 'Which will be soon, won't it?'

When Rosie didn't answer straight away, Seb squeezed her hand. 'The longer you leave it the harder it will become.'

William and his new wife, Caroline, were standing by the gangway greeting everyone as they stepped onboard. Rosie congratulated them, handed over her present and wished them every happiness before accepting a glass of bubbly from one of the attentive crew.

As she and Seb made their way down to the main saloon where people were gathering, she saw Olivia and Zander chatting to another couple, and at the far end Charlie was talking to a pregnant woman – and Terry and Saskia. Rosie froze. Unable to walk any further. The thing she'd been dreading, bumping into Terry socially, was about to happen.

Had Terry told Charlie as well as Seb that he was her father? If he had – how many other people had he told? Maybe he was busy telling everyone, hoping to embarrass her into acknowledging him. Was this why Charlie had pressurised her into coming this evening? Deliberately setting her up?

Seb casually placed his arm around Rosie's shoulders and squeezed her tightly, before whispering, 'Smile!' Which she did involuntarily as she saw Charlie glance their way and registered his reaction to the way Seb was holding her.

She took a large drink of her champagne before shrugging her shoulders and uttering a deep sigh.

Seb looked at her. 'What?'

'I've just realised it's twenty-seven years since both my parents have been in the same place as me. I remember they weren't speaking on that occasion either!'

Fleetingly, Rosie wondered what life would have been like if Olivia and Terry had stayed together. Would Terry have made a fortune without going to the USA? Or would he have uprooted them and taken them to live in Hollywood. Stupid to go down that road; she'd never know.

'Darling, lovely to see you here,' Olivia said, appearing at their side. 'Bit surprised to see you know who. I didn't know William and Charlie even knew Terry – sorry, Tiki.'

'Have you spoken to him?'

Olivia shook her head. 'Not yet. We've merely acknowledged each other's presence with a nod. Zander wants me to introduce him. Says they've probably got friends in common in California. Not sure I'm ready for that particular introduction, though.' She leant in towards Rosie before whispering, 'Your sister is a very pretty girl.'

Rosie nodded. 'She is. Lucky girl – must take after her mother.'

'That's a bit hurtful, darling,' Olivia said.

'Oh, Mum, I'm sorry – that was bitchy of me. But you know what I mean.'

She felt Seb's arm tighten around her shoulders briefly. 'Want to leave?'

She nodded. 'Please.'

But before they could make a move Charlie, hand in hand with the pregnant woman, was in front of them.

'Rosie, I'd like you to meet an old friend of mine, Sarah Miller.'

Was this the Sarah he'd rushed off to help weeks ago? Was the baby Charlie's?

'You remember Alan Miller from college?'

'Of course,' Rosie said, smiling at Sarah. Charlie and Alan had been best mates at college and the three of them had had some great, fun times together. The last she'd heard he'd taken up extreme sports. 'You're Alan's wife? Is he here tonight?' She looked around.

It was Charlie who answered her. 'Alan died a couple of months back. A jump went wrong.'

'Oh, Sarah, I'm so sorry,' Rosie said. 'Alan was one of the good guys.' Why the hell hadn't Charlie told her about Alan before? Save her the embarrassment of upsetting Sarah with thoughtless words. She'd have words with Charlie about that later but right now, as she saw Terry and Saskia approaching them, she wanted to get the hell off the yacht.

'Nice to meet you, Sarah, but I'm afraid I have to leave, *right now*,' she said, turning to Seb.

'Wait two seconds,' Charlie said. 'I want to introduce you to Tiki Gilvear...'

'Nice try, Charlie, but "Mr Gilvear" and I are already acquainted, as I'm sure you know. Bye.' And before Terry and Saskia reached them, she was walking in the opposite direction.

She was off the yacht and striding along the quay before Seb caught up with her.

'Don't say a word,' she said. 'I know I shouldn't have left like that. I know I owe William and Charlie an apology. But I just couldn't stay there and make small talk with him.' She brushed a tear away. 'I'm so ashamed of myself for causing a scene.'

'Stop beating yourself up,' Seb said, putting his arms around her and hugging her. 'Just do what you know you have to do.'

Rosie took a deep breath. 'Easier said than done.'

'I can come with you if you like?'

'Would you?' Rosie said, before sighing and shaking her head. 'Thanks. But I think it's something I have to do by myself. Once Terry is settled in his new villa, I'll go.'

'Fair enough,' Seb said. 'Now, Alicia is sitting with Isabella tonight and we're both unexpectedly free for the next hour, so I'd like to take you somewhere special. We just need to go back to the hotel for my car.'

Quarter of an hour later, Seb parked on the Cap d'Antibes and, holding her hand, led Rosie up the tortuous path towards the famous lighthouse beaming its light out over the Mediterranean. Rosie inhaled the smell of the tall pine trees that hung in the evening air as she and Seb reached the summit of their climb.

'Wow. This is some view,' Rosie said, catching her breath.

'You've not been up here before?' Seb asked.

Rosie shook her head. 'I've seen the light many times from sea but no, I've never been up here.'

'It's one of the most powerful lights on the Côte d'Azur,' Seb said, watching as the beam flashed out.

Standing there in the almost silence with Seb's arm around her shoulders, looking out at the panoramic view over the Cap and the Mediterranean and along the coast in both directions for mile after mile, Rosie drank in the romantic serenity of the place. The recent upset on *A Sure Thing* faded from her mind as the balmy night air rustled through the trees and she sighed contentedly.

When Seb tightened his hold around her shoulders and pulled her closer to him she leaned in to him willingly, feeling more than comfortable in his embrace and happy to stay there.

Light pollution meant the stars weren't visible but along the whole coastline, from right to left, there were lights glittering, both stationary and moving, as traffic drove along the coast road. Out at sea, too, there were lights from boats making their way across the

Mediterranean to Italy or west to Marseille. And above it all, a crescent moon hung in the sky. A perfect evening. Seb was right. It was a special place.

'It's so tranquil, there's a real spiritual feeling up here,' Rosie said quietly. Definitely a good place to come and unwind from modern-day stress, to think things through, decide what to do.

She twisted to look at the building to the right of them standing in shadows as darkness began to fall. 'Is that a chapel over there? I can see a cross.'

Seb nodded. 'Yes. A centuries-old fisherman's church. It's full of strange offerings from fishermen and their families praying for safe voyages. There are also some sad messages pinned to the walls from widows,' he added.

Rosie shivered.

'Are you cold?' Seb said.

'No, I just feel sad that this beautiful place harbours grief as well as happiness but I guess it's that blend of the two that creates the special atmosphere.'

'Well, I'm very happy to be here tonight with you,' Seb said, turning her to face him. 'How about you?'

'I'm very happy to be here with you, too,' Rosie said. 'Being here with you will be a treasured memory. It's so...' The rest of her words, 'atmospheric and romantic', were lost as Seb bent his head and kissed her.

When they drew apart several moments later Rosie knew things between them would never be the same again. The kiss had changed everything.

'This is turning out to be quite an evening,' she said, smiling.

Seb studied her face anxiously. 'In a good way, I hope?'

Rosie nodded. 'Oh, yes.'

'Rosie, we need to talk, but before we do there are things I need to sort out, things that could come between us. But tonight is not the night.' Seb glanced at his watch.

'I need to get back to the hotel. I promise you, though, once the season finishes, you and I...' He hugged her tightly before saying, 'Things will work out, I promise. Trust me on that.'

Chapter Thirty-Nine

Exhausted wasn't a big enough word for how Rosie felt leaving the café one evening a few days later. Shattered, worn out, stressed. Clumped together those words maybe came somewhere near to describing how she felt. And the season was still weeks away from finishing.

With the café being silly busy over the last few days, plus looking after Isabella for a couple of hours in the evening, there was simply not enough down-time for her to recover. But tonight the official childminder was looking after Isabella and Rosie was free to go home and collapse into bed.

Yesterday, she'd confessed to Seb she'd never ever felt so tired and stressed. 'Not even when I was catering for VIPs on board the super yacht I worked on a few years ago.'

She suspected that the confession had been behind Seb insisting on booking an official childminder for this evening and telling her to go home and get an early night.

'I've been taking advantage,' he'd said when she'd protested that she was happy to look after Isabella. 'I should have realised how stressed you were. I'm sorry.'

'Hey, it's not your fault. Besides, I do get to relax on your wonderful terrace for an hour once Isabella's in bed.'

He'd shaken his head. 'It's not enough. You must get more rest.'

'But I like seeing you every evening after work,' she'd protested. It felt like belonging to a proper family, he and Isabella had become such a big part of her life.

She smiled now, remembering Seb's words as she'd left him last night. After kissing her gently, bringing the memory of the romantic hour they'd spent together out at the lighthouse alive again, he'd murmured, 'I promise life will be different for us once the season finishes.'

Leaving the beach behind and walking along the bord de mer, Rosie passed several couples with their arms wrapped around each other and kissing passionately. The French were so relaxed about showing their feelings publicly. Like the young couple in front of her now. She slowed her pace to stay discreetly behind them.

The boy had his arm around the girl's shoulders and was hugging her tightly against him while whispering in her ear. But something about their body language told her things were not right.

She heard the girl shout, '*No. I'm not going to. I don't want to. Get off,*' as she tried to shrug his arm off.

Rosie froze. That was Saskia's voice.

'It's payback time, you teasing bitch.'

Rosie watched in horror as Saskia tried to shrug off the arm around her shoulders again and pull away, but the boy violently swung her around and pushed his face into hers as he yelled an obscenity at her before dragging her towards the darkness of a shop doorway and hitting her across the face, making her scream out.

Rosie reached in her bag for her phone before lengthening Lucky's lead and charging towards them, screaming, 'Leave her alone, you bastard. I'm phoning the gendarme.' Lucky joined in, barking furiously.

'Back off, lady – mind your own business. This is between my girlfriend and me.'

'This is my business. That's my sister you're assaulting. Let her go now. And don't you even think about kicking my dog,' Rosie shouted as the boy raised his foot towards Lucky, who was now snapping at his ankles, before dropping his hold on Saskia. With a muttered curse he turned his back on them both and ran away down the street.

'You all right?' Rosie asked Saskia, looking with concern at the bruise already appearing under her left eye.

Saskia nodded. 'Please don't phone the gendarmes.'

'He should be reported. He's seriously assaulted you.'

Saskia shook her head and brushed the tears away. 'No. And please don't tell Dad. He'll be all for getting a lynch mob organised. Promise you won't tell Dad or the police what you saw tonight. '

'I'm not sure how you're going to keep it from him,' Rosie said. 'He's going to take one look at the state of your face and know something bad happened.'

'I'll tell him I walked into a door,' Saskia said. 'Please, Rosie?'

Rosie sighed. 'Okay. I think you're wrong but, if you insist, I won't tell. Come on, let's get you back to the hotel and get a compress on that eye.'

'Rosie?' Saskia paused. 'Could we go to your place rather than the hotel?'

Rosie looked at her. Maybe that would be better. She could at least keep an eye on her then in case shock set in – which it surely would.

'Okay. Come on, it's not far.'

Back at the apartment, Rosie wrapped some ice in a tea towel and told Saskia to hold it over her cheek and eye.

'Thank you for coming to my rescue tonight, Sis,' Saskia said quietly.

'I'd have done the same for anyone. I dread to think what could have happened if I hadn't been there. You know you should report it to the police – another girl he assaults might not be so lucky.'

Saskia sighed. 'I know, but please don't keep on.'

'It was one of the boys you play volleyball with, wasn't it?'

Saskia nodded. 'I thought he genuinely liked me.' Her body began to shake as she burst into tears. 'I'm such a stupid idiot.'

'No, you're not. Naive maybe, but not stupid.' Rosie pushed a box of tissues towards her. 'I'll make some tea. God, listen to me. I sound like my mother. She's always believed that tea is the first necessity in times of crisis. Although these days I think she's probably replaced it with wine or champagne. D'you take sugar?'

'No. Is your mother lovely?'

'She has her moments,' Rosie said. 'But generally, yes, she is lovely.'

'I wish I'd known my mother,' Saskia said quietly. 'I think my whole life would have been different – Dad's, too.'

Shocked, Rosie looked at her. 'What d'you mean?'

'She died soon after I was born.' Saskia sniffed and took another tissue to rub her good eye in an attempt to stop the tears.

'All the time I was growing up Dad never told me any details – just that she died when I was very young. He'd never tell me how old I was when it happened. I spent years looking at photographs of her, trying to dredge up a memory or two. Nothing. It took me a long time to realise the one picture of her and me that existed had been taken when I was maybe an hour old.' She gave a big sniff.

'That's when I made Dad tell me the truth. She'd died within forty-eight hours of having me.'

'Oh, Saskia, you poor love,' Rosie said, wanting to envelop Saskia in a hug. Before she could move closer or voice any more sympathy, Saskia defiantly took the ice pack away from her face.

'Apparently, it wasn't me that killed her. Sudden Adult Death Syndrome did that. Doesn't stop me feeling guilty, though.' Saskia took a deep breath. 'How can I miss her so much when I never knew her?'

'Have you ever talked to anyone about this? Had counselling? Talked to your Dad about how you feel?'

Saskia gave a bitter laugh. 'Rosie, I'm American, I've had counsellors for everything. Think this needs some more ice. It's warm.' She held the cloth out. The subject of her mother was clearly being closed.

'You look like you've had a run-in with Mike Tyson,' Rosie said. 'Not sure your story about walking into a door is going to be believed.'

Saskia shrugged. 'It was a big door.' She felt in her jeans back pocket and groaned. 'I seem to have lost my phone. Could I use yours, please? I was supposed to meet Dad for dinner. He'll be wondering where I am. Besides…' She hesitated. 'I don't want to upset him. He seems a bit stressed at the moment.'

'Sure,' Rosie said, taking it out of her bag. 'We'll need to phone for a cab to take you back, too.'

'Do you have to?' Saskia bit her lip as she looked at Rosie. 'Can't I tell Dad I'll see him in the morning and stay with you tonight?'

Chapter Forty

Against her better judgement, Rosie agreed to Saskia staying at her flat overnight. She felt sorry for her but she couldn't help feeling it would be better if she went back to the hotel and faced up to things. Let Terry see the state of her face. He would surely insist on her reporting the assault to the gendarmes.

Rosie pulled the sofa bed out and started to make it while Saskia phoned her father to tell him she was staying with a friend.

'Honestly, Dad, chill. I'm just spending the night with a friend. What? Female, of course. I'll see you in the morning. Love you.' She put the phone down on the table and smiled at Rosie.

'There. Now he won't spend the night worrying about me.'

'I doubt that,' Rosie said. 'He still has no idea where you are – which must be a worry for him.' She glanced at Saskia. 'You could have told him you were with me. Which may or may not have reassured him. Right, you can have the sofa bed.'

'May I have a shower first? I kinda feel dirty,' Saskia said.

'Of course. Clean towels in the bathroom cupboard.'

As Saskia disappeared into the bathroom, Rosie's discarded phone on the table played its incoming call music. Rosie answered it, expecting it to be Seb.

'Can I talk to Saskia, please?' an American accent demanded. 'And who am I talking to?'

Rosie took a deep breath. Terry. Of course he'd check up on Saskia, phone the unknown number on his phone. Like any loving father, he would not simply take her word for it that she was safe.

'Sorry, she's just stepped into the shower. And it's Rosie.'

'My Rosie?'

Refusing the temptation to snap, 'I'm *not* your Rosie,' Rosie said, 'Yes.'

'Right.' He paused. 'Okay. I'll leave you two to it.'

'Goodnight then,' and Rosie switched the phone off. She could tell from the surprise in his voice that Terry had no idea how to react to her being the 'friend' Saskia was staying with.

That made two of them then. She had no idea whether she was handling the situation the right way or not. She suspected if she'd told Terry why Saskia was with her, he'd have been on the doorstep within minutes demanding to see her and calling the police.

When Saskia reappeared wrapped in a towel, Rosie realised she needed something to sleep in and went into the bedroom to find her something.

'T-shirt okay?'

'Thanks.'

'I hope you're not hungry. I don't keep much food here, I eat mainly at the restaurant.'

Saskia shook her head. 'I'm not hungry, thanks. Can I just go to bed, please?'

'Sure. I'll see you in the morning,' Rosie said. 'I hope you sleep well.'

'Rosie? Thank you.'

Rosie waved her thanks away. 'Get some sleep.' Her phone rang and this time she looked at the caller ID: Seb.

'I'll take this in my room. Night night.'

'What's going on, Rosie? Tiki is in a bit of a state. Says he knows something is going on with Saskia.'

'Is he with you? No? Okay. Briefly, Saskia was assaulted tonight. I brought her back here and she asked to stay the night.' Rosie hesitated. 'Please don't tell Terry. She doesn't want him to know. She'll be back at the hotel in the morning and plans to play things down. Say she walked into a door or something.'

'She's not going to the police?'

'No. Although I'm hoping Tiki will change her mind about that when he sees her face.'

'Are you all right?' Seb asked. 'If anybody has hurt you, I'll personally sort them out.'

'I'm fine. Glad I was in the right place at the right time, though, to help Saskia. It could have ended up a lot worse,' she added quietly. Didn't bear thinking about.

'D'you want me to come round? Try to talk some sense into Saskia. Give you a hug?'

'A hug would be wonderful but I'll wait until I see you tomorrow. Saskia's already in bed and I'm about to do the same.'

Before she climbed into bed, Rosie opened the door quietly to check on Saskia and smiled at the scene in the sitting room. Saskia was fast asleep with Lucky snuggled into the curve of her legs.

As tired as she was, sleep evaded Rosie and she tossed and turned before eventually falling into a fitful sleep filled with dreams. Dreams that featured Seb fighting monsters on her behalf and holding her tight and promising never to let her go.

The smell of coffee woke her the next morning. Stumbling out of her room she found Saskia pouring two mugs.

'Hi. I was about to bring this in to you.' As she turned to hand Rosie a mug, Rosie couldn't hide her shock. The bruise around Saskia's eye and cheekbone this morning was large and flamboyantly coloured.

'Aren't I pretty this morning?' Saskia said. 'Don't suppose you've got any concealer anywhere?'

'A tubful won't be able to hide that bruise,' Rosie said. 'And no way is your father going to believe the damage was done walking into a door.'

'I guess not but that's what I'm going to say.'

'You should tell him what happened,' Rosie said. 'Seb says he was in a terrible state last night.'

'I can't tell him. He'll be furious with me. He'll ground me indefinitely and he'll want me to go to the police.'

'Which you should,' Rosie said. 'Even if you don't want to press charges, he should be made known to the police in case he does the same to another girl. Or even attacks you again.'

Saskia shook her head. 'I'll stay away from him in future.'

Rosie shook her head in despair.

The two of them walked together along the bord de mer to the café. Rosie did offer to ring for a taxi but Saskia said she'd rather walk. 'It's a beautiful morning. Besides, it delays the moment of facing Dad.'

'Do you want some breakfast before you go to the hotel?'

Saskia shook her head. 'No, thanks. I'd better get it over and done with. I'll see you later.'

Rosie watched her walk across the car park and disappear into the hotel and wondered what would happen next.

Half an hour later, Seb appeared in the kitchen, engulfing her in a bear hug and placing a kiss on her head.

'You okay, ma cherie? That's some bruise Saskia has on her face. Tiki is beside himself with anger. Made worse because Saskia just keeps saying she walked into a door and won't tell him what really happened. It's obvious to him she's been assaulted.'

'My sister appears to be a very stubborn girl,' Rosie said. 'I did try to get her to change her mind and tell him the truth.'

'Tiki was wondering whether there were witnesses who could tell him the truth and report it to the police.' Seb raised his eyebrows as he looked at her.

Rosie stiffened. 'There was only me and I promised Saskia I wouldn't tell either Terry or the gendarmes.'

'How much did you see?'

'All of it,' Rosie said quietly. 'Horrible.'

Seb hugged her tightly. 'Maybe it's a promise you shouldn't have made?'

Chapter Forty-One

Eight o'clock in the morning and GeeGee stood in the empty office, watching the agency printer spewing out her new business handouts. A stack of business cards was already neatly boxed up on her desk.

Waiting for the printer to do its stuff, she glanced around the office. As a shop window for an upmarket, modern, successful business, the sparse black-and-white style worked but she'd never felt really comfortable here. Too intimidating. She definitely wasn't going to miss coming here. She'd miss the printer, though.

She picked up one of the business cards. Dark-green printing on white card simply stated her mobile number and the words 'Georgina George. Home and Property Management Consultant'. Plain and professional. Carefully, she placed it on top of the envelope marked 'Jay' she had on her desk. The printer finished and GeeGee began to place the last batch of handouts into one of her new files.

She took a deep breath as she heard the door being unlocked. Jay? Or one of her co-workers? She'd hoped to have finished and left before anyone turned up.

'Morning, GeeGee. You're early. Couldn't sleep?' Jay said as he walked towards her.

GeeGee put on a bright smile as she looked up at him as she continued to pick up her printouts. Showdown time. She picked up all her bulging files, put her bag over her shoulder, and handed Jay the envelope and card before picking up the boxed business cards.

'What's this then?' Jay said, looking at the card. 'A spot of moonlighting?'

'There's a cheque for the rent I owe you in the envelope.' She held up her hand to silence him as he went to speak. 'I'm out of here as of now.'

'You can't just walk,' Jay said. 'What about the clients? And I want a month's rent in lieu of notice.'

'My clients. I'll continue to deal with them. As for money in lieu of notice – forget it.' GeeGee began to walk towards the door. The last thing she wanted was a scene or an outright row with Jay. She just wanted to get on with her life and new business.

'I've left the office keys on the desk. I guess I'll see you around.' She stopped herself from slamming the door closed. That would be just plain childish.

Whoo. She'd done it. Suddenly she felt light-headed at the enormity of it all. She glanced at her watch. She'd love to go and have breakfast down on the beach but she had an airport run booked in an hour's time. A party of twelve guests for a wedding that needed both Bruno's large people carrier and her car to go to one of the big hotels in Antibes, Eden Roc. Breakfast at the airport would be better. She'd treat herself to a paperback or glossy magazine to read while she ate.

Half an hour later she wandered into the big newsagents. In among all the magazines and paperbacks there was a section of 'How To...' books. One bright cover extolled the virtues of EFT (Emotional Freedom Technique). 'Tap Tap your stress and phobias away.' Despite herself GeeGee was curious and picked one up.

Standing there, reading about how tapping on certain parts of the body could help banish stress and phobias, GeeGee decided she needed this book. Anything that could help relieve the stress the next few months were sure to bring would be good.

Buying a coffee and croissant, GeeGee settled down to wait for Bruno and the 11.40 plane to land. She was deep into the book when Bruno sat down beside her.

'How's things?' he said, placing his own coffee on the table.

Silently, she handed him one of her new business cards. 'What d'you think?'

'Not going to be stealing my clients, are you?' he said. 'I'm joking,' he added quickly as he saw the look on her face.

'No, of course I'm not, but I am hoping you'll think of me for any, let's say, overspill you might have. You know, extra airport runs, maybe a holiday apartment that doesn't fit in with your area?' She looked at him hopefully. 'Work together.'

Bruno nodded. 'What about your desk in the agency?'

'Given up. Fully independent as of today.'

'Anything to do with Jay returning?' Bruno asked quietly.

'He was the catalyst but it's more to do with earning a big commission that will be landing in my bank account about now,' GeeGee said. 'Large enough to give me a security cushion for a few months while I expand. It's a bit of a 'do it now or it'll never happen' time really.'

'Get it right and you'll have a good life and business. I'll certainly carry on getting you to help out with airport runs,' Bruno said. 'As for overspill, well, we've been asked to handle one or two new apartments that we're hesitating over. Let me talk to Patsy tonight, okay?'

Speechless, GeeGee gazed at him in delight.

'Right now, though, I think we'd better go and do a spot of meet and greet. The flight appears to have landed early,' Bruno said, standing up and pointing to the arrivals monitor on the pillar behind them.

Chapter Forty-Two

Erica knew it was premature of her to start packing things before she'd even had an official offer on the house, let alone found one she wanted to buy, but she was determined to be ready to move. She didn't want any last-minute panic. Eight years of living in the house meant there was a lot of sorting out to do. She was unprepared for the current emotional roller coaster she found herself on, though.

She'd thought she was beginning to heal. Almost twelve months on, both she and Cammie had survived the hurt. She no longer woke in the middle of the night and sobbed uncontrollably into her pillow, praying that Cammie wouldn't hear her. She'd stopped crying out in despair, 'Why did it have to happen to Pascal?'

They'd had so many plans for their lives. Another baby – maybe two – siblings for Cammie. Now Cammie would always be an only child and she herself was unlikely to produce any more babies.

Cammie, too, was better in so many ways. Her teachers had told her they noticed an improvement week by week. More like the child she'd been before the accident. No longer withdrawn and thumb-sucking but still not wanting to get in a car. Although there had been a couple of times recently, when Erica had suggested it, that Cammie had appeared to hesitate before shaking her head. Erica knew she had to work on this; that it was the key to Cammie going forward to being whole again.

Having promised Cammie that, 'Yes, Daddy's things will come with us to the new house,' Erica knew she had to tread carefully sorting out his things. Anything she disposed of would have to be done out of sight of Cammie.

She still missed Pascal like crazy. His clothes still hung in the wardrobe, pushed to one side, admittedly, as she couldn't face seeing them every time she opened the wardrobe door, but knowing they were there and clutching them in her arms, inhaling their scent, had given her some comfort in the early days. Sorting through them and taking them to a local charity had been something she'd delayed and delayed. But the time had come. She'd start with the clothes, hoping that Cammie wouldn't notice their absence in the new house.

Jumpers and T-shirts she could wear went in one pile; trousers, suits, shoes, all went in black bags.

Finding the photo in the breast pocket of a linen jacket Pascal had worn on summer evenings, Erica couldn't hold back the tears. She'd forgotten about this photo.

Taken the weekend of her birthday last year, the three of them had gone to Marineland in Antibes. She remembered, at the end of the day, Pascal asking a passing stranger to take the shot, refusing to settle for just a selfie on his phone. 'No, I want a nice picture of the three of us,' he'd insisted. 'Something to treasure.'

They'd stood by the penguin enclosure, arms around each other, Cammie in front of them grinning happily. Such a lovely day. Erica put the photo down on the dressing table. Something to treasure indeed. She'd find a frame for it later.

GeeGee arrived home as she was dragging the bags downstairs. 'Hi, you ready?'

Erica looked at her. 'Hell, I'd totally forgotten we were house-viewing this evening. Give me five minutes,' Erica said. 'And could we drop these off at the charity shop on our way?

'Sure. You go freshen up and I'll put them in the car.'

The villa GeeGee drove them to had ticked a lot of boxes for Erica when she'd seen the brochure. Even Cammie had said it looked nice. The reality looked good, too, as GeeGee parked on its private driveway.

Situated in a narrow lane off a steep hill above the coast road, the villa and gardens had wonderful views of the Mediterranean. The gardens were a manageable size and, as GeeGee unlocked the front door, Erica felt a frisson of anticipation.

'How long has it been empty?'

'About three weeks. English couple had to return unexpectedly – family problems,' GeeGee said, opening the first pair of shutters in the kitchen.

Sunlight filled the large room, illuminating its terracotta floor and Provençal blue-and-yellow-tiled work surfaces. Erica could see herself and Cammie happily cooking together there. French doors led out onto a small patio – perfect for eating breakfast al fresco.

Excitement began to bubble up as Erica followed GeeGee from room to room. The sitting room ran the length of the villa – its front wall consisting of several sets of French doors, which all opened onto a large terrace overlooking the swimming pool, its waters glittering in the evening sunlight.

Wandering through the rest of the house – four bedrooms, three bathrooms, a utility room, cellar, Erica knew she'd found the place for her and Cammie. It just felt so right.

'I should come back with Cammie to make sure she likes it, too, but I love it. So much room for all three of us.'

'Three?' GeeGee said.

'One of the bedrooms with the en-suite has your name on it,' Erica said, turning to look at her friend. 'No arguments. Have you got the papers on you? I want to sign.'

'Without showing Cammie?' GeeGee said, surprised. 'You do get a seven-day cooling off period, but...'

'We'll bring her to look but I just don't want to risk anyone else buying it from under me. I know she's going to love it as much as me – especially if I tell her there is definitely room for a dog,' Erica said. 'Come on, let's go get her.'

GeeGee dropped Erica off to collect Cammie from Madeleine's and, as they walked home, Erica told her about the new house.

'We'll drop your things back home, and then we'll walk over there for you to see. GeeGee has the keys and will meet us there.'

'Is my room big? Can I see the sea from it?' Cammie said. 'What kind of dog can I have?'

Erica laughed. 'We'll have to move in first before we think about a dog.'

When they got back to the villa GeeGee was waiting for them with bottles of rosé, orange juice, water and some plastic cups.

'I nipped into the supermarket on the way back. Thought we'd celebrate by having our first picnic down by the pool,' GeeGee said as an excited Cammie ran around looking at things. 'The pizza should be here soon.'

'Are we really going to live here?' Cammie asked as she flopped down exhausted by Erica and dangled her feet in the pool.

'Yep, as soon as the notaires do all the paperwork,' GeeGee said. 'Think I can hear a motorbike with our pizza delivery.'

While GeeGee went to fetch the pizza, Erica asked Cammie. 'So you think you'll like living here then?'

Cammie nodded. 'Yes. Which bedroom are you having, Mummy? Because I'd really, really like that one.' And she pointed to the bedroom window at the far end of the villa. Erica, working out that it was the one she'd planned on giving to her, couldn't resist teasing her a little.

She pulled a face. 'I like that one, too.'

Cammie shook her head. 'The big one in the middle with the little balcony is better for you. You can sit out there and read when you can't sleep. Nobody will see you in your PJs.'

Erica smothered a smile. Sometimes Cammie reminded her so much of Pascal with her instant observations and grown-up statements. 'Okay. That's settled. GeeGee can have the other big bedroom at the back of the house.'

An hour later, sitting on the terrace having devoured pizza, watching the sun set, with her daughter cuddled into her, Erica felt happy and optimistic for the first time in months. This villa represented a new beginning for both her and Cammie. Things could only get better from now on.

She shifted her weight and gently shook her sleeping daughter who had dozed off leaning against her. 'Come on, sleepy head, time to walk home.'

'I can take you,' GeeGee said sotto voce. 'If she's asleep...'

Erica shook her head. 'No. I can't do that. She has to decide to get in a car herself. I'm not tricking her into it.' She shook Cammie gently again. 'Wake up, sweetheart. Time to go home.'

'I'm tired,' Cammie said irritably as she stood up and yawned. 'Don't want to walk. Can't GeeGee take us in her car?'

Shocked, Erica looked at GeeGee before scooping her daughter up in her arms and making her way towards the car parked in the driveway. Today was turning out to be very eventful.

Chapter Forty-Three

It took four vases to hold the huge bouquet of flowers that arrived for Rosie at the café. The card told her they were from 'A grateful Tiki who desperately needs to talk to you. Please, please, contact me'.

Seb walked in as she was placing the last vase on the restaurant bar. 'I'm guessing Tiki?'

Rosie nodded. 'Over the top, really, but they are beautiful, aren't they?' She handed him the card to read.

'He's leaving the hotel today. He's persuaded the lawyers to get their fingers out and complete the villa purchase urgently.' Seb looked at her. 'He's also told Saskia she's not going anywhere without an escort – even talking about hiring a bodyguard.'

'Saskia was afraid he'd overreact,' Rosie said. At least she wouldn't have to worry about him coming into the restaurant, or bumping into him unexpectedly on the beach if he'd moved into his new house.

'So, when are you going to see him?'

'I'll ring him later and find an evening when it's convenient,' Rosie said. 'Let him settle in first.'

'Good luck with that,' Seb said. 'Honestly, you have no idea how upset he is. He needs answers and he's not a patient man.'

'Well, he's going to have to wait,' Rosie said. 'I've got the café to run.'

'If you don't want him turning up here you'd better ring him sooner rather than later.' Seb kissed her gently. 'I've got to get back to the hotel. I'll see you after lunch.'

Rosie took her phone out of her pocket. She definitely didn't want an angry Terry turning up and causing a scene. This time Terry recognised her number.

'Rosie. Thank God you've rung. I thought I'd have to come to the café to see you. Can we talk this morning? Ten o'clock would suit me.'

'I'm afraid it doesn't suit me. The earliest I can make it is seven o'clock this evening. You're busy moving today anyway, aren't you?'

'Yes, but I have people taking care of all that,' Terry said. 'Okay. Tonight. I'll send a car for you.'

'You don't have to do that. I can make my own way,' Rosie said, but she was talking to empty air. Terry had hung up.

The limo that Terry sent to fetch her that evening was long, sleek and luxurious. Rosie sat back looking out at the Mediterranean as the chauffeur negotiated his way along the traffic-filled bord de mer, taking deep breaths in order to calm herself.

Terry wanted to talk about Saskia's assault but the chances that he would bring up the subject of her and Olivia afterwards was high. The first she could cope with rationally, but Rosie knew she'd have to fight to stay calm when the conversation turned to events of nearly twenty years ago. If only the drive could go on forever. Or preferably the driver could get lost and take her home instead.

Ten minutes was all it took to arrive at the villa with its dark-green and gold-leaf-highlighted wrought-iron gates that silently swung open at the touch of a button.

A short drive curved its way through banks of oleander before the car stopped in front of a flight of shallow steps leading up to the Provençal villa, its numerous windows glinting in the evening sun, the grounds around it immaculate.

Rosie caught her breath. The pictures in the brochure she'd seen at Seb's had, like he'd said, failed to do it justice. It was like driving into a film set. Surreal.

As the chauffeur opened the door for her and she stepped out, she saw Terry at the top of the steps waiting to welcome her. In the few days since she'd last seen him walking past the café, he appeared to have aged.

She realised with a shock, too, that his ponytail had gone. His hair had been cropped into an old-fashioned crew cut. His clothes, black jeans and a white shirt, were as immaculate as ever but he'd definitely lost weight and they hung on him. Stress over Saskia? Or was his illness becoming worse?

'Rosie. Welcome to my new home.'

Thoughtfully, Rosie followed him as he led the way out onto a terrace at the back of the villa overlooking an enormous swimming pool. The view along the coast was spectacular. Cane chairs with small teak tables were dotted around the terrace. On one, a bottle of Moet in an ice bucket was waiting to be opened.

'I'll give you a tour of the house after we've talked,' Terry said, gesturing to her to sit before he sank into a chair opposite her.

'Impossible to believe you only moved in today. Everything is so organised,' Rosie said. 'Thank you for my flowers, by the way. They are beautiful. But there really wasn't any need. Is Saskia here?'

'Right now she's sorting out her room. She'll maybe join us later.' Terry looked at Rosie, his face serious.

'Neither she nor I can thank you enough for the other evening.'

'I only did what anyone would do.'

'So far she refuses to report it,' Terry said. 'Or tell me exactly what happened. I'm hoping you'll fill me in on the details?'

Rosie shook her head. 'Sorry. It's down to Saskia to tell you, not me.'

'You're both as stubborn as each other. Must be in the genes,' he added with a sideways look at Rosie. When Rosie ignored the comment, he sighed.

'I don't know what Olivia has told you about the past, but things aren't always black and white, you know.'

'Don't you dare blame Mum. She never said a bad word about you to me when I was growing up. If anything she defended you, not wanting me to believe you'd stopped loving me as well as her. It was your own words and indifference when I rang you that made me hate you.'

The silence that followed her words was long and painful to both of them. Rosie, looking at Terry's ashen face, regretted saying them so harshly but there was no way she'd let Olivia take the blame for anything. 'I'm sorry but that's the way it was.'

Terry bit his lip as he nodded sadly. 'I'm sorry, too.' He hesitated before asking, 'Do you still feel that way?'

'I'm not seventeen any more, so no. These days I do try and think about things more objectively rather than leaping to conclusions,' Rosie said. 'Something I've been told I do too readily,' she said, remembering Seb telling her off. 'But to be honest, I'm not sure how I feel about you at all these days.' She shrugged. 'Indifferent probably sums it up. You disappeared out of my life so long ago that it's difficult to believe you want back in.'

'To be fair, Rosie, in the beginning I didn't disappear out of your life so much as you wouldn't let me stay in. I'm praying it's not too late to try and change things because this time you have a sister who needs your help.'

Guiltily, Rosie remembered the cards and presents she'd refused to have anything to do with. Had he ever mentioned Saskia in the letters she'd thrown away unread?

'A sister I never knew existed until this summer. Why should I care?' Even as she spoke, Rosie realised she did in fact care a great deal about Saskia, nevertheless. 'Did you tell her about me as she was growing up? Or did you keep quiet about your family in England?'

'I told her I had another daughter who I loved very much but hadn't seen for a long time and that I hoped one day she and you would be friends,' Terry said quietly. 'I realise now I was wrong not to return to Europe years ago and have the two of you meet. Get to know each other. But life, like it does, conspired to get in the way. And now it's tied another knot in the mess of mine and Saskia's lives.'

'Her life isn't a mess because of the assault. Luckily, I happened to be in the right place at the time to help. If you can persuade her to tell you about the assault and report it to the gendarmes, I'll go with her as a witness,' Rosie said.

Terry shook his head. 'Thank you but this isn't just about the assault. It's about protecting Saskia from yet another blow in her life.' He took a deep breath. 'Like you she has been brought up by a single parent. Her mother died hours after she gave birth.'

'I know,' Rosie said quietly. 'She told me the night she stayed with me.'

'She did? What she didn't tell you – couldn't, as she doesn't know – was that it happened the day you rang telling me about Olivia's problem and wanting me to come back.'

Shocked, Rosie stared at Terry. 'Why didn't you tell me that at the time? At least I would have had a concrete reason for being upset rather than just feeling I had been thrown aside as someone of little importance in your life. I thought you didn't care about me in any way, any more.'

'So, so not true,' Terry said, rubbing his forehead with a shaking hand. 'I wasn't thinking straight right then. All I knew was that I had a newborn child to take care of and her mother was dead.'

Instinctively, Rosie reached out and touched his arm. 'It must have been a terrible time for you.'

'At least Saskia knows nothing about that horrendous time and I've tried to do my best for her ever since, to make up for everything,' he said, his voice breaking. 'It's a task I'm hoping I can delegate to you, Rosie.'

Nervously, he fiddled with his watch strap before looking up at her. 'I have a heart problem. Currently, it's under control but I need you to promise me you'll look after Saskia if anything happens to me? Be her official guardian, if necessary? It's the main reason I'm buying a house over here. You're the only blood relative Saskia has and I need to know you'll be there for her.'

Chapter Forty-Four

Terry insisted on his driver taking her back to town and Rosie sat in the limousine as it drove her home, deep in thought.

So many of her beliefs about her father shattered. Learning the truth about long-ago circumstances had turned everything on its head. Feelings of guilt now clouded everything. If she hadn't selfishly rebutted all Terry's attempts to contact her and they'd talked things through years ago, both their lives could have been different. Their father-daughter relationship could have survived. Now it was going to take time to salvage.

Seb had been right to urge her to see Terry. If she'd learnt everything Terry had told her this evening after his death, she would have had to live with the guilt for the rest of her life. At least this way she had a chance to make amends.

Her mobile pinged as the car neared the beach. Seb texting to ask how her meeting had gone and to tell her that supper was waiting for her. Rosie quickly texted back: 'Walk on the beach first? Need to clear head.'

He was waiting for her on his usual rock and after a hug and a kiss they began to walk together along the shoreline as Rosie told him about her meeting.

'Have you forgiven Tiki?' Seb asked. 'Are you friends now?'

'We have to get to know each other again as adults before we can become friends,' Rosie said. 'I do understand now why he did what he did, and I think he understands my reaction.' She scuffed some sand with her trainer. 'Whether I'm up to doing what he wants me to do is another question.'

Seb caught hold of her hand. 'Which is?'

'Get to know Saskia and be there for her if anything happens to him. Become Saskia's official guardian if she's still underage when he dies.' Rosie sighed. 'Which he hopes won't be for some time but the reality is he doesn't know how long he's got.'

Seb squeezed her hand but didn't speak.

'I've agreed to see more of him and to do "sisterly" things with Saskia – whatever he means by that. He wants a family dinner at the villa one evening next week. I know you can't come to the dinner but you will come along later, won't you? After you finish at the hotel?'

'Of course.'

Rosie sighed happily. 'Thank you. Talking of food. Did you say something about supper? I haven't eaten for hours and I'm starving.'

'Come on then.' Seb whistled to Lucky, busy chasing seagulls at the far end of the beach. 'Time I got back anyway. One of the waitresses was babysitting Isabella for me. I have something to talk to you about, too.'

Rosie looked at him intrigued but he shook his head.

'It can wait until we're back at the hotel.' As he put his arm around her shoulders and held her tight as they walked, Rosie instinctively placed her arm around his body. It felt so good walking together like this.

Sitting out on Seb's hidden terrace above the hotel watching the lights twinkling along the coast, Rosie took a large sip from the glass of rosé Seb had given her while he fetched their supper from the kitchen. Looking eastwards along the coast, Rosie wondered if any of the lights she could see belonged to Terry's villa or was it hidden away on the other side of the promontory?

Terry and Saskia had given her a tour before she left and she had to admit to being stunned with the sheer beauty of the place. The recent renovations had somehow captured the nostalgic atmosphere of the villa's heyday. The simple act of turning a mother-of-pearl, round door handle to enter rooms that still held the air of the roaring twenties was exciting.

The two Jean Cocteau sketches lovingly preserved on the walls of the sitting room had taken her breath away. If Woody Allen had appeared, haphazardly directing his latest film, Rosie wouldn't have been surprised. All that had been missing was the noise of a saxophone moodily playing somewhere in the grounds.

Seb pushed the trolley out onto the terrace. 'Supper.'

'Nobody has ever spoilt me with food like you do before,' Rosie said. Previous boyfriends had tended to be fearful of her cooking skills and she'd either fed them or they'd eaten out. Having a chef prepare food for her was something she could get used to – especially if Seb was the chef.

'I've never seen asparagus served like this before,' Rosie said, taking a bite of a spear wrapped in a chive-seasoned omelette with a slice of parma ham holding it all together. 'Mmm. I think it's just become my favourite starter.'

The mushroom terrine and green salad Seb handed her next was equally delicious. As she swallowed the last mouthful, she sighed. 'You're good, you are. You deserve any number of stars.'

'Why thank you, ma'am,' Seb said. 'Rhubarb and raspberry tart?' he asked, picking up a knife and cutting two slices.

'Later. I'm full right now. A drop more rosé would be good, though, and then you can tell me what you wanted to talk about.'

Seb topped up both their glasses before saying, 'I've had a letter from Zoe. She's having such fun she's staying out east. Might be back before Christmas but might not.'

'Have you told Isabella?'

Seb shook his head. 'Not yet. I don't want to rock her world in case the news upsets her. She seems happy, doesn't mention Zoe much – in fact she talks about you more than her mum at the moment. Lucky-dog figures in her conversation a lot, too.' He fiddled with the stem of his wine glass.

'I've applied to the court to become Isabella's official guardian. The notaire says he can't see a problem because I'm obviously a responsible father and Zoe isn't even in the country.' He looked at Rosie. 'How d'you feel about me being a full-time father?'

'Is this one of the things you said you had to sort out that evening at the lighthouse?' Rosie said.

Seb nodded.

'You'll be a brilliant full-time dad – you are already,' Rosie said. 'Isabella loves you to bits. I don't see a problem.'

Seb waved his hand, dismissing her words. 'Rosie, you're missing the point. I want you in my life, too. I want us to be a couple.' He took a deep breath. 'But I'm coming with baggage.The question really is, how do you feel about being a full-time substitute mum to Isabella? If you can't handle it, I'm not sure where we go from here.'

He regarded her anxiously in the brief silence that fell between them before Rosie finally smiled. 'Oh, I see. Well, I've always wanted a family of my own so I don't have a problem with treating Isabella like my daughter.'

'You sure?' Seb said. 'You promise you won't do a Zoe and run out on us in a few months?'

'I promise that will never happen. Besides, don't forget I've now got baggage you're going to have to live with, too, in the shape of Terry and Saskia.' Rosie leant across and kissed him. 'I think I'm ready for my dessert now we've got that out of the way.'

Wordlessly Seb placed a slice of tart on a plate, smothered it with cream, and to her surprise, instead of handing it to her, began to spoon-feed her.

'You know where Lucky-dog is?' he asked.

With her mouth full, unable to answer, Rosie shook her head.

'She's curled up on Isabella's bed,' Seb said, scooping up another spoonful.

Rosie swallowed quickly. 'Oh, I'm sorry. I'll call her and...'

'Stop talking. Open your mouth,' Seb interrupted, and placed another spoonful in her mouth.

'Seems a shame to disturb her. Probably wake Isabella if we did. She'd be upset. Might even cry. Much better if you stay here tonight, don't you think? Make everyone happy.'

Chapter Forty-Five

Rosie was enjoying a beautiful dream involving her and Seb honeymooning on some tropical island. Seb was urging her to come and see something he'd discovered on the white beach outside the luxury cabin they were staying in.

'Rosie, Rosie, darling. Please wake up.'

She came to with a jolt. Seb was kneeling by the bed, shaking her gently.

'What is it? What's the time?'

'Nearly midnight. Saskia's phoned. She's at the hospital with Tiki. She wants you there.'

Rosie was out of bed and pulling on her clothes. 'Can you call me a taxi?'

'I'll drive you.'

'What about Isabella?'

'Alicia's on her way. I've told the night porter. Ready? Let's go.'

There was traffic along the bord de mer and several red traffic lights that conspired against them, but fifteen minutes later, Seb pulled into the hospital car park.

The nurse in A&E directed them to a small waiting room near where Tiki was being cared for. Saskia, slumped in a chair in the corridor, jumped up when she saw Rosie and ran to her.

Rosie hugged her. 'How is he?'

'I don't know. They won't let me see him.'

'I'll go find us some coffee,' Seb said, 'and also see if I can find out anything.'

'I'm glad you're here,' Saskia said, still standing in Rosie's embrace.

'What happened?' Rosie said.

'After you left we had supper on the terrace and just sat there chatting for an hour or so. He was so happy that he'd sorted things out with you and planning all sorts of things for us to do together. Then, he just sort of keeled over. It was horrible, Rosie.'

Rosie hugged her tighter.

'I just wish they'd tell me what's happening.'

'I expect they're busy helping him. We'll just have to wait. They'll come and tell us as soon as they have some news,' Rosie said.

Seb returned with three coffees. He shrugged as he handed them out. 'Apparently, somebody will be along soon.'

Rosie glanced at Seb. 'D'you need to go home for Isabella?'

'I'm staying with you,' Seb said. 'Isabella will be fine with Alicia.'

It was half an hour before a tired-looking doctor, accompanied by a nurse, came to tell them that Tiki was stable.

'Can we see him?' Saskia asked.

'One of you. Briefly. Then go home and get some sleep. Come back in the morning.'

Rosie gestured to Saskia to go with the nurse.

'Can you tell us what happened?' Seb asked the doctor. 'Something to do with his illness?'

'No. He suffered a minor stroke this evening. We'll be able to tell you more in the morning.'

When Saskia returned she was crying.

'Come on, lets get you home,' Rosie said, looking at Seb. 'I think my apartment rather than the villa.'

Seb dropped them both at the apartment. He kissed Rosie goodnight, and gave Saskia a gentle hug before saying, 'I'll see you both in the morning,' and leaving.

Rosie made two mugs of hot chocolate and she and Saskia sat side by side on the sofa, each lost in their own thoughts. Saskia broke the silence.

'Dad is going to be all right, isn't he?'

Rosie shook her head. 'I don't know but I hope so – he and I have a lot of catching up to do. He's in the best place for help.'

'I know he's not been well but I thought all that was under control and now this happens.' Saskia's voice trailed away. 'He's all I've got. I don't want to be all alone in the world.'

'If the worst does happen you won't be alone. You've got a big sister now, remember?'

Saskia smiled weakly. 'I hadn't forgotten, really. It's just that its only ever been Dad and me. My sister was this horrible unknown person living in Europe who didn't want anything to do with us.'

'That's because I didn't know about you. Now I do, I promise you I'm going to be around for you. I take my new role of big sister very seriously.'

'Should think so, too. It's a very important role,' Saskia said. 'Where's Lucky-dog? She slept on my bed last time and it was lovely.'

'She's having a sleepover at the hotel with Isabella,' Rosie said. 'She adores her,' she added, trying to make it sound like a regular occurrence rather than something that happened for the first time tonight.

'Were you having a sleepover, too?' Saskia said. 'Is that why you and Seb arrived together?'

'Yes,' Rosie said. No point in denying it. 'Come on, I think we'd better try and get some sleep. It's been a long day and tomorrow will be, too.'

As they made the sofa bed up, Rosie found her thoughts turning to Terry and what would happen if he did die. Saskia, for all her brave words, would be heartbroken. Having a big sister take the place of a beloved father wouldn't be much consolation, would it?

Saskia pulled the duvet over herself before looking up at Rosie. 'Night night. I'm glad my new brother-in-law to be is going to be Seb. He's nice.'

'Not so fast.' Rosie laughed. 'It's not official yet.'

'But it will be. Can't wait to tell Dad. He likes Seb.'

As Rosie climbed into her own bed she could only pray that Terry would live long enough for Saskia to tell him the news.

A busy week in the restaurant meant Rosie had no chance to think about the changes happening in her life. Changes she knew would inevitably cause far-reaching upheaval in her future. Some welcome, some not.

She phoned the hospital every morning before starting work. Terry was holding his own, with slight improvements every day. Conversation during her evening visits was becoming that of friends – both she and Terry were slowly letting the past drift away and focusing on their future relationship.

During the day, Rosie concentrated on keeping Café Fleur running smoothly, organising the final preparations for Tansy and Rob's wedding, making sure Saskia was eating, walking Lucky-dog. The list went on.

The days took on a new routine dictated by busy lunchtimes, normal day-to-day café work, followed by hospital visits. Looking after Isabella had been taken out of her hands by Seb.

'I've hired a full-time nanny from the agency. You've enough to do without worrying about fitting in childminding,' he'd said.

Seb employing the nanny had fanned her guilt. If Isabella was going to be her daughter Rosie wanted to be involved with her care – no matter how fraught life was. Besides, she missed seeing the little girl. The fact she didn't have the energy to argue with Seb told her how tired she was. The end of the summer season wasn't far away, and she promised herself she'd make it up to both of them then. In the meantime she just had to go with the steamroller effect of current events in her life.

To Rosie's surprise, Olivia turned up at the café late one afternoon as she was preparing to leave for her daily visit to Terry. She'd phoned and told her about Tiki's stroke the day after it happened and Olivia had made her promise to keep her updated with his progress.

'I thought I'd come with you tonight,' Olivia said now. 'I sort of feel I should. He played a large part in my life – without him I wouldn't have you. If you think he's strong enough for the shock of me appearing that is?'

'I'll check with him first,' Rosie said. 'He's a lot better. He keeps badgering the doctors to discharge him but they keep insisting they need to do more tests. He's not their easiest patient, that's for sure.'

Olivia laughed. 'No, he's always been too impatient for his own good.'

As Rosie opened the door of his private room, she overheard Saskia say, 'So, with a wedding to look forward to, you've got to get better.' Terry was lying back on his pillows, a happy smile on his face.

'Hi. How're things today?' Rosie said, giving him a kiss on the cheek.

'The docs have finally finished their tests. Hoping they'll let me leave soon,' Terry said. 'Saskia's been telling me about you and Seb. I'm so happy for you – Seb's a good guy.'

'Nothing official yet,' Rosie said. 'But yes, Seb is a good guy. Umm, Dad?' She stopped, selfconsciously realising what she'd just said. The word had somehow slipped out, maybe because of what she was about to suggest.

Terry smiled as he looked at her. 'Yes?'

'Mum's outside. She was wondering if you were up to a visit? She's fine about it if you're not.'

Terry smiled. 'Olivia's here to see me? Wow! That's unexpected. But good news. Show her in.'

When Olivia walked in, Terry smiled and held out his free arm. 'Can't give you a proper hug,' he said, indicating the intravenous drip in his left hand. 'It's good to see you. And isn't it great news about our daughter and Seb?'

Olivia looked at Rosie and raised her eyebrows. 'Well, you heard that news before me,' she said, smilingly, 'but, yes, it's wonderful news.'

'Before you get told off for having too many visitors, Saskia and I will leave you two to chat for a bit. Be nice to each other, won't you?' Rosie said, knowing the interrogation from Olivia about what was going on with her and Seb would come later.

As Rosie and Saskia sat in the tiny café in the hospital grounds, Saskia said, 'Good of your mum to come and see Dad.'

'I'm not sure what prompted it,' Rosie said. Maybe it was Olivia's way of showing her she was glad the rift between father and daughter was over. Maybe she had her own reasons, too, for wanting to put things right between herself and Terry.

Whatever the reason it was good not having warring parents after all these years.

Chapter Forty-Six

GeeGee treated herself to a large iced coffee and made her way to her usual table at the Café Fleur, thankful for the shade of the two large eucalyptus trees on the edge of the terrace.

Setting up her laptop to take advantage of the shade she began to check her emails. Bruno and Patsy had generously passed on the contact details of three new apartments they'd been asked to handle and which they'd declined, saying they were already stretched to their limit. Two of the contacts had signed with GeeGee and the third had said he didn't want to go with a start-up company. Fair enough, but two out of three wasn't bad and GeeGee was pleased.

Since leaving the agency she'd done the rounds of places and people she hoped would take her flyers and business cards. Erica, of course, had a stack of cards on the counter of The Cupboard Under the Stairs and slipped a flyer into the bag with every purchase.

Seb, too, handed her card out to any guest who indicated they were house hunting. The bookshop in town had not only taken some flyers but had expressed an interest in her managing their two holiday apartments next year. She hadn't asked Rosie yet to help spread the word. She couldn't when Rosie's life was in such turmoil.

GeeGee sipped her coffee and looked around. Her own life seemed to be on a high for once. Enquiries for managing holiday properties were coming in, airport runs were keeping her busy, and the cash flow was brilliant. Taking a percentage every month from handling holiday properties instead of selling them would ensure her a more reliable income from clients who signed up for her services.

Leaving the agency and going solo had been a good move. Selling two villas in quick succession had been a stroke of luck and had to be a good omen for her future. The relief of having some money behind her while she established things was immense. And there was still the commission to come from the villa Erica was buying. Commission she was determined to use to pay Erica back in some small way for everything.

She'd overridden Erica's 'no way am I taking rent off you' by refusing to agree to move into the new villa without paying the going rent for a studio room.

'If you don't want it, pay it into an account for Cammie for when she's eighteen.'

Today she planned on emailing clients she had on file who had bought places off her in the past six months, asking them to consider her as an agent if they ever wanted to let them out. One of the first names to come up on the 'Recent Sales Spreadsheet' was Tiki Gilvear.

Like everyone else she'd been amazed when the news broke that Tiki Gilvear was Rosie's father. To hear he had been taken ill so soon after buying the villa she'd found strangely upsetting. She remembered how thrilled he'd been with the place the first time she'd taken him to view it.

He'd confided in her it was the type of home he'd dreamt of owning as a boy growing up in the inner city.

She sincerely hoped he'd get to enjoy living there with Saskia. Maybe Rosie would move in, too?

She clicked on the mouse and moved the cursor down the spreadsheet to the next name. Dan Brewer, apartment 4c. She smiled, remembering the afternoon he got the keys and the way he'd kept his promise about buying her a coffee.

Dan had been carrying a large rucksack when he arrived at the notaire's office, and once all the formalities were dealt with and he had the keys to the apartment in his hand, he'd turned to her. 'It's coffee time. Come on.'

Instead of making for one of the nearby pavement restaurants, they'd gone straight to the apartment. Once there he'd taken an espresso machine out of the rucksack, placed it on the kitchen work surface and plugged it in. Coffee capsules, cups, plates, milk and sugar had been pulled out of the rucksack in quick succession and placed alongside.

GeeGee couldn't stop laughing as she watched him. 'You look like a magician pulling stuff out of a hat!' she said as he pulled the final item out of a side pocket: A boulangerie paper bag.

'I hope you like squashed pain au raisin,' Dan said, opening the bag and sliding two sorry-looking cakes out onto plates. 'Let's go out on the terrace. If you take these, I'll bring the coffees.'

The previous owner had left two rickety chairs up on the terrace and sitting there, drinking coffee and eating the squashed cakes, she and Dan got to know each other as well as talking about his ideas for the apartment. Ideas that appeared to be similar to the way she'd decorate the place if it were her own.

GeeGee raised her cup in a toast. 'Here's to you and 4c. I hope you'll be very happy here. Will working on the yacht make it difficult to spend time ashore?'

Dan shook his head. 'No, I finish at the end of this season. Working on the yacht was only ever temporary while I decided what to do next.' He glanced at GeeGee.

'I worked in the City for ten years. Then I got burnout,' he said. 'Marc suggested I become a yachtie like him. Said the sea air would do me good. So I sold my London flat and the obligatory Porsche and took a year off. I've enjoyed it but, as careers go, it's not for me.'

'So this is going to be your holiday apartment then?' GeeGee said, disappointed. She'd been hoping Dan would be around during the winter months. That maybe they could become friends; get to know each other better. Her heart lurched, though, at his next words.

'No. It's going to be my permanent home. I just have to find a job that can use my financial expertise but doesn't take over my life.' Dan shrugged. 'Meantime, I'm going to enjoy sorting this place out, making new friends. And getting to know you,' he added, looking at her.

GeeGee smiled at him. 'Sounds like a plan.'

Dan had sailed away to Greece the next day and she'd started counting the days till his return. Which should be soon; sometime next week according to his text two days ago.

An email pinged into her inbox, bringing her back to the present.

Bruno: 'Possible to do an airport run today at three o'clock?'

She quickly typed: 'Yes. Name etc?' and pressed the Send button. She loved the spontaneity of her new life. Every day was different. Things would slow down in October and over winter, she knew, but that was weeks away. Weeks where she'd still be earning money unlike in other years. She'd spend winter advertising the business and spreading the word so that, come next spring, she'd be ready for a bumper summer. And Dan would be back living in town. A definite bonus.

Her email pinged again. Expecting it to be Bruno with the airport details, her heart flipped as she saw Dan's email address:

'Returning earlier than expected. Will be home tomorrow. Can't wait to see you. L. xxx'

Chapter Forty-Seven

The call came at ten to six in the morning. Rosie, more than half asleep as she answered the phone, struggled to take in the quiet words that were telling her Tiki had died.

Saskia appeared in the bedroom doorway. And knew instantly that her beloved father had gone. She sobbed uncontrollably in Rosie's arms as Rosie repeated the hospital's words.

'He had a major stroke at five-thirty. The medical staff could do nothing. It was over very quickly in the end.'

'But he was getting better,' Saskia sobbed. 'He was coming home at the end of the week. Talking about things the three of us were going to do together. And I didn't get to say goodbye.'

Rosie could only sit there and hug her sister.

'We'll still do things together.'

'But it won't be the same,' Saskia said.

'No it won't, but we'll do them anyway,' Rosie said.

Rosie sat holding Saskia, lost in her own thoughts. She and Terry had become friends again while he'd lain in his hospital bed but longer had been needed to change the relationship back to one of father and daughter. Time she'd been denied.

As Saskia gradually became calmer and stopped shaking, Rosie said, 'I need to make some phone calls, and then how about we get dressed and go find Seb at the hotel?' She personally needed a hug and Seb's comforting presence. He'd know, too, what she and Saskia had to do now.

When they got to the hotel Seb wrapped both of them in a fierce hug. 'I'm so sorry.' He insisted on them having coffee and croissants. 'You need something.' Saskia drank her coffee but crumbled the croissant into crumbs on her plate.

Olivia arrived mid-morning and took Saskia off for a walk on the beach, giving Seb and Rosie the opportunity to start notifying the various authorities and doing all the formal paperwork connected with Tiki's death.

Saskia had popped out for a coffee one evening when Rosie had visited Terry in hospital and he'd insisted on talking about what he wanted if he was to die. A private funeral and cremation.

'My agent will arrange a memorial service, no doubt, back in America, but here I want just family and for you and Saskia to scatter my ashes in the grounds of the villa.'

When she'd tried to stop such morbid talk, he'd squeezed her hand. 'It's important you know what I want. So promise me.'

Rosie was grateful for Seb's matter-of-factness as she relayed the conversation to him. 'That's what I'll help you arrange then.'

Saskia and Olivia returned from their walk on the beach arm in arm, with Saskia looking more composed. White but composed.

'Your mum is a lovely person,' she said to Rosie after Olivia had left. 'She says if I want to I can treat her like a surrogate mum.' Saskia looked at Rosie. 'She said if she'd known about me she'd have insisted you kept in contact with Dad so we could have met before. Sisters deserve to know each other, she said.'

Wordlessly, Rosie hugged Saskia as she inwardly promised to tell Olivia how much she loved her. Something she'd lost the chance of saying to her Dad ever again.

Over the next few days, as the funeral plans began to come together, Rosie realised with a sinking heart the funeral was going to take place just two days before Tansy's wedding.

The morning of the funeral, Rosie went down to Café Fleur early and pinned a notice to the door: 'Closed due to exceptional circumstances. Please forgive any inconvenience.'

She picked up some junk mail and an official-looking letter from the floor. Franked across the top of the expensive envelope was a notaire's name. The one dealing with the accusation of food poisoning.

Rosie stared at it. All summer she'd been waiting for this and it had to arrive today. No way was she going to open it this morning. Today belonged to Terry.

She pushed the letter into the depths of her tote-bag. Later would be too soon.

There were only five of them at the crematorium. Saskia, Olivia, Zander, Seb and Rosie. Rosie was surprised to see Zander arrive with her mother, but watching the tender way he took care of Olivia opened her eyes to the fact that he was most definitely a fixture in her mother's life.

Seb insisted they all return to the hotel for a drink to celebrate Tiki's life. A bottle of vintage champagne was opened and it was Olivia who led the toasts to her former husband.

'Exasperating he may have been, boring he never was. Here's to a life well lived. RIP, Tiki Gilvear, formerly known as Terry Hewitt.'

It was then that Rosie's tears started to fall. The sheer futility of it all. Finding her father only to lose him again so quickly and so permanently this time. Seb took her into his arms and held her tight, as she buried her face in his shoulder and sobbed unreservedly for all the things that could now never be rectified.

Chapter Forty-Eight

'There, that's another box packed,' Erica said with a big sigh. 'Think that's enough for this evening. Time for a drink and something to eat up on the terrace.' She reached for her phone. 'Thought I'd order a couple of takeaway pizzas if that's okay with everyone?'

'Can I have a four-cheese one, please, Mummy,' Cammie said instantly.

'Me, too,' GeeGee said, wrapping an ornament in some bubble wrap.

'Sounds delicious,' Amelia said, folding in the flaps on the box she'd been packing and dragging it across the room to join the other ones.

Tiredly, Erica looking around the sitting room now full of cardboard boxes, empty shelves and cupboards. Working all day in The Cupboard Under the Stairs and then coming home to start packing ready for the move was exhausting. Amelia's offer to come down and look after Cammie while Erica was at the shop and help pack up the house had been accepted with thanks.

'I can't believe how much stuff I've accumulated,' she said. 'We've barely started and already I've run out of cardboard boxes.'

'I'll pick up some more tomorrow,' Amelia said. 'We can have a break until the weekend and then get stuck in again.'

'I can't believe how quickly everything is going through,' Erica said. 'Less than a fortnight before we move and so much to do.'

'Oh, about that...' GeeGee said, 'I forgot to tell you that the notaires have asked to bring the completion date forward by two days.'

'Did they say why?' Erica asked as her heart sank.

'No. Just that they had several properties to deal with that week, and as yours had been so straightforward...' She shrugged. 'It's not a problem, is it? Just means you'll be in your new home quicker.'

Erica bit her lip. She couldn't expect GeeGee to remember the significance of the date – it wasn't her husband who'd died a year ago on that day. Looking at Amelia's face she knew that she too had realised the significance of the date. Before she could say anything, the doorbell rang announcing the arrival of their pizzas and the moment was gone .

Sitting out on the terrace half an hour later, finishing their pizzas, GeeGee glanced across at Erica before saying, 'Dan's having a bit of an apartment-warming party at the weekend. Would love you to come and meet him.'

'Oh, I'd love to finally meet Dan,' Erica said. 'But I'm not much of a party girl these days. Why don't we meet down on the beach at Rosie's for lunch instead?'

'We can do that,' GeeGee agreed. 'But I still want you to come to the party. It would do you good to start socialising again. You go to work, go to the beach with Cammie, even visit the occasional vide grenier, but basically you avoid having a social life these days.'

Even as she went to protest, Erica realised GeeGee had spoken the truth. She'd shied away from meeting new people for months.

'I agree,' Amelia said. 'You do need to get out more. And while I'm here to look after Cammie you don't have any excuse.'

Seeing them both look at her expectantly, Erica sighed. 'Okay, I'll think about it but I'm not promising anything.' It had been bad enough forcing herself to return to work and talk to customers in the shop after Pascal died, but at least there she was able to talk about the things she was selling.

Making small talk with strangers at a party was something else. Something she wasn't sure she was ready to tackle.

'Right,' GeeGee said. 'The airport calls. I'll see you in the morning.'

There was a short silence as GeeGee left before Amelia spoke. 'There's something I'd like to ask you, too. Please may I take Cammie home with me for a few days before school starts again?'

'Please, please, Mummy. Can I go with Granny?' Cammie jumped up and down with excitement.

Erica smiled and took a deep breath. The answer just a month ago would have been a definite 'no', however much Cammie had begged.

'I don't see why not. So long as you promise to behave.'

Cammie let out a loud 'Yippee' and ran around the terrace excitedly. 'And when I come back we can get our dog!'

Erica laughed before saying quietly to Amelia, 'However much one wishes one could change things, life itself simply keeps pulling one along, forcing acceptance and moving forward, doesn't it?'

Amelia nodded. 'It's not easy but accepting it is what it is, is the only way I've found of getting through life.'

***

The evening of Dan's party, Erica left home to walk to the apartment, leaving Cammie and Amelia happily watching *Frozen*. A first for Amelia but Erica had lost count of how many times Cammie had seen it.

People were out enjoying the last of the evening sun, wandering along the narrow streets, sitting at pavement cafés enjoying moules and frites, wandering through the artisan night market buying holiday souvenirs.

Approaching Dan's apartment along the narrow rampart pavement, Erica hoped GeeGee would remember her promise to keep an eye out and be there for her the moment she arrived. But there was no sign of her, and the street door to the four apartments was firmly closed. The intercom had an 'hors service' notice taped across it so was useless.

As she stood there wondering what to do, a well-dressed man came striding up and swore under his breath when the door failed to open for him.

'Looks like we've been locked out,' he said. 'You going to Dan's party, too?'

Erica nodded. 'Haven't even got Dan's number on my phone so I can't ring him.' You could ring GeeGee, though, a little voice in her head whispered.

'We could cross the road and try shouting to attract their attention,' the man suggested.

Erica looked at him. 'You could. But I'm going home. I kept my word to come to the party. Not my fault if I can't get in.' She turned to leave just as the door opened and GeeGee looked out.

'You made it. I was afraid you'd chicken out,' GeeGee said.

'It did cross my mind,' Erica said, smothering a sigh. Ten more seconds and she'd have escaped.

'Hi,' GeeGee said, turning to the man. 'Come on up, both of you.'

The man bounded up the first flight of stairs ahead of them, his long legs taking two at a time and disappeared from sight. Following GeeGee upstairs to the top floor Erica tried not to tense up as she heard music and loud laughter drifting down the stairs. She'd never suffered from shyness before but it was so long since she'd gone to a party as a single woman.

Back then, too, she'd usually gone with a crowd of girlfriends and it had been all about meeting Mr Right and having a bit of an adventure. Now she'd met, loved and lost her Mr Right, parties had lost their attraction. Had turned into an ordeal, not an adventure.

'Dan, this is Erica, my best friend,' GeeGee said, taking her across to the table where drinks had been placed.

'Hi, Erica. Nice to meet you,' Dan said, pouring a glass of wine and handing it to her. 'Give me five minutes to check on the food situation in the kitchen and I'll be back to get to know my girlfriend's best mate.'

Erica smiled at GeeGee as Dan made for the kitchen. 'He's nice. So you're officially his girlfriend then?'

GeeGee nodded. 'Seems like it. Come on, let's go out on the terrace and mingle. Find someone out there you can chat to while I go and see if Dan needs any help.'

'Oh, I don't know...' Erica started to say, but the look on GeeGee's face silenced her and she obediently followed her out onto the terrace.

Candles and solar lights had been placed in strategic places, creating shadows and a glamorous ambience as dusk fell. Three or four people were grouped around the wrought-iron table in the corner, while a couple were standing by the parapet, listening to the sound of the sea below, and talking in low voices. Several other couples were standing, arms around each other, moving languidly to the music.

Before GeeGee could drag her over to introduce her to anyone, Erica walked over to and stood behind a large potted palm tree with fairy lights wound around its trunk.

'You go and help Dan,' she said. 'I'm fine here,' she then added as GeeGee went to protest. 'Go. I'm happy to wait here, sip my wine and do a spot of people-watching. I promise I'll mingle with you later, when I've relaxed a bit and got this inside me,' she said, indicating her wine.

Standing there partly hidden from general view she looked out over the Mediterranean and watched the lights twinkling on various yachts as they sailed along the coast. The view from the terrace at home was inland and lovely in its own way but a sea view was always magical. The view from the new house out over the coast was going to be like this one. Sea and boats and sky. Lots of sky. Thoughtfully she sipped her wine. Life was about to change again, only this time she was setting things in motion.

'Can I interest you in one of these?' Standing in front of her holding out a platter of nibbles was the man who'd arrived with her.

'Thanks.'

'Were you really going to run away back down there, if GeeGee hadn't opened the door?' he asked.

'Yes. I'm not much of a party animal these days,' Erica said. 'Unless it's a children's party.'

'You have children?'

'A little girl, Cammie. How about you?'

'No wife. No children. My sister, on the other hand, has several. Five at the last count. The kids love me to bits. Tell me I'm their favourite uncle.'

Erica laughed. 'I bet that means you spoil them rotten and let them do things any sane parent would forbid instantly!'

'Got it in one. Every child deserves an eccentric relative. And everyone deserves to be spoilt occasionally.' A wicked smiled accompanied his words.

He swallowed a mouthful of wine before looking at her seriously. 'I'd love to spoil you. Banish that sad look from your eyes.'

Erica stiffened. Up until that moment she'd been enjoying his company but now she didn't know how to respond. Was he flirting with her? Or just trying it on. And did her eyes really look sad these days?

'I'm Laurent, by the way.'

'I'm E—'

'Erica, yes I know. GeeGee told me.'

'What else did she tell you about me?'

'I only asked what your name was. I was hoping you'd tell me more over dinner tomorrow.'

'Why would I have dinner with you? I don't know you,' Erica protested. 'And you have no idea about who I am.'

'Having dinner together would be a good starting point,' Laurent said. 'There's a wonderful restaurant I know just over the border in Italy. I'd love to take you there.'

Erica shook her head. 'I'm sorry, Laurent, but...' She paused. 'I'm so out of practice at all this. I'm not sure I'd make a very interesting dinner companion.'

'I, on the other hand, am sure you will make a delightful one,' Laurent said. 'Please, let me have the pleasure of finding out.'

Erica sipped her wine and regarded Laurent, thoughtfully. She couldn't think of one real excuse why she shouldn't have dinner with him. Just her fear of the unknown. Her fear of moving forward; leaving the past behind. She took a deep breath and smiled at Laurent before saying, 'Thank you. I'd love to have dinner with you tomorrow evening.'

Chapter Forty-Nine

The months since she'd agreed to host Tansy's wedding party seemed to have disappeared in an instant to Rosie. If she could have anticipated the events that would be happening over summer, particularly in the week before the wedding, she would never have agreed in the first place. But she had agreed and now the day was here. As tired and emotionally spent as she was, she was determined to give her best friend a day to remember.

Thankfully Tansy and Rob had settled for a low-key civil wedding in the local Mairie in the end with just their respective parents, followed by a champagne and cake tea for immediate family and friends at Café Fleur.

'No more than a dozen of us. Then a beach barb-b-q party in the evening for other friends who want to come and celebrate with us.'

After a busy lunchtime, Rosie closed the restaurant and sent Tansy home to get ready.

'Off you go and get married then,' she said, kissing Tansy on the cheek. 'We'll see you and your new husband back here at six o'clock for your wedding tea.'

Alicia had finished icing the cake weeks ago, and had promised to be responsible for setting it up ready for the tea. Seb was coming over to help decorate the restaurant, while Saskia had offered to make up some favour bags and decorate the tables.

Rosie had worried whether she should suggest Saskia let Alicia take over the decorations but decided doing something creative and keeping busy would be better for her. Keeping busy was her own current modus operandi for getting over Terry's death. Hopefully, it would work for Saskia, too. The two of them may have lost the same father but their individual reactions to the loss of him from their lives couldn't but be miles apart.

Saskia had lost a beloved father whom she'd always remember with love. Rosie, more upset than she'd professed she'd ever be to Seb all those months ago, found her own sorrow was fuelled more with regret and anger than love at the moment.

Regrets and recriminations that could never now be allayed. Anger at the lost opportunity to heal both their wounds. The bridges between her and Terry had only been half rebuilt. Her growing relationship with Saskia would have to be the bridge completed in memory of their shared father.

Seb, when he arrived, was smiling. He picked Rosie up as he kissed her and swung her round.

'Good news: I'm officially Isabella's full-time guardian. Zoe didn't even contest the case. And I have it in writing so she can't simply change her mind on a whim.'

'That's wonderful,' Rosie said kissing him, before remembering the letter in the bottom of her tote. 'I need you to read something for me. Although maybe we should leave it until tomorrow in case it's bad news.'

She pulled the now-crumpled envelope out and handed it to Seb. 'It came the day of Terry's funeral and I didn't want to open it then.'

She waited anxiously as Seb took the letter out of the envelope and began reading. 'What does it say?'

'That a pizza my clients bought at your establishment caused them serious stomach problems, meaning they had to book extra hotel nights, couldn't fly home...' Seb stopped reading and looked at Rosie who was dancing around punching the air.

'Yes! Yes! Yes!'

'What?'

'Think about my menu, Seb. Where on it does it offer pizzas? Nowhere. It never has. And I can prove it with my food diary. You were right when you said you thought it could be a scam. I haven't poisoned anyone. Café Fleur is safe.'

A few hours later, the beach wedding party was in full swing. Seb had generously set up the hotel barb-b-q in front of the Café Fleur and sent over a couple of his sous-chefs to do the cooking for the evening.

Rosie, watching from the restaurant doorway, thinking about Seb and how her life had changed over the last few months, jumped as Charlie and Sarah appeared at her side.

She'd known Tansy had invited Charlie to the beach party but seeing Sarah with him was a surprise.

'Sarah, how are you?'

'Be better when this little monster is in the world,' Sarah said, lovingly stroking her stomach. 'And we can settle down to being a family.' She glanced at Charlie.

Rosie looked from one to the other in surprise. 'You two are together now?'

Charlie nodded. 'Getting married next month. I hope you wish us well.'

'Charlie, I couldn't be happier for you,' Rosie said sincerely.

'I hear you and Seb...?' Charlie looked at her. Rosie smiled and nodded and he leant in and kissed her cheek. 'Be happy, Rosie.'

As Sarah and Charlie moved away, Rosie smiled again as she saw Seb and Saskia with Isabella swinging between them walking towards her.

Life may have thrown her a couple of a curved balls this year but somehow she'd caught them and now she had something she could never have anticipated at the beginning of summer: a sister and a ready-made family with Seb and Isabella – an extended family she was looking forward to getting to know, and finally burying all the hurtful memories from the past with hopefully a multitude of good ones from the future.

She took a deep breath. Life was finally starting to give her the things she'd dreamt of for so many years.

'Rosie, darling, could I have a word? I have something to tell you,' Olivia said, appearing at her side unexpectedly. 'Zander has just asked me to marry him. And I've said yes, of course.'

If you loved *Rosie's Little Café on the Riviera*
then turn the page for an exclusive extract from
The Little Kiosk by the Sea, another sparklingly
brilliant romance from Jennifer Bohnet!

EARLY SEASON

Chapter One

For as long as anyone could remember the kiosk on the quay had been part of the town's summer street furniture. A focal point for the locals as much as the holiday-makers. Every 1 March, the wooden hexagonal hut re-appeared without fuss or fanfare on its designated place on the embankment between the taxi rank and the yacht club, it's wooden struts and panels gleaming with freshly applied paint. Red, white, blue and yellow – all bright summer colours, which, come October, would have been bleached and faded away by the summer weather. The jet-black orb on the top of the domed roof was a favourite with the gulls, who perched there serenely surveying the scene before swooping down and stealing ice creams and pasties from unwary holiday-makers.

As well as its annual paint make-over, the kiosk had occasionally been refurbished inside. These days it boasted an electric connection for the necessary computer, a kettle, mugs, a round tin that was never empty of biscuits and a small electric heater to keep the occupant warm in early and late season when the wind off the river blew straight in through the half open stable door.

There was a small shelf unit for holding tickets and the cash box, a cupboard for locking things in, space to the left of the door for the outside advertising boards to come in over night and three fold away canvas director chairs for sitting outside in the sun with friends when business was slow.

The whole atmosphere of the town changed as the locals welcomed the re-appearance of the hut which signalled the imminent arrival of the holiday-makers, the second home owners and the day trippers. Maybe this would be the year fortunes would be made. If not fortunes at least enough money to see the families through winter without getting deep into overdrafts. The last thing anyone wanted – or needed – was another wet season.

This summer though, 1 March came and went with no sign of the kiosk. All winter, rumours had rumbled around town about its demise and locals feared the worst: the council had never liked it and wanted it gone – not true the mayor said. Health and Safety had condemned it as an unfit workplace - but nobody would give details of the problem. The rent for the summer season had doubled and Owen Hutchinson, owner of the pleasure boats he operated through the kiosk, had refused to pay. A fact he denied.

Then, two weeks before Easter, without any warning, the re-painted kiosk appeared in its usual place. Collectively the town heaved a sigh of relief. Panic over. Time to enjoy the summer.

Chapter Two

Sabine

'Two tickets for the afternoon river trip? No problem,' Sabine said, smiling at the young woman standing in front of the kiosk.

'Here you go. We cast off at 2.30 today so make sure you're back here at least 15 minutes before.'

'Definitely. We'll be here. It won't be rough will it?' the girl asked as she handed over the ticket money. 'I'm not a very good sailor. We're down on holiday and my boy f... my husband loves boats so I thought I'd treat him.' She looked along the embankment. 'He's wandered off to look at some old steam engine or something.'

'The river will be as smooth as the proverbial baby's bottom this afternoon,' Sabine promised.

'Great. I'd hate to spoil things by being sea sick.'

'On honeymoon are we?' Sabine said looking at the shiny ring on the girls left hand.

The girl flushed. 'How'd you guess?'

'Oh, something to do with the way you forgot to call him your husband? You obviously haven't had time to get used to saying it yet.'

'Two days,' the girl confided. She leant in. 'We eloped.'

'Very brave of you,' Sabine said smiling.

The girl shrugged. 'Necessity rather than bravery,' she said. 'See you this afternoon.'

Sabine watched her walk away and join her new husband who greeted her with a lingering kiss. 'May married life be kind to you,' she muttered, before turning her attention back to sorting the kiosk out for the season.

Two weeks late arriving on the quay meant there'd barely been time to set up things before the first river trip of the season. Not that there was a lot to do really but Sabine liked to have everything to hand. Ticket books, cash tin, receipt book, tide-table book, chalk, mugs, foldaway chairs, kettle, bottles of water, coffee and biscuits. That just left finding space for the first four paintings of the season.

A couple of years ago, she'd discovered the tourists liked her pencil sketches of the town and the river. One quiet afternoon she'd sat in one of the canvas directors chairs outside the kiosk and idly started to sketch the river and its boats. She'd wanted a small picture to hang in her newly decorated bathroom, with its blue and white nautical theme. A tourist collecting tickets for a boat trip had seen it and asked to buy it when finished – provided she'd sign it for him.

That initial sale had thrown her into a panic. She'd no idea what to charge for an unframed original picture. It wasn't as if she was famous or anything – or likely to be. In the end she suggested a sum and the tourist had shaken his head at her – before giving her double what she had asked, and saying, 'You really don't know how talented you are, do you?'

Sabine had taken the money, thoughtfully. Yes, she did know she had a talent. Years ago she'd been all set to go to art college but instead had to give up her place and stay at home to help look after her mother. Something that she'd done willingly.

By the time she was free to pursue a career, the time to go to art college had passed and marriage and family life had eventually taken over. If she drew anything in the following years it was simply because she fancied doing it.

After that first unexpected sale, she'd started to do a couple of drawings a week, surprised by how quickly they sold. These days she spent winter painting and drawing views of the town and the river, ready for summer. By the end of the season she rarely had any left. Her secret 'just for fun' bank account grew substantially every summer.

The one she hung now on the folded back stable door was a firm favourite with the tourists. A pen and ink drawing of the old Butterwalk with its columns and hanging baskets it sold well every season.

Once she was satisfied the picture was hanging straight, she stood with her back to the kiosk looking across the river and along the embankment, breathing deeply and thinking about the future. Was this really going to be the last season she'd be working in the kiosk? If the council carried out their threat at the end of summer forcing Owen and the other boat owners to use an unimaginative refurbished office on the other side of the road, it would be. No way could she bear the thought of working indoors all summer long. Still Owen and the Robertsons were on the case, demanding a public meeting before a decision was taken and getting up a petition.

A flash of red coming towards her caught her eye. She laughed and shook her head. Johnnie her twin brother. The old Breton red beret sitting jauntily on his head and the folder of papers he was carrying told her instantly this morning he was on the 'Save the Kiosk' war path. Five minutes later he was greeting her with his customary cheek kisses. They might have been born in the town but their French father had ensured they knew all about their French ancestry and learnt the language. For years now they'd spoken only French to each other in private.

'*Ça va?*'

'*Oui. Et tu?*'

Johnnie LeRoy nodded.

'Haven't seen that for a few years,' she said, looking at the beret. 'Thought we'd thrown it out when Papa died.'

'Never,' Johnnie said, shaking his head. 'Family heirloom. Sign of the workers solidarity this is.'

Sabine smiled. She doubted that any of the locals would realise the significance of the red beret.

'Got a few signatures already,' Johnnie said, opening the folder and handing her a poster with the words, SAVE THE KIOSK em-blazed in red across the top. 'Need you to pin this up and to put the petition somewhere people can sign it.'

'You don't think the powers that be are serious about getting rid of the kiosk?'

Johnnie shrugged. 'Don't know. Telling them we want it kept won't do any harm though. Embankment wouldn't be the same without the kiosk.'

'True. Fancy a coffee?' Sabine asked reaching for the kettle.

Johnnie shook his head. 'Not this morning, thanks. I want to drop a poster off at the yacht club and then I'm planning on giving Annie and her bottom a good going over.'

Sabine smiled at the scandalised expression on a passing tourists face. Johnnie grinned at her before whispering, 'Gets them every time!' *Annie*, named after his late wife, was Johnnie's 32-foot sailing yacht moored out on one of the pontoons in the river.

'Have fun. See you tonight for supper,' she said, turning her attention to a couple looking at the times of river trips for the week, and began to talk them into taking the afternoon trip. Gift of the gab, Owen called her sales technique. Said it was the main reason he employed her to run the kiosk. That and the fact he was in love with her. She'd lost count of the number of times he'd asked her to marry him since Dave died. Said he was going to keep asking her until she said, yes.

It had become something of a joke between them now. Only last week he'd asked her again and she'd said her usual, 'No,' adding jokingly, 'I think you'd better stop asking me Owen. Otherwise, one of these days, I might be tempted to say yes, and then you'll be saddled with me.'

'If that means there is a possibility of you saying yes, one day, I intend to keep on asking,' Owen had replied seriously. 'I've always loved you. Dave was my best mate but I could have killed him when you married him and not me.'

Sabine sighed. 'Owen, I love you to bits but not in that way. You deserve more than a one sided marriage.'

'If you were the one side, I'd take it happily,' Owen said.

Sorrowfully, Sabine shook her head at him before reaching up and giving him a kiss on the cheek. 'Sorry, Owen.' She knew she hurt him every time she refused his offer but love had to be two way thing for a marriage to work, didn't it? She'd been a single woman for so long she could barely remember what it had been like being in a relationship, let alone being married.

When Dave had died, it had been a devastated Owen who'd tried to step into his shoes and be there whenever Peter had needed a father figure, insisting that was what godfathers were for. Two years ago he'd made sure Peter had a job ready and waiting for him when he'd finished his engineering course at college. At the time she'd questioned Owen as to whether it was a genuine job at the time or one he created.

'Of course it's genuine,' he'd said. 'I need a boat engineer. Happy for it to be Peter. Besides,' he added with a grin. 'A bit of nepotism never did any harm!' It was Peter's second season this year and he'd told Sabine he loved it. Couldn't imagine doing anything else – living anywhere else.

She did wish sometimes that Peter had been a bit more adventurous – left home and seen a bit of the world before settling down in town. He'd done a couple of yacht deliveries with Johnnie but hadn't wanted to do more. Took after his father in that respect. Dave had never wanted to live anywhere else or even take holidays abroad. Whereas she had always longed to see the world. The one opportunity to do that had sadly come at the wrong time of her life.

She glanced at a tourist studying the sailing timetable.

'Can I book a ticket for this afternoon's trip?' he asked, his accent marking him as American.

'Of course.'

'Great little town you've got here,' he said, as Sabine took his money and handed him a ticket.

'Your first visit?'

'Yeah hoping to unearth some relatives,' he said with a grin. 'Grandmother was a GI bride way back in '44.

She kinda lost touch with folks here when she left. Family name was Holdsworth. Don't suppose it's yours? Know anyone of that name?'

Sabine laughed. 'Well connected ancestors you've got with that name, that's for sure. No, its not mine. And as this isn't small town America, I don't know everyone, but I don't think there are any Holdsworths currently living in town.'

'You mean there's no longer a Govenor Holdsworth in charge out at the castle? I was hoping for an invite to stay there.'

'You wouldn't be very comfortable if you did – Windsor Castle it's not.'

'Shame. Good job I booked into the Royal for a week or two then. See you later.'

By the time Sabine helped Owen and Peter to cast off that afternoon, the boat was three quarters full and she watched it depart pleased the first of the seasons sailings was so full.

As the *Queen of the River* began to make its way upstream, Sabine started to close up the kiosk. Life for the next few months would be ruled by the tide tables and the need to open the kiosk everyday to take advance bookings. Today though it was early enough in the season with few people around, she could close up and go home for an hour or two before the boat returned and she had to be on hand to help the passengers disembark.

A chilly March breeze was blowing off the river and Sabine was glad of her fleece as she made for her cottage halfway up Crowthers Hill one of the old roads leading out of town into the back country.

The house in Above Town she and Dave had bought together as a newly married couple had been too full of memories for both her and Peter to stay there happily without Dave. Far better to have a new start in a different house – one that she and Peter and could build into a home, so twelve years ago she'd bought the cottage when Dave's insurance money had eventually turned up.

Johnnie and Annie helped with getting the place habitable – it had been empty for two years and took weeks of hard work from the three of them to make it habitable - and she and Peter had lived there ever since.

Johnnie alone was responsible for the attic conversion three years ago. Sabine had watched in despair as her lovely kind compassionate brother all but followed his wife into an early grave. Finding him, bottle in hand, wandering around town at two o'clock one afternoon barely able to stand, she threatened him with dire consequences if he didn't stop.

'Did you see me doing this when I lost Dave? No. It's hard but you've just got to get on with it.'

'You had Peter,' he'd muttered. 'Perhaps if we'd had a child I'd have something to live for.'

'You think it was easier because I had a child? Dream on. It was harder. A constant reminder of what I'd lost. He needed to grieve too. You've still got a lot of life to live so don't give me that bullshit about not having anything to live for. I'm still here loving you and so is Peter.'

Shouting and yelling at him to get a grip hadn't made any difference so in the end Sabine had taken action the only way she knew – she gave Johnnie something practical to do. Not daring to think about him drinking when he was away on a trip, she cancelled all his yachting work for six months. Then she bullied him into doing her attic conversion, insisting he moved in with her while he did it. That way she could monitor his alcohol, keep an eye on him and feed him regular meals.

Nine hard months it took but at the end he'd hammered and sawn his way out of his grief and Sabine had a studio in the attic with a view of the river. More important Johnnie was on his way back to living life. These days he lived mostly on board his boat despite still owning the cottage he and Annie had bought tucked away in the old part of town.

Lack of exercise over winter meant she was panting by the time she pushed her key into the front-door lock. Still, the summer routine of walking into town and being on her feet for most of the day would soon have her fit again.

After organising supper for her and Johnnie – Peter was out with his girlfriend tonight – she made a mug of coffee and went upstairs to her studio. Her favourite place in the house.

Pressing a button on the cd player, Sabine sank down onto the settee and let the relaxing sounds of her favourite Miles Davis recording wash over her. Missy her old tabby cat immediately left the comfort of her basket in the alcove and sprang onto her lap.

A light and airy room courtesy of the dormer window she'd fought hard to get planning permission for, the room was exactly as she'd dreamt. A comfy two-seater settee with creamy loose covers over it and its feather filled cushions, a book case down one wall holding her collection of art and teach yourself books, a wooden cabinet whose drawers and shelves held her paints, paper and other arty stuff as well as a combined radio and cd player. A small cane coffee table standing on a scarlet scatter rug on the wooden floorboards polished and varnished to the nth degree by Johnnie added a splash of colour to the room. An easel with her latest painting on it stood to one side of the dormer-type window and a few framed family photos were pinned to the ceiling beam that ran the width of the house. A small wood-burner on the side wall kept the room cosy in winter. Stacks of finished paintings were lined up wherever there was wall space.

Tristan at Churchside Gallery had offered to hang half a dozen or so of her paintings in an local artists exhibition he was planning for May. For the last few months, she'd been working on getting enough to sell over the season and to have some different ones to offer Tristan. It would be the first time her work had ever been hung in a proper gallery. Tristan had asked her to do some larger paintings of the river, 'Romanticise the scene,' he'd said. 'People can't get enough of pictures like that. An old boat or two is good – go for a nostalgic feel.'

Sabine had enjoyed painting the larger scenes and as she'd grown more confident she'd painted a couple of bright abstract ones not knowing how Tristan would receive them. If he didn't want them she'd give one to Johnnie and one to Owen.

Absently Sabine stroked Missy. Normally, in March, she was full of energy and looking forward to the season. This year though, all the talk of the kiosk closing had unsettled her. Making her question what the future might hold. And, if she were honest, made her feel old. Which was ridiculous. She still had plenty of years ahead of her. It was just a question of deciding how she was going to live them.

After all, her life so far had failed to be anything spectacular so that was unlikely to change. The one chance she'd had to change things had come at a wrong moment in her life. Now it was too late. The opportunity gone forever. Owen at least had never given up on her. Owen, apart from Johnnie, was the one person Sabine knew she could call in any emergency and know he'd be there for her. He would have made a wonderful father she knew from seeing him with Peter – she'd even deprived him of that. Had never married anyone else. If only he'd met someone else, the pressure would have been off her but, no, Owen had proved steadfast in his love for her. Sabine remembered with gratitude Owen 'being there' for her and Peter down through the years. He was a good man, Still quite fit in his individual rugged way.

Sometimes in the studio late at night when she felt lonely and vulnerable, she fantasised about accepting his proposal. Mrs Sabine Hutchinson had a good ring to it, but resolutely she always pushed the thought away. It wouldn't be fair to Owen.

* * *

Back down on the quay an hour later, she waited as the *Queen of the River*, with Peter at the helm, gently draw up alongside the pontoon.

Owen followed the last of the passengers up the pontoon gangway, leaving Peter and the other crew member to take the boat out to its mooring in the middle of the river.

'You got time for a quick drink?' he asked. 'Something we need to talk about.'

'Sounds serious,' Sabine said, her heart sinking. The beginning of the summer was not a good time for Owen to need to talk. 'Why not talk here?'

Owen shrugged. 'Rather sit in the pub in comfort. Besides, this way I get to enjoy your company for longer.'

'Have to be a quick one, Johnnie's coming for supper.'

'Won't take long what I've got to say,' Owen said. 'Ready?'

Ten minutes later with a glass of Chardonnay in front of her and a pint of beer in Owen's hand, Sabine looked at him. 'Well, what's this all about Owen?'

'Will you marry me Sabine?'

She shook her head. 'Sorry.'

'In that case, its just two things. Peter and Hutchinson River Trips is the first.'

Sabine took a sip of her wine and waited. Was he regretting offering Peter a job and wanted out?

'I've been talking to the solicitor about Peter inheriting the business.'

It took a few seconds for his words to sink in.

'You want Peter to have the business? You're not ill are you? You don't look ill but...'

'No, I'm not ill,' Owen said.

'Thank God for that.'

'I just want to get things sorted, and Peter's like the son I've ever had to me.'

'Does Peter know about this?'

'Not yet. I wanted to make sure you didn't have any objections. Accuse me of forcing him to stay put before he's seen the world.'

'He's a real home bird,' Sabine said. 'I can't see him ever leaving for a life somewhere else. Besides he loves his life on the river. But what about your dad's relatives? Surely there's a cousin or two out Stokenham way, who have a claim to the family business?'

Owen shook his head. 'No. So what d'you think? Good thing or not?'

'I think it's an incredibly generous action on your part Owen,' Sabine said. 'But I hope he doesn't get to inherit too soon.'

'So do I, darling, so do I.' Owen laughed before taking a swig of his beer. 'Right, I'll get on to Trevor Bagshawe to do the necessary. Once that's done, we'll tell Peter, Okay?'

Sabine nodded. 'You said there were two things – what's the second?'

'I've been talking to your Johnnie about all the places he's been. The sights he's seen. I've decided I've missed a lot so...'

'You're going to become a yacht deliverer?'

'No, of course not. At the end of the season, I'm off touring Europe for six months.' Owen looked at her, a serious look on his face.

'Want to come with me? No strings. Just two old friends having an adventure together before its too late.'

Acknowledgements

First, thanks must go to the team at HQ – in particular, Charlotte Mursell, who clearly has the patience of a saint when dealing with needy authors!

Thanks must also go to my online author friends, who are always ready to offer sympathy and send virtual gin and chocolate when the editing gets tough (you know who you are).

Finally, but by no means least, a huge thank-you to everybody who buys and reads my books.